DREAM OF VENUS

Pamela Sargent published the first novel in her "Venus" trilogy, *Venus of Dreams,* in 1986; that book about a generations-long terraforming project was followed by *Venus of Shadows* (1988) and *Child of Venus* (2001). *Publishers Weekly* described the three novels as "a masterful SF trilogy...Sargent brings her world to life with sympathetic characters and crisp, concise language."

For the first time, *Dream of Venus and Other Science Fiction Stories* collects the short fiction set against the background of Sargent's Venus novels, stories written after the trilogy had been completed; as Sargent writes in her introduction, "characters and stories existing in the interfaces of the novels began to speak to me." These are stories that can be enjoyed both for themselves and by readers who want to revisit the world of the Venus trilogy.

> "If you have not read Pamela Sargent, then you should make it your business to do so at once. She is in many ways a pioneer, both as a novelist and as a short story writer.... She is one of the best."

> —Michael Moorcock

Borgo Press Books by PAMELA SARGENT

Dream of Venus and Other Science Fiction Stories

DREAM OF VENUS

AND OTHER SCIENCE FICTION STORIES

PAMELA SARGENT

THE BORGO PRESS
MMXII

DREAM OF VENUS

FIRST EDITION

Published by Wildside Press LLC

www.wildsidebooks.com

DEDICATION

All three of my Venus novels were dedicated to *George Zebrowski*, who gave me essential editorial and moral support while I wrote them, so this collection is dedicated to him as well.

CONTENTS

ACKNOWLEDGMENTS

"Introduction: Dreaming of Venus" and the "Afterwords" are published here for the first time. Copyright © 2012 by Pamela Sargent.

"Venus Flowers at Night" was first published in *Microcosms*, edited by Gregory Benford, DAW Books, 2004. Copyright © 2004, 2012 by Pamela Sargent.

"Follow the Sky" was first published in *Space Stations*, edited by Martin H. Greenberg and John Helfers, DAW Books, 2004. Copyright © 2004, 2012 by Pamela Sargent.

"Dream of Venus" was first published in *Star Colonies*, edited by Martin H. Greenberg and John Helfers, DAW Books, 2000. Copyright © 2000, 2012 by Pamela Sargent.

"Utmost Bones" was first published in *Envisioning the Future*, edited by Marleen S. Barr, Wesleyan University Press, 2003. Copyright © 2003, 2012 by Pamela Sargent.

The above stories are reprinted here by permission of the author and her agents, Richard Curtis Associates, Inc., 171 East 74th Street, New York, NY 10021.

INTRODUCTION:
DREAMING OF VENUS

Sometime during the early 1970s, the idea of writing a novel set on the planet Venus came to me. I can even recall where I first had the idea; I was sitting on the porch of the old Victorian house where I was renting an apartment, had just finished a game of chess with a friend who lived down the street, had been reading Carl Sagan's speculations about the possibility of terraforming Venus, and had an impulse to write a lengthy and profound family saga along the lines of Thomas Mann's first novel, *Buddenbrooks*. I'd already had the experience of writing a novel that was something of a family saga (my first novel, *Cloned Lives*, which was published in 1976), but this time wanted to write about several generations of a family.

I might have set such a story on an invented planet, but that didn't appeal to me; why make something up when the solar system already offered a variety of fascinating settings? And the scope of a terraforming project—decades, most likely centuries, of efforts to make an inhospitably world habitable by humankind—required a story that would have to encompass generations.

From the start, I unconsciously realized that trying to write such a novel would take some time and demand a long-term commitment. I didn't foresee that the one long novel I first imagined, *Venus of Dreams*, would grow into three massive tomes, require almost twenty-five years of writing and rewriting (about half of my adult life by the time the third volume, *Child of*

Venus, was published in 2001), and eventually need successive agreements with four different publishers in the U.S. alone to get all of the volumes into print. I contracted with Pocket Books for the first book, *Venus of Dreams*, had that contract cancelled shortly before Pocket's Timescape science fiction imprint was discontinued in the early 1980s, sold a trilogy including *Venus of Dreams*, *Venus of Shadows*, and *Child of Venus* to Bantam, saw *Venus of Dreams* published in 1986 and *Venus of Shadows* in 1988, had the Bantam contract abruptly cancelled while I was in the middle of writing the third volume in the early 1990s, and finally sold the orphaned *Child of Venus* in the late 1990s to HarperPrism, a division of HarperCollins, which brought it out under the Eos imprint acquired by HarperCollins after it took over William Morrow and Avon. The entire trilogy is now available, in both print-on-demand trade paperbacks and electronic editions, from E-Reads (http://ereads.com/).

This winding and uncertain course of publication put me through much stress, depression, and soul-destroying angst; had I known what lay ahead, I would have abandoned *Venus of Dreams* the day after the idea first occurred to me. But writers often sense that the writer is only a device for a story or novel to get itself written, and that what happens to the writer doesn't much matter to the story. The Venus novels got themselves written, and that the process took as long as it did was partly because of the immensity of that task, partly because of broken promises by publishers, and partly because life does go on, and there were other things (including other books and stories) demanding my attention during those years.

I might have set my generational saga on Mars instead of Venus, but enough masters of science fiction had used Mars as a setting to make me feel I should head toward relatively unexplored fictional planetary territory. (Kim Stanley Robinson had not yet embarked on his masterful trilogy about the terraforming of Mars, nor had Greg Bear written *Moving Mars*, but H. G. Wells, Ray Bradbury, C. S. Lewis, Robert A. Heinlein, and legions of other masters had already dealt quite well with the Red Planet, and Joe Haldeman has recently inhabited it for his novel *Marsbound*.) Venus also offered opportunities for female imagery and for using the hellish environment of Venus, with its runaway greenhouse effect, to make some points about the increasing climatic threats to our own planet. But I didn't expect, a decade after the last Venus novel was published, to feel as though I am now living through the early stages of the future history that I invented for those novels.

I got lucky with some of that future history. I call it luck because carefully considered futuristic extrapolations and forecasts have a lot less to do with my writing than instincts, unconscious processes, and often feeling that using one detail rather than another will make for a better story. Because I had read Soviet dissident Andrei Amalrik's book *Will the Soviet Union Survive Until 1984?*, I assumed that the Soviet Union would have fallen apart sometime before the beginning of *Venus of Dreams*, a novel that begins some five hundred years from now. I was vague about when this fragmentation took place (a good rule for science fiction writers is: know when to be vague) and by the time I traveled to Russia, after *Venus of Shadows* was published, the Soviet Union's disintegration was already under way and I could congratulate myself for being prescient.

Another notion that appealed to me was creating a future Earth dominated politically and culturally by Muslims. This had less to do with extrapolating a possible future and more to do with my desire to create a future that felt connected to our present and our past while also being convincingly strange and different. A story or novel for me almost always begins with a character (sometimes more than one character) trying to tell me a story. The character who began speaking to me when I first thought of writing *Venus of Dreams* was a young woman in North America trapped among the well-meaning but ignorant members of her family, with apparently no way out and no way to become part of the effort to terraform Venus. Only after I had written about her, and had completed a rough early draft of the novel, did I begin to get a fuller picture of her world.

This future Earth was made up of nomarchies, provinces with a certain amount of cultural individuality and political autonomy but dominated by a council based in the Middle East and largely made up of Muslims. It seemed reasonable to assume that people there and in remnants of Russia and the East might pick up the pieces of an Earth ravaged by climate change and earlier conflicts that I called the Resource Wars. I didn't lay out the background of my novel, the future history, charts of governmental and Venus Project hierarchies, maps, a chronology, and all the rest until I'd finished that first draft, which is normal for me even if it seems to be doing things in the wrong order. I have to let my characters clue me in, and only then can I dig into the details of their histories and cultures.

Given this backwards way of working, I've found myself surprised that I seem to have done a better job of prognosticating than I thought possible. The future history of climate change, diminishing resources, failing educational systems (most of the people in the Venus books, those who are not among the elite who have gained their power through the control of both resources and information, are illiterate or close to it), mosques dotting the American landscape (accompanied unfortunately by a rabid xenophobia that I hadn't anticipated), deepening political divisions, and diminishing expectations is rushing upon us more quickly than I envisioned, and I am not at all convinced that it will lead to a terraforming project like the one I imagined or indeed to a promising or sustainable future.

But I can hope.

I was sure that I was finished with the Venus terraforming project and also any fiction even slightly related to the trilogy once *Child of Venus* was written (I estimate that the published novels contain some 750,000 words), but as I've said, stories will get themselves written however they can. The stories in this book were not part of the Venus trilogy, but were written after I had finished *Child of Venus*, when characters and stories existing in the interstices of the novels began to speak to me. These are stories that can stand alone outside that context, but

I hope that they will allow some readers to revisit those books and perhaps others to discover them.

—Pamela Sargent
Albany, New York
December 30, 2011

VENUS FLOWERS
AT NIGHT

The escarpment to his northeast was the sheer face of mountains taller than the Himalayas, a range of peaks sustained by the upwelling of Venus's mantle. Karim gazed up at the vast wall of the cliffside. Masses of dark gray clouds hid the top of the escarpment, but patches of mossy green were visible against the black and gray face of the cliff. To the west, a pale glow could be seen behind the thick clouds; the sun was rising.

The scarp was the southwest side of the Maxwell Mountains. To the north lay the high plateaus of the land mass of Ishtar Terra. Life, although precarious, had already come to the cliffs; soon people would travel to the Venusian surface to live in the enclosed settlements of the high plateaus.

No, Karim thought, and the cliffside disappeared.

Now he stood on a rocky shore, looking out at a wrinkled gray ocean. In the east, the setting sun was no more than a smear of white light against the thick gray mist of the sky; another month would pass before it disappeared below the horizon. No birds flew above this shore; no life lived in this sterile and acidic sea.

No, Karim thought again, and the gray ocean vanished. He lifted his arms and removed his silver linking band from his head.

He sat in the small room that adjoined his sleeping quarters aboard the *Beverwyck*. The floor rocked almost imperceptibly under his feet. He would have preferred a large hovercraft, or perhaps an airship, for this journey, but Greta had insisted on hiring the *Beverwyck*. The small watercraft's functions were controlled by an artificial intelligence, so its crew of three would be all they required, meaning that he and Greta would have more privacy. Greta also believed that the citizens of North America's Atlantic Federation would be more reassured by a visiting Mukhtar who was traveling slowly upriver in a simple vessel and spending time at places along the way, instead of speeding past towns and villages in a hovercraft or floating above them in an inaccessible airship, stopping only to talk with the occasional high official.

"You have to show some sensitivity and respect," Greta had told him. "Many of the people in my home Nomarchy still haven't forgotten what their place once was in the world."

Karim al-Anwar usually heeded his wife's advice on such matters, having learned that her political instincts were often superior to his own. But he suspected that Greta also preferred a journey aboard the *Beverwyck* because that would allow her more proximity to the places of her childhood. Greta Gansevoort-Mehdi had grown up along the Hudson River, in a home that overlooked the Albany port, watching ships move up and down the waterway while dreaming of her escape from a region of Earth that now counted its wealth in history and monuments to the past and little else.

I should go to sleep, he told himself. Instead, he crossed the sitting room and climbed the short flight of steps to the deck.

A small human form topped by a mass of dark curls was silhouetted against the railing; Lauren, the female steward, was on watch tonight. She turned toward him.

"Is there anything you require, Mukhtar Karim?" she asked in badly pronounced Arabic.

"No, thank you." He leaned against the railing. They had passed under the Verrazano Bridge and come through the narrows and now lay at anchor in Upper New York Bay. In the moonlight, he was able to glimpse a long low black wall astern of the *Beverwyck*: the dikes of Staten Island. That morning, he had paid visits to the seawall workers in Asbury Park and Perth

Amboy along the Jersey shore, and recalled the wary, suspicious look he had glimpsed in the eyes of many in the crowd as their supervisor introduced him, how they had stared blankly at him as he assured them of the Council's good intentions and their concern for the people of North America.

After their arrival in Washington several days ago on a suborbital flight, he and Greta had taken a train to Atlantic City, where they had boarded the *Beverwyck* after a reception hosted by that city's officials and a town meeting with some of its citizens. They were given a private car on the train from Washington; their sitting chairs had holes in the red upholstery and the blue and red carpeting was nearly threadbare. The car had rattled as it moved, sometimes so loudly that he and Greta had to shout at each other to be heard. The Atlantic Federation and its sister Nomarchies on the North American continent had the worst trains in the world, perhaps because so many of these people clung to their electric and ethanol-powered automobiles, personal hovercraft, and other forms of private transportation, still holding on to the illusion of being entirely free to go anywhere at will.

"How long have you served aboard the *Beverwyck*?" Karim asked the young woman.

"Served?" At first he thought that she had not understood that word. "But we own the *Beverwyck*," Lauren continued, switching to Anglaic, "my brother Zack, my bondmate, and myself. Zack and I bought her five years ago, and not long after that Roberto and I made our pledge, so Zack and I cut him in for an equal share."

"I see," Karim replied in Anglaic, wishing that Greta had told him the three young people were the craft's owners and not just a crew hired to see to their comfort. But perhaps his wife had not known that. He would have to adjust his manner, treat them with a bit more friendliness and a little less reserve.

"But it is assuredly less of a drain on our purses for us to look after our passengers ourselves instead of hiring others." Lauren had switched back to Arabic. "There is not so much to be made with the *Beverwyck* that we would be able to amply reward any hirelings."

"Please." Karim gestured with one hand. "I don't mind if we speak in Anglaic, and the practice will be useful for me."

"Doesn't sound to me like you need much practice, Mukhtar Karim, but your Anglaic's a lot better than my Arabic." Lauren cleared her throat. "As I was saying, we don't make all that much, but it isn't such a bad way to live your life, going up and down the Hudson, taking our time and going slow and not rushing to get up to Troy in a day with a cargo, and we've had some interesting passengers. None so interesting as you, of course."

"I am flattered," Karim said.

"Your wife drove a hard bargain, but a fair one. It also can't hurt us to have such a prominent passenger. It'll certainly be good advertising."

"I'm grateful to be of some small service to you, then."

"Sure there's nothing I can do for you, sir?" Lauren asked.

"No, thank you." He should go back below, force himself to get some sleep.

Karim left the deck, descended the steps to the sitting room, and closed the door behind him. He had left his linking band on the small table next to his chair; he sat down and put the thin band around his head once more.

"Mukhtar Karim," the soft alto voice of the *Beverwyck*'s cybermind whispered, "do you wish to call up another mind-tour?" The voice was faint; he was still having some slight trouble interfacing with the artificial intelligence properly through his band. "I have quite an extensive archive of virtual experiences," the mind went on. "Most of them are far more entertaining and detailed than what you have been accessing."

"No doubt they are," Karim said. His mind-tours of Venus were barely more than sketches and rudimentary designs he had pulled together by himself, and he knew only the rudiments of mind-tour production. His vision lived more fully inside him than in his mind-tours. He wondered if it would ever live in reality.

"You also need not limit yourself to the subject of the planet Venus," the AI continued.

"Ah, but that's the subject of most concern to me these days," Karim replied.

"Perhaps you will tell me why."

"Because Earth is of so much concern to me."

"That does not seem to cohere with your retreat into your mind-tours," the AI said. "Nor does it seem consistent with your present assignment of visiting parts of this Nomarchy to assure the people here that the Council of Mukhtars has their best interests at heart."

"That assignment," Karim said, "was given me partly to get me out of the way."

The AI had nothing to say to that. Karim thought of how delicately Mukhtar Hassan Tantawi had broached the subject of this tour. Someone had to be sent to the Atlantic Federation, and perhaps to a couple of the other Nomarchies of North America after that, on a diplomatic mission, the object of which was to listen to any grievances and appeals for additional aid and to report any interesting observations. Given that those particular regions of Earth were still among the more suspicious and distrustful of the New Islamic States, they were especially in need of reassurance, and the appearance of a member of the Council would do much to convince them that the Mukhtars who now ruled Earth wanted only to cooperate with them and see that their needs were met.

Karim did not doubt the purpose of his mission, only the reasons Mukhtar Hassan had given for choosing him to carry it out. He was fluent in Anglaic, but several other members of the Council knew that language well, and most educated people had at least some familiarity with the tongue. His wife had grown up in the Atlantic Federation, which could be useful, but the fact was that Greta's presence on this trip was not really necessary.

The truth, he admitted to himself, was that he and his allies were losing their influence on the Council to a group of younger, more practical men. More farmland was being lost to climatic changes, and more coastal areas to the rising oceans fed by the melting polar icecaps. The Council had to see that Earth's people were fed, clothed, housed, and trained for the work to which their individual talents were best suited, and to indulge in other dreams was a luxury they could not afford, especially a dream as grandiose as the one Karim harbored. People with the task of healing their own wounded planet could not be distracted by the vision of transforming another world, especially one that presented the challenges of Venus. Even Mukhtar Ali bin Oman, once a strong ally of Karim's, had seen which way the sands were drifting and had begun, however gently and shamefacedly, to mouth the phrases of the doubters.

The Council had not sent him here only to soothe the North Americans, a task any of the Mukhtars could have performed and for which at least a few of them were better suited than he. His mission was also a warning to him, and Hassan's words, however artfully phrased and ambiguous, had delivered that warning: You will have a chance to think and reconsider your thoughts while we will be free of your efforts to win more supporters for your cause. If you return and insist on pressing for your dream again, we can find another mission for you, perhaps one not as pleasant. And if you persist after that, then, God willing, it may be time to relieve you of some of your responsibilities.

Karim did not fear expulsion from the Council or exile, or even the disgrace such a punishment would bring to his family; the stronger among his brothers, sisters, and cousins would eventually overcome the dishonor, and the weaker would glean what crumbs they could for themselves, as they always had. It was powerlessness that he feared, being deprived of any influence, unable even to hope that the Council, soon or in times to come, might come to share his vision.

"We can't go on this way, you know," he murmured through his linking band to the mind of the *Beverwyck*, "just trying to repair the damage and living in the fantasy that we are the future, that human history has at last passed into our hands.

We're certainly better off than we were a century or two ago, but maybe our past sufferings have so marked us that we're willing to settle for what we have and be grateful we have survived."

"Human beings have not only survived on this planet," the AI said, "but also in space."

"The habitat-dwellers have survived in space," Karim replied. "Some among my brothers on the Council would say that they have already diverged from the stream of human history, and others would call them cowards and traitors to their kind. But they are looking outward, beyond simply conserving what they have, while we stopped looking outside ourselves some time ago. Maybe when we were a poor people and still fighting for the scraps the more powerful threw to us, that was necessary. When we were salvaging what we could from this world and doing the work of rebuilding, we had no choice but to concentrate on practical matters. But if we never look to anything greater...."

"...your culture will stagnate," the AI interrupted. The mind had heard him say that often enough, aloud and through the band, during the trip from Atlantic City, and now it repeated his words. "It will again become a backwater. You are immersing yourself in your mind-tours in order to convince yourself that the great endeavor you dream of is possible."

"Oh, I can convince myself," Karim said, "or at least I can do so intermittently. It's how to convince others that's the problem."

* * * * * * *

He was aboard a small shuttlecraft, moving away from the space station orbiting Venus toward the parasol shading the planet from the sun. Constructing the parasol had cost both resources and lives, but now, after nearly a century of effort, a hyperthin umbrella of aluminum would allow the hellish planet to cool.

As his craft approached the parasol, Karim could make out a series of slats designed to reflect sunlight outward and away from Venus. To design the parasol, to build it, to stabilize it so that the vast umbrella would neither drift closer to the sun nor threaten Venus, had been the greatest feat of construction ever undertaken by humankind, and yet it was only a first step in the work of terraforming Venus.

"And also only the first step," a voice added, "in mastering the tools we may need to restore Earth's biosphere." The disembodied alto voice speaking to him was that of the shuttlecraft's AI, and yet it sounded oddly familiar.

It would take some two hundred years for Venus's surface temperature to drop enough to allow for surface settlements, and even then the first settlers would need to live in protected and closed environments. An effort to terraform Mars would have proceeded more quickly; if Karim had not lived to see the end of such an effort, his children or grandchildren surely would have. But the refugees from Earth, the habitat dwellers, had claimed Mars for themselves, making habitats of its two satellites, bases from which they occasionally ventured forth to explore the Red Planet.

Once Karim had resented the claim of the habitat dwellers to Mars, but he had eventually come to understand that Venus might be better soil for the flowering of his dream. Venus might have been another Earth, might have more closely resembled humankind's home world during the first five hundred million years of their planetary histories; to terraform Venus would be to restore her to what she might have been. Human settlers born there in the distant future would not become exiles from their home planet, since Venus's gravity was close to that of Earth, but any Martian settlers would be exiles; their bodies, adapted to the gentler gravitational pull of Mars, would cut them off from ever being able to return to Earth.

His shuttlecraft passed through the umbra of the shadow cast by the parasol, and then a spear of light caught him. Karim covered his eyes reflexively as the viewscreen darkened, then peered at the screen again.

"One of the parasol's fans has begun to drift away from the shade's main body," his craft's AI said softly as more light filled the screen. "Do not fear. This craft is not in danger."

But the Venus project is, Karim thought apprehensively. The fan would have to be replaced; more resources and lives would be lost to that work. That of course was assuming that the parasol did not become unstable and begin to drift away from its L1 point between Venus and the sun. If it moved closer to the sun, more of the planet would eventually be left unshaded; closer to Venus, and the metallic umbrella would be caught and torn apart by fierce winds—if the sulfuric acid of the poisonous atmosphere did not dissolve the parasol first. He trembled in his seat. They might have to rebuild the entire shield.

"My calculations tell me—" the shuttlecraft's mind began.

"No," Karim replied, and the shuttlecraft suddenly vanished.

For a moment, he did not know where he was, then recognized the familiar surroundings of the *Beverwyck*'s sitting room. He felt the pangs of disappointment and loss.

"You asked me," the *Beverwyck*'s mind whispered through his band, "to provide you with an emotional sense of a past in your sketches, so that you would experience each mind-tour as an achieved reality."

"Yes, I remember that now."

"But I did not anticipate that you would become so disoriented. May I suggest that—"

"I don't want any suggestions," Karim said, then called up his next scenario.

He followed a path of white flagstones past a grove of slender willows. Greta was waiting for him outside a small pavilion. As he came up to her, she took his arm. They kept to the path that led to the edge of the island, passing a greenhouse and then another pavilion. Five people sat at one of the tables under the pavilion, sipping tea from cups and eating from a large bowl of fruit. One man raised his hand to Karim and Greta, silently inviting them to join the group; Karim smiled and shook his head.

Overhead, the wide disk of yellow light at the center of the dome that covered the island was growing dimmer; the silver light of evening would soon be upon them. This artificial island, and the others that now drifted in the upper reaches of Venus's atmosphere, had been built on vast platforms made of metal cells filled with helium and had then been enclosed in impermeable domes. Few people lived on this island, no more than a few hundred, and there were even fewer on the other islands, but more would come, more of the specialists and workers needed for the next stage in terraforming the planet below.

The path ended at a low gray wall, about one meter high, that marked the edge of the island. This wall now encircled the entire island, but Karim could recall coming to the island's edge years ago, just after arriving here from Earth, to peer through the transparent dome at the darkness beyond: Venus cloaked in the parasol's shadow. There had been no wall then, only the blackness, and for a moment he was suddenly afraid that he might step off the island's edge and through the dome, to fall through the thick and poisonous clouds. The wall had been built to prevent that feeling of vertigo that so many of the first arrivals had felt, and Karim now often took evening walks to the island's edge with Greta.

Another team, a group of engineers, was scheduled to arrive here soon; Karim had heard that several hours ago, just after first light. They were already inside the space station that orbited Venus, where the freighters and passenger torchships from Earth had to dock. From the station, a shuttlecraft would carry them to the one Venusian island that functioned as a port, where they would board an airship bound for this island. Here, in the upper reaches of the atmosphere, helium-fueled dirigibles were the most convenient form of transportation between islands.

"...vulnerable," Greta was saying, and he had the odd sensation that she was reading his thoughts.

Karim turned toward his wife. "What were you saying, my dear?"

She gazed at him in silence with her long dark eyes, then said, "Our airships are useful, but they also leave us vulnerable. Consider this—we can only leave these islands on shuttlecraft, and can only travel to Earth from our Venusian space station. That means a risk of being completely cut off from Earth at two points, our island port and at the space station, and then we'd have only our airships, which have to remain in the atmosphere. We could be trapped here, cut off completely from the outside."

"That's a possibility," Karim said, distressed that she would spoil the mood of their stroll with such concerns, "but a very distant one. We've built enough redundancy into our systems to—"

"I wasn't thinking of a systems failure," Greta said. "I was thinking of a siege, or a blockade."

Karim almost laughed. "A blockade?" He shook his head. "But why? For what possible reason? The Mukhtars want only success for this project."

"Yes, that's true at the moment. But what if those who follow us here begin to hope for a looser hand on the reins? We're here to make a new world, and part of that is allowing that world to develop in its own way. We're terraforming a planet, probably one of the most revolutionary undertakings of our species, so we shouldn't be surprised if that provokes people to entertain rebellious ideas in the future. Some here already talk of being free from many of Earth's restrictions. The Mukhtars might not care for such independence, and they could easily enforce their will. All they would have to do is cut us off completely by allowing no shuttlecraft to enter or leave our port."

"They wouldn't risk destroying their own project," Karim objected, "not after spending so many resources on getting us this far."

"But they wouldn't be destroying the project. The parasol would still shade Venus, and seeding the atmosphere could proceed. All they'd have to do is wait out the island settlers, who would eventually have to bow to Earth's will or else face a slow death, and it would be a slow death, Karim. They could survive for a while on greenhouse crops, and the life support systems can be maintained, but sooner or later crucial components of our systems would fail, ones the islanders would be unable to replace. After all of the sacrifices Earth has made for this project, to ensure that their culture will take root on another world, do you really believe that they will ever let us go our own way?"

She was voicing some of his own fears. He pressed his hands against the dome, felt the surface yield, and found himself sitting in a chair, his hands gripping the armrests.

"Where am I?" he called out.

"Aboard the *Beverwyck*," a voice replied, and then he remembered. "I suggest," the AI continued through his band, "that you reset your mind-tour specifications, Mukhtar Karim. You can enjoy your scenarios while still remaining somewhat aware that you are experiencing a mind-tour. You do not have to put yourself into a temporary amnesia, to forget that you are living here and not there."

"Ah, but then the experience would not be nearly as convincing."

"It does not have to be convincing, only diverting."

"I prefer the sense of reality." In his scenarios, however briefly and imperfectly, he could capture the conviction that the terraforming he dreamed of could succeed. He needed to hold to that conviction even more now.

* * * * * *

Karim had suggested that, after the welcoming ceremony and his meeting with the mayor of New York City, he and Greta invite Lauren, her brother Zack, and her bondmate Roberto to dine with them at the New World Trade Center's rooftop restaurant.

"No, Karim," Greta had replied. "Forgive me, but I don't think that would be at all appropriate. It might offend some people's sensitivities. There are certain episodes in our history we've never forgotten, even if they did happen over a century and a half ago."

He understood, given the long memory of his own people,

and had settled for giving the *Beverwyck*'s owners the day off and permission to use his credit while they dined at the restaurant by themselves.

A small city hovercraft was sent to take him and Greta to City Hall. The mayor, Donata Grenwell, met him with three members of the city council, then led him to her office while the council members took Greta on a tour of the building. Karim and the mayor sipped coffee while Donata spoke of the city's need for more engineers to design and supervise the construction of more dikes, and for more physicians and vaccines against the viruses and tropical diseases that afflicted so many in New York. Karim assured her that the Council of Mukhtars would do everything possible to help her.

Donata Grenwell stood up, and seemed about to lead him to the door, then hesitated. "I wish—" she began as she adjusted the scarf around her head that she had worn in deference to his people's customs.

"Yes?" he said, waiting.

"I wish there was something else to do besides just shoring up what we have, repairing the damage." She gazed at him steadily with her pale gray eyes, then looked away. "How we used to push ourselves in the old days. I'd hear the stories from my grandmother—she was just barely old enough to remember. Always on the move, she said, always impatient, knowing nothing would stay the same from one year to the next, always having to keep up with everything and be fast on your feet, always having something to look forward to and be optimistic about. That's how it was for us once."

"I understand," Karim murmured.

"But the Council of Mukhtars has more important things to worry about," Mayor Grenwell said. "You have to keep things going and keep them from getting any worse, and if we manage to accomplish that much, it'll be a job well done."

"God willing," Karim said, "but I wonder if we can do that without also looking forward and dreaming of something new."

The mayor arched her brows, looking surprised, then showed

him to the door.

* * * * * * *

Two aides to the mayor took him and Greta on a short tour of the lower Manhattan waterways and canals. Their watercraft, a small flat-bottomed boat with a canopy to shade them from the sun, wound its way among canals crowded with waterbuses, gondolas, and motorboat taxis; a police boat carrying five officers followed them. The air smelled of sulfur and brine; the shouts of the vendors who had set up shop on docks and small barges were nearly drowned out by the sound of the traffic. Occasionally a small personal motorcraft sped past the slower vessels, rocking Karim's boat in its wake. The steep cliffs of highrise apartment buildings and commercial establishments loomed on either side of the canals. The beaches south of Brooklyn had been lost to the rising sea before the dikes and seawalls had been raised on higher ground, and the oceans were also gaining on lower Manhattan. As long as the water could be channeled into canals, and the buildings here remained accessible to workers and residents, better to expend their ever scarcer resources elsewhere; so Donata Grenwell had told him.

They arrived at the pier near the plaza of the New World Trade Center before noon, but already the hot weather of late March was making Karim sweat under his white ceremonial robe and headdress; the humid air seemed as thick as soup. Even Greta, who had grown up in such a climate, looked uncomfortable as she dabbed at her pale damp face with a handkerchief. Karim picked up the wreath of lilies he had brought with him and stepped onto the dock, with Greta just behind him. The wreath had been his wife's recommendation, and now he felt the rightness of her advice.

The police in the boat behind them disembarked; the lieutenant walked with Karim and Greta across the wide plaza toward the glassy buildings on the other side. Other people were gathered in the plaza, some talking among themselves, but most silently watching him and his party pass. Karim was nearly at the memorial, a latticework of metal and twisted beams that surrounded a black wall bearing thousands of names, when the apparition he had been expecting to see began to take shape.

The hologram flickered into existence, and then he saw the two tall towers, translucent and ghostly, take form behind the shorter structures that had replaced them. Karim thought he heard a sigh from the people nearest him. He looked up at the towers, imagining for a moment that they might become solid, that he would be able to enter them and climb up to where they seemed to graze Heaven.

Karim whispered a prayer, then knelt to lay the wreath at the base of the memorial.

* * * * * * *

Shading Venus with a parasol had cooled the planet enough for a steady rain of carbon dioxide to begin. Over the next century and a half, oceans had formed until much of the low-lying Venusian surface was covered with carbon dioxide seas.

It's only a beginning, Karim thought. If the planet was kept in the parasol's shade, the precipitating carbon dioxide would change from rain into snow and ice. He thought of people living on the surface, enclosed in domes like those that covered the islands floating in the Venusian atmosphere, looking out at a dark frozen world that would not be a new Earth, but only a prison.

Even as that thought came to him, he found himself looking through the transparent wall of a dome at a plain of ice illuminated only by the light from inside this dome and another that glowed in the distance. Suddenly angry, he struck the dome with his fist. Why had he come to this settlement only to imprison himself?

But he knew the answer to that question. The alternatives he and his fellow Earthfolk faced were fairly stark. They could live here, gaining a precarious foothold on Venus until they solved the new set of problems the terraforming project had presented, or they could return to an Earth growing ever hotter and ever more unlivable.

Earth, he thought, might eventually resemble the Venus that had existed before terraforming began, with its oceans boiled away, an atmospheric pressure great enough to crush an unprotected man, and temperatures hot enough to melt metals. He imagined feeling such heat even as he gazed out at Venus's icy wastes.

"Karim," Greta said.

He opened his eyes. He was lying on a bed in a darkened room; his beard seemed damp. Greta leaned over him; strands of her graying hair had slipped from under her scarf. The air around him had grown so warm that he was sweating under his light cotton robe.

"The homeostat wasn't working," Greta went on, "but Zack fixed it just a few minutes ago. The temperature in our rooms should be back to normal in less than an hour. By the way, he and the others told me that they very much enjoyed dining in the city today." She spoke in Anglaic, as she always did when they were alone; her Arabic was fluent without having ever become truly eloquent or poetic. She moved closer to the edge of the bed and gently slipped his band from his head. "You were to rest, not lie here accessing cyberminds."

"I was taking another of my mind-tours."

"Are you all right?"

"Just a bit disoriented," he replied. "Where are we?"

"The *Beverwyck*'s just north of the George Washington Bridge. Zack decided that we should stop at the docks here for the night. We'll leave before sunrise, before the traffic gets too heavy. I hope you'll be able to keep away from your mind-tours long enough to enjoy a view of the Palisades."

"I wonder if that view will be as impressive as the one I saw in a mind-tour some time ago," Karim said as the remembered image of a ridge of unbroken rock came to him. That simulation had been of the Palisades as they might have appeared four hundred years ago, but the waters had risen since then, creeping higher up the sides of the cliffs.

"Mind-tours." Greta sat down on the bed and reached for his hand. "I've never seen you so caught up in such entertainments. You've had your band on during almost every free moment we've had since we landed in Washington."

"I haven't been seeking mere diversion, Greta. I'm still exploring my terraforming scenarios."

"Venus. I see." For a moment, he expected her to voice the objections he had heard from her before. "I could tell you to give up such hopes," she continued, "but you wouldn't listen to me anyway, and maybe I'm no longer so sure of my reasons for arguing against your dream in the past. The effort would be costly, but that has to be measured against the possibility of making an entirely new habitable planet for ourselves. It might be better to leave Venus alone in order to learn what we can about it, but we'd also learn much about that world during any terraforming project."

"There is the possibility of failure," Karim murmured.

"Of course. There always is. Still, we could fail at making Venus another Earth and yet make many important advances in technology and science. We might even learn enough to restore Earth's ecology many centuries from now. And—" She was silent for a while. "I think it'll be easier for you to know that you never have to doubt my loyalty."

"If I push too hard," he said, "you know what the consequences will be."

"I don't care about exile. I don't care even if they force us to move to some desolate place with just enough to keep us alive, because if the Council punishes you simply for dreaming, there isn't much hope for any of us anyway."

"My dear—"

"I just wish that you wouldn't keep escaping this way."

"It's not an escape," he said, "at least not entirely. You seem to have gained more faith in my dream at the same time I've been in danger of losing some of my own. I'm trying to regain my convictions, Greta. I'm afraid that some of the other Mukhtars' doubts have begun to creep into me."

"I hope not, Karim." She clutched his hand more tightly. "I don't want to see what you would be like without your dreams."

* * * * * * *

To seed the atmosphere of Venus with microorganisms that would break down its atmosphere of carbon dioxide was a formidable task, but the biologists working on the Venusian islands had lived up to Karim's expectations. After enough failures to dampen even his confidence, a team of biologists headed by his wife had developed new strains of red and green algae that were capable of ingesting the sulfur dioxide of Venus's rains, and also a strain of cyanobacteria that could survive without sunlight while oxygenating the atmosphere. Greta's report had minimized the frustration and expense of all the failed strains, all of the bioengineered microorganisms that had shown early promise only to fail and die in the lethal atmosphere.

Years had passed since the first seeding, and the new aerial ecosystem of algae and bacteria had survived, even thrived. Karim still saw the same familiar darkness outside the translucent dome of his island station, and the misty acidic rains continued to fall, condensing as the planet cooled, but changes had already been measured—small decreases in the level of sulfur dioxide in the rains and the presence of more iron and copper sulfides, of more carbon dioxide broken up into carbon and oxygen.

The biologists had begun their bioengineering of new strains of algae at about the same time as a team of engineers, under the direction of Hassan Tantawi, had begun to aim giant tanks of solid compressed hydrogen at Venus from their station orbiting Saturn. As oxygen was freed by the changes in the Venusian atmosphere, hydrogen would be needed to combine with the oxygen to form water. But setting up the Saturnian station and building the giant skyhooks that siphoned off the hydrogen had taken too great a share of the project's resources. Karim was beginning to worry that some on the Council of Mukhtars might halt the process of terraforming at the stage they had already reached. They would never admit openly that the project had grown too costly, that they might put an end to its work altogether; the Council was much more likely to make noises about "suspending operations temporarily" and "conducting more studies." The Mukhtars would tell themselves that something could still be learned from what had already been accomplished.

"I'll tell you what the problem actually is," Ali bin Oman said. Karim abruptly found himself sitting on a cushion in front of a low table. Ali sat across from him, sipping from a cup.

"The problem?" Karim asked.

"Why this project is stalled. Why we're likely to be here just long enough to see the next stage through to its conclusion before they suspend operations and haul us back to Earth. It's as I've always said—sooner or later, we'll have to reach out to our brethren in their space habitats. They wouldn't have been able to survive and to build their habitats without developing technologies superior to ours. They could help us in our work here, God willing, if we can swallow our pride long enough to ask them for their aid."

"Our fellow Mukhtars would force you off the Council if you voiced such ideas," Karim said.

"They'd probably do worse than that to me."

"You're also forgetting that the habitat-dwellers don't approve of terraforming planets."

"That may be overstating the case," Ali said. "They don't see the need for such efforts, since they're able to engineer their own environments in their artificial worlds. But I think they might be interested in contributing to a project that would add to their store of knowledge. That would be their only reimbursement from us—what they might learn. We have little else to offer them."

"The Council would never agree to that," Karim said. "This project was to be our refutation of that space-dwelling culture, our jihad, our moral equivalent of a war against them. To turn to them now means to admit that we've failed."

Ali grew translucent, then faded out. The room slowly darkened, and became again Karim's cabin aboard the *Beverwyck*.

* * * * * * *

Karim watched from the prow with Greta until the basalt cliffs of the Palisades were behind them, then went below as more boat traffic began to crowd the waterway—ferries crossing between New York and New Jersey, water buses moving north and south, sailboats, small hovercraft, patched-together vessels riding so low in the water that it seemed they might sink.

Lauren's bondmate Roberto was in the sitting room, drinking coffee. The young man got to his feet and bowed slightly, pressing his fingers to his forehead.

"Please sit down," Karim said as he settled himself on the couch across from Roberto. "It's good that we got an early start," he continued. "The traffic is going to slow us up."

"Only for a while, sir. This is rush hour, but in a couple of hours, we'll have clear passage. You'll be at West Point by midafternoon, if not sooner." Roberto poured more coffee for himself and a cup for Karim. "Uh, I have to ask you for a favor, Mukhtar."

Karim waved a hand. "Ask it, then."

"Of course you're free to refuse it."

"Of course."

"I had a message this morning from my brother Pablo. He's been living in Poughkeepsie for the past two years, but he's been offered a position in Albany. He asked if he could come aboard and travel there with us."

"What kind of position?" Karim asked.

"Designing educational mind-tours for the New York Museum and the Albany Institute. He trained as an engineer, but he got interested enough in mind-tour design to learn something about that and do some work on the side for a couple of tour producers." Roberto sipped his coffee. "He wouldn't be in your way, and Zack said he'd put him up in his room. And there's no black marks on his record, so you can clear him with the police if you're worried about security."

Karim frowned. "I am here on a mission of friendship," he said softly. "My wife is a native of this region. I have no worries about our personal safety." He tactfully refrained from mentioning the implant in his arm that would summon both medical personnel and a squad of Guardians to his side if danger threatened, and the pin-sized camera on his headdress that would preserve images of any assailant.

"But if you'd rather not have Pablo aboard, we can just go upriver as planned and head back for him later after we leave you and your wife off."

Karim raised a brow. He had not expected the stolid Roberto to have an educated brother. "Would Pablo lose his chance at his new position if he didn't travel with us?"

"No, sir. He wasn't supposed to start his new work right away. It's more that he wanted time to find new quarters and get settled. Anyway, I shot a message back to him saying I'd ask, but I didn't promise him anything."

Karim made his decision immediately. "Tell your brother that he's welcome to come aboard."

Roberto grinned, then stood up. "Thank you, Mukhtar Karim." He bowed deeply from the waist. "You don't know how much—"

"It's nothing." Karim retreated from the young man's effusive gratitude into the bedroom.

* * * * * * *

If Venus was ever to acquire Earthlike weather patterns, the planet would have to rotate more rapidly; keeping the Venusian "day" of two hundred and forty-three days meant an inhospitable world of hot and cold extremes. Any human beings living there would have the undesirable alternatives of either living in completely enclosed environments or being constantly on the move in order to stay within a narrow habitable band between scorching heat and excessive cold, in the twilight between sunlight and darkness.

Ali bin Oman and Greta occupied themselves with a game of chess while Karim perused the report they had presented to him. The choices proposed by the engineers to solve the problem of Venus's climate seemed equally problematic. The parasol could continue to shade Venus entirely while a soletta and mirror orbited the planet to provide reflected sunlight, or a large asteroid or object of similar size could be hurled at Venus to speed up its rotation.

When Karim looked up from his screen, Ali and Greta were watching him, ignoring their game. "The soletta and mirror design is ingenious," Karim began, "but it would require constant maintenance by a civilization that would have to endure over millions of years while sustaining its interest in this project. That's expecting rather a lot of a species that's managed only a few thousand years of continuity in its cultures at most."

"A continuously maintained artificial environment," Greta murmured. "That's what we'd have, not a natural Earthlike world. That isn't what our terraforming project was supposed to be about."

"Then we should aim an asteroid at Venus," Ali said, "and when it hits, God willing, the impact increases its spin." He peered at his pocket screen. "If it hits near the equator—"

"That powerful an impact would dissipate a lot of energy," Karim said, "perhaps enough to destroy what we've accomplished so far. That is unless we settle for a Venusian day that would last for a couple of months or even longer."

"What we need," Greta murmured, "is some sort of planetary spin motor that can greatly speed up the rate of rotation but without damaging Venus."

Karim shook his head. "In other words, a technology that doesn't exist."

Greta and Ali flickered, then disappeared. Karim stood at the edge of the island, gazing down at shadowed Venus. A bright spot suddenly appeared near the equator, then blossomed into a flare. His pocket screen was still in his hands, but he already knew what the screen would tell him. Venus was beginning to turn more rapidly, but the crust near the impact point was melting. How long would it take for the heat generated by the collision to dissipate? Long enough, perhaps, to stall the work of terraforming until an increasingly impatient Council decided to abandon it altogether.

We've failed, he thought; after all this time, we've destroyed our work.

Something brushed against his hand. "Karim," someone said from far away; he recognized Greta's voice, and remembered. He lifted his band from his head, returning to the *Beverwyck*.

"Karim," Greta said again. She wore a long blue robe, dark blue tunic, and scarf; she took the linking band from him and handed him his formal headdress. "It's time to go."

"Yes, I know." He was already dressed in his formal white robes. He stood up and followed her out to the deck.

* * * * * * *

General Michael Yamamura, the commandant at the West Point Military Academy, was a small gray-haired man with erect posture and a piercing gaze. He met Karim and Greta at the north dock just beyond a sharp bend in the river, listened without comment as Karim rattled off his ceremonial greeting, then left them with two cadets to guide them on a tour of Kosciusko's Garden. Karim and his wife were still there admiring the roses when General Yamamura rejoined them. The two cadets left with Greta while the commandant outlined their upcoming schedule of events: dinner that night with the commandant's staff, a luncheon the next day with a few members of the faculty, a question-and-answer session with their most promising cadets.

Throughout the dinner and the walk back to the hotel near

Gees Point where Karim and Greta were being housed, the commandant avoided any mention of the issue that had to be uppermost in his mind. Karim finally had to bring up the subject the next day, just before lunch. Although the graduates of West Point were to be absorbed into the Guardian force that served the Mukhtars, the Council would not interfere with either their course of study or with Academy custom. The cadets would be free to wear their gray uniforms until they won their commissions and donned the black uniform of the Guardians. Any officers serving at the Point would also be allowed to wear gray, and the Council had no objection to their continuing to fly their ceremonial flags, even though the country represented by the red, white, and blue banners no longer existed. The commandant had not been able to completely conceal his gratitude and relief.

Greta was part of his audience in the auditorium with the cadets, at which Karim was peppered with so many questions by the young men and women that General Yamamura finally had to declare the session over. Even after that, several cadets followed Karim and Greta back to the *Beverwyck*, anxious perhaps to impress a Mukhtar who might later consider them for a post on his staff. Their questions, on various subjects, had soon revealed the central concern of the cadets: that as officers in the Guardians, they might be reduced to being little more than part of an international police force, there to keep the peace and rein in anyone who threatened their world's precarious security. Even those officers who eventually won their way to a post on one of the orbiting space stations would not be looking beyond their own world, as their predecessors had done. They would be there only to monitor resources and changes in the weather, to repair satellites and to patrol spaceports and industrial satellites; their only purpose in looking to the heavens at all would be to track and divert any interplanetary body that might threaten Earth. Their mental universe would forever be enclosed by practicalities.

* * * * * * *

The sea to the south of Ishtar Terra was a wrinkled gray surface that only occasionally swelled into waves. A patch of dim yellow-white light, all that could be seen of the sun through the open slats of the parasol that still shaded Venus, was reflected by the ocean. Karim could walk along the shoreline without having to fear the crushing atmospheric pressure that had once existed here, but he supposed that any future settlers would have to wear much the same protective clothing as he did. His suit protected him from the heat of the day, because even with the parasol limiting the amount of sunlight that reached the planet, a day that lasted two months meant a steady rise in temperature, while the equally long night resulted in frigid cold. The helmet over his head and the tank on his back were necessary because the atmosphere was still too rich in carbon dioxide to be breathable.

There was life in the Venusian ocean, a stew of microbial life forms, but he wondered how many would ever evolve on the dry and barren land masses. Hundreds of years for this, Karim thought, and vast numbers of lost lives that he would not care to enumerate, and what they had won for themselves was a sterile world, not the new Earth of their dreams.

Venus would change in time, become something else, but not soon enough for the Council, for whom a wait of thousands of years might as well be a million. They had wasted resources and lives in remaking this planet, and now, as if to punish Venus for their failure, they had turned it into a prison. The domes on the plateaus of Ishtar Terra had quickly filled with those who offended the Mukhtars, who were a danger to others, or who were simply inconvenient. If Venus was to be ugly and barren, the Council would make it uglier still, and any people exiled here would never escape.

No, Karim thought, and tore his band from his head.

He was still in the *Beverwyck*'s sitting room, but found himself standing in front of his chair. He sat down again and thought of the kind of report he might write when he had completed his tour of this Nomarchy. He could write of the Washington functionaries whose lives had shrunk to the management of ever-decreasing resources, the Jersey seawall workers whose labor was largely designed to postpone the inevitable, the New York mayor who looked forward to little, the West Point cadets who would never see glory or true accomplishment, and of the need for a dream that might give all of them some hope and enlarge their universe. Or he could note that the Atlantic Federation was under control, that its people had finally come to see the necessity for being ruled by the Council, that the old hatreds and animosities had finally died in their defeated hearts.

He knew which of those reports his fellow Mukhtars would prefer, and which report was likely to guarantee that his old age would be one of powerlessness and exile.

* * * * * * *

In Poughkeepsie, Karim was scheduled only for a brief meeting with the mayor and a town meeting with a few hundred of the small city's residents and anyone else who cared to participate on the public channels. Unlike the cadets of West Point, the citizens of Poughkeepsie asked few questions, and most of their inquiries were about practical concerns: renewed efforts to rid the Hudson of the pollutants that had plagued it even before the Resource Wars, insect control and disease prevention, aid for their rapidly failing farmlands. Karim assured them that the Council was already drawing up plans to help them.

His day ended at the riverfront, where, north of an old bridge that spanned the river, the *Beverwyck* was docked next to several ramshackle boats. A few people were on the decks of their sailboats and cruisers; they stared at Karim and Greta with the same lack of interest they had shown that morning. Out on the Hudson, a sloop with triangular sails glided past, a graceful reminder of an earlier age.

Karim let Greta board first, then followed. Lauren and Zack

nodded at them from the stern. "We'll have our supper after we're underway again," Karim said to the couple, "and perhaps my wife and I will dine on deck." It would be a pleasant way to pass the evening, moving slowly past the forested hills while dining.

"I wouldn't advise that, sir," Zack said, glancing heavenward. "It looks like we might get a storm." Karim looked up and then noticed the thickening clouds. "I'm thinking of waiting here to see how it goes."

"I'm supposed to be in the town of Hudson tomorrow by noon," Karim said.

"You needn't worry about that, Mukhtar Karim. Storm isn't likely to last all night, and if it was going to be a bad one, they would have put out a warning and told us to get you ashore. We'll be on our way before dawn with plenty of time to spare." Zack brushed back a strand of his long blond hair. "Roberto's below with his brother. It was mighty kind of you to say he could come along."

"It's no trouble at all." He went below, Greta just behind him, to find Roberto in the sitting room with another tall, broad-shouldered, dark-skinned man who strongly resembled him.

The two quickly rose to their feet. "My brother, Pablo Mainz-Aquino," Roberto said. "This is Mukhtar Karim al-Anwar." Karim was about to extend his hand when Pablo bowed slightly and touched his fingers to his forehead. "And his wife, Greta Gansevoort-Mehdi." Pablo nodded in her direction.

"Please sit down," Karim said. The two men sat down again on the sofa. Karim and Greta seated themselves in two of the chairs.

"I'm grateful you let me come aboard, sir," Pablo said.

"Your brother is part owner of this craft. I wasn't about to refuse passage to one of his people as long as there was room. He tells me that you will be working as a mind-tour designer."

Pablo nodded. His gaze was more direct than his brother's, the expression on his broad brown face more alert. "It's what I've always wanted to do, but the only way you can actually train for it, at least now, is by working with a producer and picking up skills along the way."

"I suppose that's why you studied engineering," Karim said, "so that you would have something to fall back on."

"That's part of it, sir, but it was mostly because I thought some training in mechatronics and bioengineering might make me a better designer. Any real knowledge a designer can bring to a mind-tour, whether it's engineering or biology or a background in history, can help him bring more detail and reality to his creations. Most of the mind-tours we've got are either adventure scenarios or virtual tours of museums and other sites, and most of them are put together by people who are largely trained in audio and visual arts."

"There are a number of educational mind-tours," Karim said.

"I'd call most of them training sessions rather than educational virtuals," Pablo said, "since they're designed to take someone through the steps needed to perform certain tasks. And the others, the historical mind-tours and such, are mostly variations on adventure scenarios. All they teach you is how to escape while pretending you're actually learning something. Serious students don't spend much time with them." He paused. "We're still a long way from what mind-tours might become as an art form."

"An art form?" Greta asked.

Pablo nodded. "We've reached the point where the mind-tourist doesn't run into as many of the glitches that destroy the illusion of reality, where the experience almost seems as detailed as the actual world. That's an accomplishment in itself, but there's still the potential for much more."

"And what sort of art do you envision?" Karim asked.

"It's hard to put it into words." Pablo frowned. "I think what I'm looking for is a way to create a virtual world that doesn't exist, that never existed, but that we might bring into being someday, that's actually possible to create. That may sound like I'm just talking about an elaborate sort of modeling process, and that's part of it, but maybe it would also inspire—"

Roberto was making surreptitious gestures at his brother with his hands. "Excuse me, sir...ma'am," Pablo murmured. "I'm taking up too much of your time." Outside, there was the low rumble of thunder. "And I'd better help the others secure the boat before it rains."

"When would you like your supper served, Mukhtar Karim?" Roberto asked.

"After you've finished whatever there is to do," Karim replied.

"That'll be about an hour, sir. I'll bring it to you here." Roberto went up the steps, his brother at his heels.

* * * * * * *

The storm was upon them by the time Karim and Greta were in bed. The boat rocked under them; the small porthole in the bedroom was suddenly white with light, and then a crack of thunder made his wife start and reach for his hand.

"It's all right," Karim said.

"I know." As a girl, Greta had lived through having her childhood home destroyed by one of the fierce late spring storms that sometimes ravaged New York and Massachusetts; storms had made his wife nervous ever since.

He held her hand until he knew she was sleeping, then lay there listening to the thunder growing more faint. He thought of Pablo and his ambitions for mind-tour designing. The young man was the first person he had met in some days who actually looked beyond what was around him, who seemed hopeful.

Karim slipped from the bed and put on a robe over his long tunic, then went out to the sitting room and up the steps to the deck. The rain had already stopped; the air was still humid, but cooler. Two lanterns were on in the stern, where a man was folding up a tarp. Roberto, Karim thought; and then the man turned and he saw Pablo's face.

"Salaam, sir," Pablo said. "I told the others to get some sleep while I took care of this. Zack'll get up in a couple of hours and have us on our way to Hudson."

"Good."

"Is there anything I can get for you? There's some iced tea in the galley."

"No, thank you." Karim sat down in a deck chair while Pablo stowed the tarp in a large chest. "I would like to ask something of you, though." He was silent for a few moments, choosing his words. "For a few years now, I have spent some of my spare time doing mind-tour designs myself. Not that I was able to do anything that would measure up to the efforts of a professional, needless to say."

Pablo sat down in a facing chair. "I don't suppose you can call any of us professionals," he murmured, "not in the usual sense, with formal courses of study and certificates. It's not anything anyone can train for except by actually doing the work, at least not yet."

"In other words," Karim said, "you serve an apprenticeship."

"You could put it that way. And then you find out if it's something you can do well or not, and if you can't—well, you see why I got my degrees in engineering." Pablo leaned back in his chair. "What sorts of mind-tours have you been working on?"

"This may strike you as odd," Karim replied, "but my subject has been the planet of Venus. I began with depictions of Venus as it is now, based largely on data from our probes."

"Then I assume most of the data is a few decades old, since near space exploration isn't one of our higher priorities these days." Pablo smiled. "I took an interest in space exploration at the university, but knew I wouldn't find any work in that field."

"Unfortunately, you're right. Yet I persist in this notion that human beings aren't at their best, aren't going to accomplish anything worthwhile and lasting, until they look beyond themselves to something greater. It's an idea that is somewhat at odds with the prevailing opinion of the other members of the Council of Mukhtars, who grow ever more concerned with more practical matters."

Pablo nodded. "But why Venus? As the subject of your mind-tours, I mean."

"There is much we can learn from Venus, and not only by sending more probes, although that is certainly something we should be doing. For some time now, I have been proposing to my fellow Mukhtars that we consider a detailed study of the feasibility of terraforming Venus—in other words, altering its biosphere and geology enough to make it an Earthlike world, God willing, one where our descendants might be able to live."

The young man let out his breath. "You don't dream small, sir."

"I have presented a number of practical arguments for undertaking such an ambitious project, the primary one being that we might, in centuries to come, need the knowledge gained from terraforming to restore Earth to what it was before the greenhouse effect became so troublesome. But I also think that it's necessary for other reasons, one of them being that need of human beings to look outward. We've become so preoccupied with this world, with sustaining its life and trying to keep things from getting any worse, that we're in danger of forgetting that there's anything beyond it."

Karim had meant to tell Pablo only a little about his preoccupation. Instead, he found himself speaking of his growing conviction that a terraforming project might offer rewards that would far outweigh the huge cost in resources and the long-term commitment to an end that even their grandchildren would not live to see, a project that had to be measured in centuries, perhaps even in millennia if the obstacles along the way proved too great.

"I put together a number of mind-tours," Karim concluded, "because I thought that perhaps they might be useful in presenting my case. At least that's what I told myself, but I suspect that I was trying to convince myself as much as anyone else. And as it turns out, they've become a private pursuit of mine. The scenarios fail at some point—that's the problem. And I keep thinking—" He paused, having little more to say.

"Sir," Pablo said after a while, "would you mind if I took your Venusian tours?"

"Definitely not. I was going to ask you if you would take a look at them. I've tried to make them as detailed as possible, but they may seem crude to you, and they are personalized, since I tended to use people I know in certain of the roles. They don't come anywhere close to capturing my vision."

"Maybe you just need someone to take a fresh look at them." Pablo folded his arms. "I'll see if I can come up with any design of my own that might be what you want."

"I would be most grateful. And now, I had better get some sleep if I am to be ready for my appearances tomorrow." Karim got to his feet. For the first time in several days, he had no desire to escape into one of his virtuals.

* * * * * * *

In Hudson, Karim was scheduled for a meeting with the town council, a stop at the local train station, a question and answer session with several of the town's merchants, and an afternoon picnic in a riverside park with schoolchildren. Apparently the people of Hudson were determined to get as much out of his visit as possible, since no Mukhtar had ever traveled there before. He heard much the same kinds of remarks as he had in other places, found himself repeating most of his earlier statements, and saw the same sorts of passive, resigned looks on the faces of the people.

Greta had been at his side throughout the day. The sun was setting behind the mountains to the west as they returned to the *Beverwyck*; out on the wide river, he saw a lighted riverboat, decks crowded with passengers, gliding past the darkened hills. The pale blue sky was vivid with the streaks of purple and salmon-colored clouds. He did not see anybody aboard his craft, but the *Beverwyck*'s owners had spent the day in Hudson seeing old friends and had mentioned plans to have dinner with a few of them.

"I'll go to the galley and make us some supper," Greta said to Karim.

"Don't bother, my dear. I ate too much at the picnic. The people of Hudson were too hospitable. I didn't expect them to serve us so much food."

"I imagine that was largely for the benefit of the children. It's probably the best meal most of them have had in a while."

He followed her down the short staircase into the sitting room. Pablo was there, sitting at the desk, a band around his head and a pocket screen lying on the desk. Karim cleared his throat softly, so as not to startle the young man; but Pablo was still and seemed completely absorbed.

Karim sat down on the sofa, Greta at his side. At last Pablo took off his band and turned away from the desk. "I hope we didn't disturb you," Karim said. "I thought you might have gone into Hudson with the others."

"I looked at your tours. I can come back to Hudson another time." Pablo rested his arm on the desk. "For someone who calls himself an amateur, Mukhtar Karim, you haven't done so badly. I'll have to look at more documents on the subject of terraforming—"

"There aren't that many," Karim interrupted.

"Then it shouldn't take me long to read them. Anyway, I'm beginning to think that your problem here isn't in your depictions, but in your assumptions. You assume that most of the science and technology required for a project of this magnitude is at least within our grasp now, even if it doesn't yet exist, that given enough time and resources, we could bring it into being and use it in terraforming Venus. What you haven't done is anticipated new technologies and new knowledge and allowed for them in your scenarios."

Karim frowned. "I thought of that, but I don't see how I could create something at all plausible by factoring in unknowns."

"And I don't see how you can't," Pablo said. "You have to assume that each stage of any terraforming project is likely to yield something new."

"Of course." Perhaps he was too used to thinking of limits and of what could not be accomplished during his years on the

Council of Mukhtars.

"What I suggest," Pablo continued, "is that I sketch out a mind-tour by beginning at the end and working backwards from there."

"What exactly do you mean?" Greta asked.

"I'd begin with a vision of Venus as an Earthlike world, already terraformed," Pablo replied, "but while being rigorous about making sure that anything depicted in the scenario doesn't violate any known physical laws. What that should give us is a vision of an actual possibility even if we can't show exactly how it might come about at each stage. With mind-tour design, I've found, you have to have a strong sense of where you're headed. You can't just hope you'll end up with something convincingly real."

"I have a sense of where my scenarios should be headed," Karim said. "The problem is getting there."

"And I still think that's because your assumptions are too limiting. But it's pointless to talk about it this way. I'd like to see what I might do, but I don't know how much time I'll have."

Greta glanced at Karim, then at Pablo. "We'll be in Albany tomorrow," she said. "I'll be visiting my family while my husband puts in his appearances, but he'll be staying aboard the *Beverwyck* for three days and then we're to go over to Boston by airship. You're free to stay here for that long. Will that be enough time for you?"

"I think so, ma'am. It's worth a try."

"Then try it," Karim said, feeling the unfamiliar emotion of anticipation.

* * * * * * *

He did not expect Pablo to come up with a sophisticated virtual in so little time, yet Karim found himself buoyed by the young man's absorption in his efforts. When he and Greta left the *Beverwyck* in the morning, she for her brother's estate just south of the city and he for his scheduled events, Pablo had already been up for a while, gulping coffee as he called up documents on his screen, fiddled with the desk console, or accessed the *Beverwyck*'s mind. Karim had given him complete access to all of his records and had promised to cover any expenses out of his credit.

Probably nothing would come of it; at most, Pablo might be able to send Karim a rough of a Venusian tour later on. Even so, the interest Pablo took in the project had lifted Karim's spirits. He would finish his travels in the Atlantic Federation and return to the New Islamic Nomarchy ready to demand that the rest of the Council reconsider his hoped-for Venus project, at least to the extent of funding a preliminary study. He would find ways to get more of the Mukhtars to support him, and if he failed at that, perhaps he could make enough of an impression during their deliberations to move a future Council member to take up the cause. And if he offended enough people or frightened enough of them into thinking that he was obsessed and mad enough to deserve exile, he would console himself with the thought that he had fought as hard as he could for his vision.

His more hopeful mood lent more eloquence to his speeches and brief remarks; his improved disposition seemed to elicit more friendliness and warmth from the people he encountered. Hiram Marcus, the governor of New York, a figurehead of little power who still maintained an office in the decaying rococo splendor of the State Capitol Building, gave Karim an impromptu tour of the skyscrapers and marble expanse of the Empire State Plaza; soon the panhandlers and sellers of cheap goods who usually set up shop there were calling out greetings to the Mukhtar and governor. The curators of the New York Museum guided him through their library and archives, and he found himself encouraging them to develop exhibits that would look forward as well as back in time.

During the second day of his visit, Karim was taken on a tour of a few of Albany's historic mansions, and soon collected a crowd of interested people who followed his driver and van from place to place. On the third day, more people were waiting for him on the pier when he left the *Beverwyck*. He offered a few lengthy remarks about the five-hundred-odd years of their city's history, grateful for all the stories Greta had told him about her long lineage of Dutch, Irish, and South Asian ancestors who had settled here, while the city officials who had come to fetch him to a luncheon fidgeted and glanced at the timepieces on their fingers and wrists. "Too bad you aren't running for mayor," one of them said to him later. "You'd nail the election."

Greta rejoined him that afternoon in Albany's Washington Park, where they viewed tulips of various colors already in full bloom from an open trolley; the city was celebrating its annual Tulip Festival. "In the old days, long before my time, we held the festival in May," the city council president explained to Karim and Greta, although they already knew that. "But of course the tulips bloom much earlier in the spring now."

The day was warm, but not overly humid; a gentle and persistent breeze cooled Karim's face. People strolled along the roads and walkways or sat on the grass near tulip beds; at the park's small lake, children were feeding the ducks. Karim and Greta watched them from a small arched bridge, and he suddenly wished that he could remain here for a few more days.

They returned to the *Beverwyck* in the evening. The trolley carried them down the steep hill below the State Capitol, where men and women in Dutch costumes were sweeping the sidewalks, and let them off; they walked slowly along the riverfront toward the port, trailed at a discreet distance by three policemen. An old sailing ship was moored at one dock; another old vessel, a twentieth century battleship, was tied up at another dock. The port was quiet, the day's visitors gone. The Hudson River flowed past, dark gray in the evening light, and he imagined it becoming finally cleansed of the chemicals and wastes that had poisoned it for so long.

Lauren, Zack, and Roberto were waiting on the *Beverwyck*'s deck. Karim thanked them for their services and told them that a hovercraft would be there early in the morning to take him and Greta to the airship port.

"Glad to hear it, Mukhtar," Lauren said. "We'll have time to look at the tulips before we have to pick up our new passengers in Troy."

"You're free to wander around the city tonight if you like," Karim said. "We won't need anything this evening."

"Thanks, sir." Roberto offered a quick grin. "My brother's still aboard. He says he's finished with that job you gave him."

The three left, hurrying down the dock; Karim and Greta went below. Pablo stood up as Karim reached the bottom of the stairs. "I think I've got something to show you, Mukhtar Karim," Pablo said.

"I didn't expect you to finish this soon," Karim replied.

"Well, I'm not actually finished. There's more I could do with the sound, and the details need more work. Plenty of detail adds to the verisimilitude, and I was very careful not to get caught in any contradictory assumptions. But I hope—" Pablo looked away for a moment. "The longer I worked on it, the more interested I got. I think—but maybe you should take part of my tour before I say any more."

"I shall." Karim sat down in an easy chair. Pablo made a few adjustments on the desk console, then handed Karim a band.

"Are you prepared, Mukhtar Karim?" the voice of the *Beverwyck*'s AI asked.

"Yes." Karim slipped the band around his head.

Almost immediately he found himself gazing out at the expanse of a blue-gray ocean. Waves rolled toward him, lapping at the shore; he sniffed the air and smelled only a hint of salt and another, more acidic odor he did not recognize. Large white-feathered birds wheeled overhead, with wingspans as wide as those of golden eagles; he watched as one dived toward the water, then flew up with a silvery fish in its beak.

The ocean, he remembered, had been seeded with algae and plankton centuries ago, and the lifeforms that lived in the Venusian seas now were bioengineered variants of many of Earth's species that could survive in the shallower and more briny oceans of this world. But over time, they would evolve and find their own peculiar niches in this new biosphere. Karim still thought of Venus as new, even though people had been arriving here as settlers for a few centuries now, and there were generations of families who had known no other home.

He looked up at the overcast sky and knew that nearly two hours had passed since dawn. There was light behind the pale gray clouds in the west; sunlight had returned to Venus, but part of the parasol remained in place to prevent too much sunlight from reaching the planet. Night would come twelve hours from now and last for fourteen hours. Antigravitational pulse engines had increased the spin of the planet; Karim could remember hearing of the decades of work by artificial intelligences and machines in erecting those massive engines at Venus's equator. There had been more quakes after Venus had begun to spin more rapidly, and its many volcanoes had become even more active, but there had been no lasting damage, only the tectonic throes of a world at last coming to life.

A boulder as bright and hard as a diamond sat near him on the reddish-brown sand and rock of the shore. Other shining stones were on the shore, some nearly as large as the boulders, others small bright gems. He picked up one of the tiny stones and knew the jewel for what it was, a bit of calcium carbonate that had been precipitated out of the Venusian atmosphere.

He turned and saw the sheer escarpment of the Maxwell Mountains to the northeast. Patches of green covered the rock; through the mists that veiled the top of the scarp, he glimpsed more green. Forests, he thought, inhaling the cool air, and understood then that the self-replicating machines of the project, tiny devices no larger than molecules, were still at work on the high plateaus of Ishtar Terra turning the Venusian regolith into soil. The history of this terraformed planet was alive inside him, coherent and whole.

He saw then that he was not alone on the beach. A few meters to his right, a man, woman, and child were walking toward him. The woman had long light brown hair, much like Greta's in her youth, while the child clinging to her hand had the man's black hair. The three were strangers, and yet he felt that he should know them.

"Greetings," the woman said as she approached; the man smiled at Karim. "I see you're out for an early walk, too." She looked away to gaze out at the ocean. "We're still not used to it here," she continued, "but the others say it's always like that for new settlers. One moment it's our being awed by how much like Earth it is here, and the next being struck by the differences."

"It's new," the man said. "That's how it feels to me, entirely new."

Karim was about to ask them where they lived, and then it came to him: they were from a community on the Lakshmi Plateau, one of the newer settlements that had been raised in the young forests near the old settlements that were still enclosed by protective domes. Some had remained in the old settlements, preferring their unchanging climate and managed environments, but more people were leaving them, while the newer arrivals embraced living in the unspoiled outside world. The family standing with him had come to the shore in a small flying craft, to acquaint themselves with this part of their new home.

"Come with us," the child said to Karim, and suddenly he was inside their craft, flying south over the ocean. They sat in a half-circle, viewing the outside through the craft's wide windows. The wrinkles of the tesserae that had marked this area of Venus were hidden under the grayish-blue ocean; the volcano of Tellus Regio was now a black mound, red at its center, surrounded by green. They left the island of Tellus behind and flew on.

There was another continent on Venus besides the highlands of Ishtar Terra, and that was Aphrodite Terra, a scorpion-shaped land mass on Venus's equator. As that thought came to him, Karim caught a glimpse of green land to the south. Frost sometimes came to the highest parts of Ishtar, but Aphrodite was a tropical land of heat and jungle and the feral descendants of once-domesticated creatures. Aphrodite was a place for visitors and adventure seekers, not for settlers.

"Not yet, anyway," the woman said, "but that will change.

People will settle here, too." Their craft descended—

—and he was standing on a hill, amid a profusion of flowers, surrounded by the engorged blossoms of orchids, by bright red peonies, by beds of pink, blue, and yellow roses and tulips. The air was filled with the fragrances of lilacs, roses, traces of cinnamon, and an elusive musky scent.

No, Karim thought, and his vision seemed to sharpen. These flowers were not the ones he had known on Earth, but only resembled those plants. The roses were much too large; the orchids were fading from purple to lavender and then darkening again.

The sky was growing dark, too; night was coming to Venus. The brown-haired woman who reminded him of his wife stood near him, near a vine-covered tree. "There's nothing more for us to do here," she said, "except to take root here with all the other life of this world, the life we've transplanted and the life that has developed here, and to live out our lives as part of it all."

"That was the hope long ago," Karim said, "to make this a world that could ultimately sustain itself without our intervention. But we're not there yet, not as long as the parasol is needed. That will require maintenance, and if it ever fails, the increase in sunlight may return Venus to her earlier self. The oceans might boil away again. The atmosphere—"

"The parasol won't fail," she said. "The artificial intelligences maintaining it will see to that." She laughed. "And maybe a time will come when we won't need the parasol, when we'll have the power to move Venus into a new orbit farther from the sun. Our work would be completed then. Venus could truly become the sister of Earth and follow her in her orbit around the sun."

Again he recalled all the centuries of effort that had brought him to this world, and to this garden. He lifted his head as the sky darkened, and wondered if, when this side of Venus was turned away from the shield of the parasol, he would be able to glimpse the stars, if he would see Earth.

Then the garden vanished, and he was again in his chair.

Karim lifted his band from his head. Greta was murmuring

a few words to Pablo; she fell silent as they both looked toward him.

"I hope that was enough," Pablo said, "to give you an idea."

"More than enough," Karim replied. "You have exceeded my expectations, Pablo. It's quite beautiful even in this form."

"Beauty's part of what'll give this tour its punch. I'll have to do more, of course, work in more of the history. That's what will give it more of the sense of reality, being able to feel yourself in the future, but a worked-out future, looking back, remembering each part of the history, having it be more than just the passing illusion of reality. The mind-tourist becomes convinced it can be real, and maybe that can inspire others to work toward making it real."

"It's my fellow Mukhtars that I'll have to convince," Karim said.

Greta shook her head. "No, my dear, not only them. Your project would have to be something in which everyone can share."

His wife was right, as she so often was. That was also part of what he had sensed at the edges of Pablo's tour, that sense of a new world open to everyone, in which people were finally free of the old boundaries.

"I'd like you to continue working on this," he said to Pablo.

Pablo looked pleased. "I'd be honored," he said.

"I can't offer you any official position, at least not yet, so you'll have to work on it in your own time. But I'll see that you get everything you require, God willing, along with enough credit to make it worth your while."

"That might be better for me," Pablo said. "I might be able to find a way to make it part of a museum exhibit eventually, so that others can share it. That's what you want—to build a constituency, so to speak."

"Yes," Karim said.

"They might make a mind-tour about you some day," Greta said. "Karim al-Anwar, master planner in a ruined world, reaching out to encompass his dream of progress in the terraforming of Venus. We see his heroic and creative journey reviving his world as his people win a new world and use that knowledge to resurrect the old."

"That sounds most farfetched, Greta," Karim said, but allowed himself to feel his pride and hope fully. He would fight for his dream, and if he failed, others would reach out for it, younger Mukhtars and all of the people who would experience the realized world of Pablo's completed mind-tour and look beyond it. "And now," he went on, "if you don't mind, I think I would like to return to the gardens of Venus for a few moments."

He slipped on his band. For a few seconds, he was lost in the darkness, and then he saw the flowers again, their colors faded but still visible, as night came to Venus and swallowed the light.

Only for a while, he thought; the dawn would come again.

AFTERWORD FOR "VENUS FLOWERS AT NIGHT"

In their introduction to "Venus Flowers at Night" in *Year's Best SF 10* (Eos, 2005), David G. Hartwell and Kathryn Cramer wrote that this story "introduces the idea of terraforming Venus, using the equally wonderful idea of virtual reality technologies, all while managing to relate a complex future history after the United States has lost its dominant place in the world. It recalls Gene Wolfe's 'Seven American Nights.' We read it as a metafiction about the potential of SF."

This was yet another story that came upon me backwards, as it takes place long before the beginning of *Venus of Dreams*, where Karim al-Anwar appears only as a legendary historical presence. I began writing it in the late summer of 2001, and it occurred to me that Karim, a powerful figure in the future history I had written, might have had reason to travel to North America. This gave me an excuse to set the story in New York and along the Hudson River, in a landscape familiar to me and where I could show some of the possible effects of climate change. (The Albany Tulip Festival mentioned in "Venus Flowers at Night" is an annual event that's been going on for over sixty years and normally takes place in May, not in March as it does in this story.) On the morning of September 11, 2001, Malik had made it to Upper New York Bay and was near lower Manhattan when a phone call interrupted me in the middle of my writing. It was my sister, calling from her office to tell me that the World Trade Center was under attack. I turned on my television just as the second of the towers came down.

This so unnerved me—my made-up future world seemed insistent on casting its shadow into my present—that I wasn't able to continue writing until at least a month or so later. But I got past that, and finished the story.

As it happens, the opening pages of *Venus of Dreams* mention the World Trade Center, when one of my characters tells another about a trip to Manhattan, by then a drowned island with only the tops of its skyscrapers above water. My prognosticating abilities obviously failed me there.

FOLLOW THE SKY

Alonza's earliest memory of her mother was also her last.

They crouched together in a shadowed space near a wall, Alonza and her mother Amparo, looking out at a brightly lighted corridor filled with people. Men and women hurried past them, a few chattering at the people nearest them, others striding along without speaking while staring straight ahead. On the other side of the corridor, holo images of meat pies, pastries, fruits, flatbreads, and colorful bottles appeared over the heads to the passers-by, hung there for a few seconds, then vanished. Occasionally a hovercar filled with people floated past, scattering the crowds with a sharp whistling sound.

Amparo clutched a small satchel. Her hand trembled slightly as she handed her daughter a bracelet. "Listen to me," she whispered to Alonza, leaning closer. "Hang on to that bracelet for now—don't drop it."

Alonza tried to put the bracelet on, but there was no clasp, and she was unable to bend the thin band of metal tightly enough to secure it around her wrist. "It won't stay on," she said.

"It doesn't have to go on. Put it in your pocket—just make sure you hang on to it until—"

"Amparo," Alonza said, suddenly afraid. Her mother's forehead glistened with sweat, and she was panting, gasping for air. Maybe she was ill. Alonza thrust the bracelet into one of the side pockets of her tunic.

"Listen to me, child," Amparo said. "Go down this corridor, and look for a bin. Make sure no one sees you when you ditch the bracelet, then keep walking. When you get tired, sit down somewhere and act like you're waiting for somebody. I'll find you later. Got that?"

Alonza nodded.

"Then go." Amparo pushed her toward the stream of people.

Alonza darted among the forest of trousered legs, and was almost struck in the face by an arm swinging a small bag. There was no clear path through the throng. She slowed her pace, but kept going, breaking into a sprint whenever a space opened up, then slowing down again.

Amparo had sent her after the woman whose satchel they had taken. Alonza had gone up to the woman to distract her while Amparo got ready to grab the stranger's bag, but this time something had gone wrong. Amparo had moved too quickly, knocking the woman to the floor. The woman had tried to get up and had struck Amparo in the knee, and then Amparo hit her over the head with the pouch full of small stones and pebbles she usually carried in case she had to stun somebody from behind with a quick blow. Alonza remembered her mother standing over the woman's still body, looking angry and then frightened.

Sometimes Amparo just grabbed a duffel or a bag from her target right away. Sometimes she waited nearby while Alonza pleaded with the mark for directions to a gateway or whimpered that she was lost and couldn't find her mother, and then Amparo swiped the bag while her mark was still talking to Alonza. Once in a while, Amparo was able to back someone into a corner and threaten her victim into giving up an identity bracelet and personal code before knocking the mark out with a drug implant slapped against an arm. That kind of job was riskier, but often more rewarding.

"Always pick somebody smaller than you who looks nervous and afraid," Amparo had explained to a couple of her younger friends who were visiting a few nights ago. "Best luck I've had is with students who look like it's their first time away from home, or with old people. They're so scared of getting hurt that they'll give you their codes as soon as you ask."

Alonza thought of the time when her mother had come back to their room with three necklaces and two jackets bought with the credit and codes of a stolen identity bracelet. Usually Amparo might be able to make one or two purchases before a victim came to and reported a bracelet stolen, but there had been more loot that time. Amparo had been in the middle of her sixth transaction when she had seen that funny look in the merchant's eyes that told her that her stolen credit was now blocked and that a security guard was on the way.

Always know when to run: Amparo had often told her that.

She had gone far enough by now. Alonza looked back; she could no longer see the place where she and her mother had been. There was a recycling bin to her right, but too many people were loitering near the shiny metal receptacle. She turned away and kept going until the corridor branched into two more long gated hallways. People were lining up at the gates for the suborb flights.

At last she came to a stretch of gates and waiting areas that were nearly empty of people. She hurried to the nearest bin and dropped the stolen bracelet into a slot, then continued down the long lighted passageway. Her feet were beginning to hurt. Amparo had traded a stolen belt for the shoes, which were made of synthaleather, but the leather had molded itself to its former owner's feet and had never fit Alonza's very well.

She was far enough away from the bin now. Alonza moved toward one of the empty waiting areas and sat down on one of the smaller cushions, wondering how long it would take Amparo to find her.

"Stay in one place," Amparo had always told her, "and sooner or later I'll find you." Alonza sat there, listening to the announcements in Anglaic, Arabic, Español, and other languages. "Twelve-twenty suborb to Toronto, gate fifty-two, now boarding." "Two zero five, suborb to Damascus, gate forty-seven, now boarding." "Sixteen thirty-one, shuttle flight to the Wheel, leaving at thirteen-oh-two from gate ninety-five."

The Wheel! Alonza thought of the space station high above

the Earth and was soon lost in a familiar daydream. Someday, when she was older, she would board one of the shuttles and travel to the Wheel herself, to wander its curved corridors and loiter in its lounges before boarding a torchship to another place, maybe Luna or the Islands of Venus. Her daydream was formed mostly of images and experiences drawn from a mind-tour called "Journey to the Wheel," one of the mind-tours anyone was free to call up without having to spend credit, even people like her and her mother who had to live on Basic and steal anything else they needed. Most of the free mind-tours she had seen bored her; either they were designed to teach some sort of skill like homeostat repair or else they were filled with action scenes that tired her out and were often hard to remember later.

But "Journey to the Wheel" was different. It kept her interested even when there wasn't really that much going on, when she was feeling and seeing what it was like to travel in a shuttle, floating weightlessly up against the harness that held her to her seat while viewing the distant pale circular tube with spokes that was the Wheel. The end of the mind-tour always left her with a tired but happy feeling of expectation, of feeling that something wonderful was about to happen to her.

Maybe people who went to other places, who didn't just do their traveling with bands around their heads so that the cybers could feed them a mind-tour's images and sensations, had that kind of happy feeling all the time. She imagined leaving the room she shared with Amparo and never having to return to the maze of apartment buildings, cubicles, and shacks where the homeostats rarely worked and the air was always too hot and smelled of sand and dust. Maybe—

"Going to Shanghai, child?" a woman's voice said in Anglaic.

Alonza looked up. A woman with short dark hair and a kindly smile was gazing down at her.

"No," she replied hastily.

"But this is the waiting area for that suborb flight."

"I'm waiting for my mother," Alonza said. "She told me to wait here." She glanced down at her hands and saw, too late, that she had forgotten to pull the long sleeves of her tunic over her wrists. The woman would notice that she was not wearing an identity bracelet. But the stranger did not look down at her hands, but continued to stare at Alonza's face.

"I see," the woman said.

"She didn't want me to get lost," Alonza added.

"Of course. Well...." The woman turned away and sat down on a cushion near the wall.

Alonza waited as more people entered the lounge and settled themselves on the cushions around her. Among them were two Linkers, dressed in long white formal robes and kaffiyehs, each with the diamondlike gem on his forehead that marked him as one of the few who had a direct Link to Earth's cyberminds; the two men sat together, and those making their way past them nodded respectfully in their direction. A few of the people were eating small rolls and pieces of fruit, and drinking from small bottles; Alonza, feeling very hungry, wondered if she could risk begging or stealing some food. Nearly every seat was taken by the time she started worrying about Amparo.

Her mother should have been here by now, Alonza thought. Soon all these people would begin to board the suborb, and somebody else would wonder what she was doing here. Already a gray-haired man was watching her with a puzzled look on his face, while a guide wearing dark blue overalls and a badge hanging over his chest had come by a couple of times already, slowing down to glance at her both times.

A space in the back wall opened. A man came through the opening and stepped to a counter as the doorway behind him closed. He wore a dark blue shirt; like the guide, he had a badge that said "Port of San Antonio" on the top and "Nueva Republica de Texas" on the bottom. Alonza knew how to read a little, and she had seen those words often enough to recognize them immediately.

The man peered at the screen of his console, apparently checking the passenger list. That meant that everyone here would be lining up in a few minutes, having their bracelets scanned and their identities and credit confirmed and then heading for the doorway that led to the field outside.

She was suddenly frightened, afraid to move from her cushion. Then she saw the guide walking toward her with another man at his side, a tall thin pale-haired man in the black uniform of a Guardian, with a stun wand hanging from his belt.

"Is your name Alonza Lemaris?" the man in the Guardian uniform asked.

She nodded. If he knew her name, it meant that her mother had been caught.

"Come with me," the man said.

They took her to a small room. The guide left them there alone, and the Guardian asked her a lot of questions, keeping his hand around his wand the whole time, but terrified as she was, she knew that Amparo would want her to say as little as possible. "I'm waiting for my mother. She told me to wait there for her. She told me not to get lost." She kept saying the same thing over and over and at last the Guardian stopped pacing and sat down in front of her.

"Listen to me, you little bitch," he said angrily. "We've already got your mother on assault, credit theft, and ident theft. If we put her to the question, we can probably get a lot more out of her, but she wouldn't be the same afterwards, and you're the only one who can stop us from doing that kind of damage to her. So you can begin telling me about what kinds of things she's been up to, and we'll find some work for her to do while she's serving her sentence that won't be too hard on her, or else we can start interrogating her until she breaks down and confesses. She won't be of much use to anybody after that. Some people get so messed up in their minds afterward that they end up killing themselves."

"I want to see her," Alonza said softly.

"You won't see her until after she's finished her time, and that's going to be long from now. Get this through your head—you'll probably never see her again. The only favor you can do for her now is to tell me exactly what she's done, what you've seen her do, what you've done together."

Amparo had always been terrified of getting caught, of being interrogated by Guardians. They would put a band on your head, her mother had told her, one of the slender silver ones like the ones people used to access a mind-tour, and then they would dig into your mind, force you to confess, find all kinds of ways to hurt you and make you scream in pain until you told them the truth. That was why it was so important never to get caught; better to be dead than in the custody of Guardians preparing to question you.

"She didn't do anything," Alonza insisted, staring at the gold lieutenant's bars on the man's shoulders. "She told me to wait for her, that's all."

The Guardian stood up and slapped her in the face. The blow shocked her more than it hurt her. "You're a stubborn one," he muttered, sounding almost pleased. "I guess we'll let you visit with your mother after all."

He led her out of the room, gripping her arm tightly. A hovercar with another Guardian was waiting for them. They rode through the hallways of the port to another room, where two more Guardians were waiting with Amparo.

Her mother was bound to a chair. A console with a screen sat in front of her. "I didn't say anything," Alonza cried out, trying to free herself from the man holding her arm, but Amparo did not seem to hear her. Then one of the men in the room stepped toward Amparo and held out a circular silver headband.

Amparo screamed. Her scream was so sharp and piercing that Alonza froze.

"Tell them!" her mother shrieked. "Tell them anything they want to know!"

Alonza told the Guardians about the woman and how Amparo had struck her and where she had ditched the bracelet they had stolen from her. The men asked her more questions about other marks they had taken things from, and Amparo, who was sobbing by then, told Alonza to answer those questions, too. When Alonza had finished telling the Guardians about what they had stolen over the past months and how they had obtained the goods, the pale-haired Guardian told her that her mother would be doing useful labor for the Nomarchies of Earth while serving out her sentence. They did not say anything about a hearing, how long a sentence Amparo would get, or how unpleasant the useful labor would be.

"What about my daughter?" Amparo asked hoarsely.

"That's none of your business, woman. We'll take care of her. She'll be a lot better off than she was with you. She'll be a better citizen of her Nomarchy when she grows up, and by then she'll forget about you."

The Guardian had been right. Alonza had been cared for afterwards, and supposed that she had grown up to be a better citizen than she would have been otherwise.

Her memory of her mother grew fainter over time. In the first years after her mother's arrest, while she was still living in the children's dormitory, Alonza had occasionally tried to find out where Amparo was being held, but the cyberminds always blocked those channels so that she could not get an answer, and then the teaching image on her screen would order her to get back to her lessons. After a while, she stopped asking about Amparo. When she was older, after the officers in charge of the dormitory had decided that she and a few of her friends showed enough promise to be sent to a school for more lessons in academic subjects instead of being trained for satellite repair, she rarely thought of her mother.

The pale-haired Guardian had been right when he told her that she would be better off in the dormitory than with Amparo. There had been the opportunity for schooling, and since the Guardians often recruited from the children housed in the dorms while their parents served time, she had eventually been trained at an officers' academy for the important work of being one of the protectors of Earth's biosphere and its peace. Had she remained with her mother, she would have grown up to be another one like her, a mosquito as they were called in their crowded neighborhood near the port, one of those who lived by stinging any unwary travelers passing through San Antonio. Had she stayed with Amparo, she would never have made it to the Wheel, certainly not as an officer and as an aide to Colonel Jonas Sansom, the commander of the Guardian detachment at the Wheel, and also the pale-haired Guardian officer who had detained her at the San Antonio port so many years ago.

* * * * * * *

Alonza Lemaris stood in the small waiting area just beyond the shuttle dock's bay. Another group had just arrived, passengers from Earth bound for Venus. Most of the people coming to the Wheel could be left to find their own way to the lounges and bays in the hub where they would wait to board their freighters or passenger vessels, but this group of travelers, who came from a camp outside Tashkent, was an exception.

Guardians were stationed at that camp to keep order, and Guardians traveled with any settlers who left the camp on the shuttle flights to the Wheel. Usually Alonza or one of the other officers met the new arrivals and ushered them to a bay near the dock holding the Habber ship that was to take them on the next leg of their journey to Anwara, the vast space station that circled Earth's sister planet, but that was not why she had come here this time.

Settlers, Alonza thought; traitors to Earth was what many would call them. She had nothing against the scientists and specialists and workers who were trained for the terraforming Venus Project, who had been chosen to go there and who had proven their worth. But the people from the camp outside Tashkent were another matter. They abandoned their homes and their work and even gave up all of their credit, to go to the camp and wait for passage until a few more workers might be needed inside the domed settlements that were being raised on the still inhospitable surface of Venus. They were, most of them, malcontents willing to leave their own Nomarchies to gamble on getting a chance at making a new world and a new life for themselves. Maybe the Project needed such people, and perhaps the Council of Mukhtars that governed Earth's Nomarchies had been wise to allow such camps as a social safety valve, but Guardians had to keep order in the camps, and Alonza considered that a waste of their resources.

A door opened and a Guardian pilot in a black uniform entered the waiting area, followed by a man and a woman who wore pins of silver circles on their blue tunics, pins that such people were required to wear in Earthspace so that anyone seeing them would know at a glance what they were. Alonza looked away from the pair as the pilot saluted her.

"Major Lemaris," he said, "how good of you to greet me. Congratulations on your recent promotion. I hear that it's well deserved."

"Thank you, Lieutenant." Looking up at him, Alonza wondered if the man was only being polite or trying to suck up to her in the hope of gaining some future favor. Hard to tell, but it did him no harm either way.

"As soon as our charges are off the shuttlecraft, my crew and I will speed them on their way to their ship," the man continued.

"I came here," Alonza said, "to tell you that their trip has to be delayed. Your passengers will have to stay here, so get them into the lift and shoot them through the spoke to Level B and the lounge next to the assistant director's office. We'll keep them under guard there until we can allow them to board their transport."

"There's thirty of them," the pilot said. He glared at the man and woman with the silver pins, as if they were to blame for the delay. "Might be kind of crowded."

"They shouldn't be there for more than ten to twenty hours," Alonza murmured, "thirty at most. They're from a camp, so they know hardship."

The pilot shrugged.

"Warn them that it'll be close to a g there," she went on, "not the half-g they've got here in the hub."

"I assume that we at least will be able to stay aboard our

ship until our departure, since I know the Wheel's space is limited." The man in the blue tunic had spoken; he was a small man, barely taller than Alonza, with short dark hair and brown almond-shaped eyes. His companion, a short dark-eyed woman with a cap of thick black hair, stared past Alonza, avoiding her gaze.

"Unfortunately, you can't go aboard," Alonza replied, "because a few components in the dock have to be replaced before it's safe to ferry anybody to your ship."

The man frowned, looking as though he did not believe her, not that it mattered whether he did or not. He and his companion were Habitat-dwellers, or Habbers as they were derisively called. Their ancestors had abandoned Earth centuries ago for the Associated Habitats, the homes they had made for themselves in space, and there were many who believed that, despite their appearance, the Habbers were no longer truly human, that their genetic engineering had far surpassed what Earth allowed among its people. Habbers might have their uses; some of them worked with the scientists and specialists of the Venus Project, and having them ferry settlers from the camps to Venus was certainly a convenience. Changing the orbits of a few asteroids so that they would come nearer to Earth and could be more easily mined had been another service of the Habbers to the home world.

Alonza could grant all of that, but loathed the air of superiority that Habbers exuded, as if the resources they provided and the necessary tasks they voluntarily undertook for Earth's benefit were little more than crumbs thrown to beggars. She thought then of how the home world must seem to Habbers, with its flooded coastlines, melting icecaps, and an atmosphere that was still too thick with carbon dioxide six centuries after the Resource Wars. They probably thought of themselves as fortunate for having abandoned what they must see as a played-out world populated by deluded die-hards. Even these two Habber pilots had that look of superiority in their eyes, the calm steady gaze of people who seemed to lack any turbulent and upsetting emotions.

"Where are we to stay, then?" the female Habber asked.

The woman probably expected to have to stay in the lounge with all the passengers going to Venus. Alonza was silent for a moment, then said, "We want you to be comfortable. I believe that our agreement with the Associated Habitats also requires us not to inflict any unnecessary discomfort on any of you. So we've found a room for you in our officers' quarters. You'll have to share it, but there are two beds, and a public lavatory just down the corridor."

"That's very kind of you," the male Habber said, and she heard a note of sarcasm in his voice. Being sarcastic was uncharacteristic of such cool and rational types as Habbers, but then this Habber and his companion were not like others of their kind.

* * * * * * *

After getting their thirty Venus-bound passengers out of the lift and settled in the lounge, Alonza led the two Habbers to their room, which was just three doors from her own quarters. In the three years since she had been assigned here, she had grown used to the gently curving and brightly lit corridors, to the gravity-like acceleration, only slightly weaker than Earth's, that was imparted by the Wheel's rotation around its hub, to the pilots and passengers passing endlessly through this station. Every twenty-four hour period brought the promise of something new—of an unusually interesting traveler, official visitors, a new detachment of Guardians with interesting tales of a Nomarchy she did not know that much about, the possibility of a mission that might take her to the L-5 spaceport, to one of the industrial, recreational, and military satellites that orbited Earth, or even to Luna. Her post here often imparted a heightened sense of expectation, of feeling that she was on a journey that would never end. It was as if she were somehow picking up that feeling of anticipation from all of those who passed through the Wheel on their way to other places.

"Your room," Alonza said to the two Habbers as she pressed the door open for them. They entered a small room bare of furnishings except for a small wall screen and two cushions in front of two low shelves. "You pull the beds out from the wall." She demonstrated by pressing a panel and pulling out the lower bunk. "And the lavatory's four doors down to your right. I hope everything's satisfactory, but if there's anything else you need, do let me know."

"We're most appreciative," the male Habber said.

"I'd be most grateful if you would both be my guests at supper in two hours," Alonza continued. She thought of asking Tom Ruden-Nodell, the physician in charge of the Wheel's infirmary and the closest friend she had here, to join them, but decided against it. She would get more of a sense of these two by herself.

The Habbers glanced at each other, apparently surprised by her offer of hospitality. "We're a bit tired," the man said. "Perhaps another time—"

"Tired? I didn't think Habitat-dwellers were as subject to our frailties. Three hours, then? That should give you time to rest. I look forward to seeing you then. I'll send a Guardian to fetch you." Alonza turned and left the room before the man could object again.

* * * * * * *

"Detain the operative," Colonel Sansom had said in his message, sent to her over a confidential channel. Alonza had seen the woman's file, stored under the name she was using. This was a matter the colonel should have handled himself, but he had left suddenly to go to an asteroid tracking station two days ago, to supervise repairs after a micrometeorite strike had damaged three telescopes, and would not get back to the Wheel for another thirty hours at least. A more easygoing officer might have sent a subordinate to the station, but not the obsessively conscientious Jonas Sansom. Tracking the orbits of asteroids that might threaten Earth was one of the most important duties of Guardians, perhaps the most important. Colonel Sansom would report to his superiors that he had seen to this task personally.

"Just get her away from the others," Sansom continued, "and into custody as quietly as possible, that's all. Best if you can handle it by yourself without bringing anybody else into it, so use your judgment."

That was all. That was more than enough. Alonza was flattered that he trusted her with this task. She must not fail him.

According to the file on her screen, the operative was using the name of Sameh Tryolla. She had supposedly grown up in the Eastern Mediterranean Nomarchy, attended and then been asked to leave the University of Vancouver in the Pacific Federation for not doing well at her studies in physics, and after that had decided to leave her work as a laboratory assistant in Ankara to go to the camp outside Tashkent. Probably everything in her file was an invention. The image of Sameh Tryolla showed a slim young olive-skinned woman with long dark brown hair and large hazel eyes; she looked frail, and hardly more than a girl.

The woman was to be detained, according to Colonel Sansom, because the Guardian Commanders who advised the Council of Mukhtars had abruptly decided to abort her mission. Alonza was to detain her as unobtrusively as possible and hold her until the colonel returned to the Wheel, after which he would take charge of the matter.

Her task seemed simple enough, but there were all kinds of possible complications in carrying it out. Perhaps this Sameh had friends among those traveling with her who might object to seeing her led away without a good excuse. Maybe the Habber pilots who were to take Sameh and the others from the camp to Venus would argue that, since she was technically in their custody until she arrived in Anwara, the Guardians had no right to keep her at the Wheel. Perhaps Sameh would demand a public hearing, claiming that the Guardian force at the Wheel was violating the implicit agreement that had been made with her by allowing her passage from Earth to Venus.

Nothing would prevent her superiors from doing whatever they wanted with Sameh in the end, but any of these possibilities would draw too much attention to the operative. The Guardian officers close to the Council of Mukhtars wanted no attention drawn to their covert activities. Better for the secret service of the Mukhtars' personal guard to be no more than the subject of unverifiable rumors, to have even the existence of such a secret service doubted by most of Earth's citizens.

Alonza closed the file on Sameh Tryolla and secured it, knowing that she would not have to retrieve it again. The whole business had bothered her from the first, and even though Colonel Sansom had not betrayed any uneasiness, she suspected that he was equally puzzled by their orders. Why not find some way to get word to the woman about the change in plans instead of confining her on the Wheel? Why take the risk of calling attention to her by detaining her? For that matter, why not put her out of the way permanently, making her death look like an accident? Why hadn't she been stopped before she got to the Wheel?

Asking such questions, though, was not part of her assignment; nor was wondering what Sameh Tryolla's mission might have been. The Council of Mukhtars had many ways of monitoring the progress of the Venus Project and the loyalty of the Cytherians, as the people who lived in the surface settlements and on the domed Islands that floated in Venus's thin upper atmosphere preferred to call themselves. Alonza had always assumed that one of the Mukhtars' methods was to plant a few spies among the settlers. She hoped that this was all the Council was doing, that the spies were no more than informers alerting Earth's rulers of possible difficulties and dissatisfactions that might require their attention.

Irrationally, something inside her insisted upon hoping that Venus might become a place where people could win more for themselves than they were allowed on Earth, that the Cytherians would make something new, that the machinations of the Mukhtars would not dampen their dreams. She had picked up such sentiments from others who had come to the Wheel, the scientists and workers and others who looked forward to the work of terraforming, even knowing that they would never live to see the results of their labors and could only hope that their distant descendants might live on the green and growing world they would create. The terraforming of Venus would redeem Earth and provide a new Earthlike planet for its people. Far in the future, the technology used to transform Venus might even be used to heal humankind's wounded home world.

Not that Alonza would let such passing thoughts interfere with her duty.

She thought of her own arrival at the Wheel, when Colonel Sansom had welcomed her to her post with a dinner in the officers' mess. "I thought you might have the makings of a Guardian," he had told her, "even back in San Antonio. You wouldn't talk, even with all the scary tales you'd surely been told about Guardian interrogations, not until we took you to your mother and she begged you to talk. First you demonstrated your loyalty, and then you showed your good sense. Adjusting well to the dorms and doing well at your assigned studies only confirmed my original judgment."

That she had never asked about her mother had likely been another point in her favor. She had learned to control her curiosity, to live with knowing that many of her questions would never be answered and that any answers, if she somehow found them, would only bring her trouble.

* * * * * * *

Alonza did not suppose that she would learn much, if anything, about Sameh Tryolla from the two Habber pilots. The woman was only another one of their passengers; it was unlikely that they had exchanged even a few words with her. But she had to know if they might pose an obstacle to her assignment.

She met them at the entrance to the officers' mess and led them to their table. Most of the low tables were in the common area, open to all officers and their guests, but Alonza and the Habbers would dine in the smaller adjoining room where Colonel Sansom often entertained visiting Linkers and other dignitaries. She wanted some privacy, so that the Habbers would feel freer to talk.

Keir Renin, the Guardian officer in charge of the camp outside Tashkent, had sent her a confidential message about the two Habbers. The woman went only by the name of Te-yu, not unusual since it was the custom among Habbers to use just one name, but her full name was Hong Te-yu. The man was known as Benzi and also had the surname of Liangharad. This was the third time that the two were ferrying people from the camp to Venus, and Keir Renin had been given the distinct impression by Te-yu and Benzi that this would be the pair's last such journey.

What was unusual about these two was that they had not been born and reared in a Habitat. They had close kinsfolk on Earth and also among the Cytherians, and had grown up on one of the Venusian Islands. But being given a stake in the Venus Project had not been enough for Te-yu and Benzi, who with several other conspirators had seized control of a shuttlecraft to flee to a Hab not far from Venus.

Few took the risks of fleeing to any of the Habitats and asking for refuge, and some had died in the attempt. Capture meant imprisonment and a forever restricted existence; other failed attempts had ended in death aboard space vessels too limited in range to reach a Habitat. Alonza had never heard of any successful refugees returning to Earth or to the regions of space controlled by the Council of Mukhtars. She wondered why these two had done so, whether they now regretted the choice they had made, if there was some way she might be able to use them.

The two Habbers sat down across from her on their cushions. Alonza folded her legs in front of her, under the table, then studied the pocket screen on the tabletop.

"Do you have any particular preferences?" Alonza asked

her guests. "With people coming through here from so many different regions, we have more variety in our cuisine than you might expect."

The woman named Te-yu shrugged.

"Please feel free to order for both of us, Major Lemaris," her companion Benzi murmured. He smiled slightly. "No doubt you know what's best."

Alonza thought she detected amusement in his smile, a hint of sarcasm in his tone. She found herself suddenly disliking him intensely, then let that feeling go. "We'll start with chili bean soup," she said, "and then some fish in a cucumber and dill sauce with rice for the main course. The fish is from one of our protein vats, of course, but it tastes almost exactly like salmon. We'll end the meal with a few fruit pastries."

"Sounds delicious," Benzi said.

"And we can offer you a selection of coffees, herbal teas, and fruit juices." The officers' mess served no alcohol, in deference to the Islamic faith of Earth's dominant Nomarchies and also to keep discipline among the Guardians and the Wheel's other personnel, although occasionally the pilots or crew members of a freighter could be bribed into surrendering a few bottles of a cargo.

"We'll have whatever you're having," Benzi said.

Alonza touched her screen to order the meal, finding their acquiescence annoying.

Te-yu's face was composed, and her dark eyes stared past Alonza. In common with the Linkers of Earth, Habbers had Links that connected them directly to their cyberminds; they could call up any data they might need from their artificial intelligences without using the slender silver headbands most people had to wear in order to open those channels. The Council of Mukhtars restricted direct Links to only a few, to the scientists, specialists, Guardian Commanders and prominent advisors to the Council who had been trained to use the Links and who had access to channels that were closed to other people. But Habbers, it was said, were all Linked, all equal in their access to their cyberminds. Perhaps Te-yu was diverting herself with some data stream or other, or picking up a message from a friend; that might account for the vacant look on her face.

How insulting of her, Alonza thought; it was as rude as coming to dinner, whipping out a pocket screen, and playing a game instead of conversing with one's companions. "I'm told that you have close kinsfolk on Earth," she said aloud, wanting to get that out of the way.

"Yes," Benzi said, "and on Venus as well."

"And do you sometimes miss what you left behind?" Alonza asked.

"You're asking if that is why I volunteered to ferry people from that camp to Venus?" Benzi drew his brows together. "Maybe so. I haven't really examined my possible motivations."

An orderly came into the small room with a tray, set down the cups of juice, then left. Having people handle such simple tasks on the Wheel was cheaper than the trouble and expense of maintaining the servos and other mechanisms that performed such jobs elsewhere. Whatever Earth might lack in other resources, it had no shortage of people.

"You might have been taking a risk," Alonza said, "even with our agreements. Ways might have been found to keep you both on Earth without violating any treaties."

Te-yu's eyes focused on her. Alonza finally had her attention. Benzi sipped some juice, then set his cup down. "We thought that most unlikely," he said.

"But still possible."

"Just barely." He frowned for a moment, then drank more juice. She wanted him a bit apprehensive; that would make him and his companion less likely to interfere with her task.

* * * * * * *

They got through the meal while saying little of any significance. Benzi and Alonza exchanged opinions on the very few mind-tours and virtual concerts they had both experienced. The dinner, better than Benzi had clearly expected, provoked them both to discuss some of their favorite foods. Alonza mentioned in passing that she had been born in San Antonio, and Benzi said that although he had grown up on one of Venus's Islands, he had been born in a small town on the North American Plains. Te-yu said almost nothing at all.

Alonza walked the two Habbers back to their room, then hurried to the nearest lift. The door slid shut silently; the cage hummed softly around her until the door opened and she knew that she had arrived at the Wheel's hub.

Alonza welcomed the half-g of the hub, where all the docks were located. She came here often, to look at the ships and imagine herself on an endless journey aboard one; such musings were one of her few indulgences.

She entered the bay area, empty except for two technicians checking some readings, and went to the viewscreen. Often Tom Ruden-Nodell joined her here after a shift of duty at the infirmary, partly because the half-g eased his minor aches and pains. He was another one like her, according to his public record, someone who had been a child living on Basic and what he could scrounge for himself until he caught the eye of a bene-factor who, impressed by his quickness and intelligence, had taken him away from his negligent parents and found him a place in a dormitory.

But they never spoke of the past. They sat in the bay and speculated about the travelers who passed through the Wheel and exchanged the stories they had each gleaned from them. There were workers in gray tunics and pants with tales of repairing seawalls and dikes near the flooded cities of New York, Melbourne, or Corpus Christi; Linkers in white robes with gossip about the sexual affairs of those close to the Council of Mukhtars; students and young scientists with stories of their future ambitions told with a mixture of youthful arrogance and insecurity. While listening to them, Alonza often thought of how far she had come from the wretched shantytown of people on Basic that nestled near San Antonio's port.

"I might put in for a change," Tom had told her the last time they were here in the hub. "I'm thinking of making a move to Luna. They'll need another physician there sooner or later, and there'd be the astronomers and other researchers to exchange ideas with and the engineers and miners to drink with. And one-sixth gravity might be just the thing for my old bones." She had noticed the deep lines around his eyes then, the graying hair, the weariness his slouch betrayed.

"You're not that old, Tom," she said.

"I am that old, Alonza," and he was right; he was eighty, and could expect another thirty or forty years if his rejuvenation therapy worked as it did for most people, but there were always exceptions, and Tom was already showing many of the signs of age. "Might not be a bad place for a Guardian officer to be posted, either," he added.

"And why is that?"

"Because there isn't much to do except keep order and look out for people's safety and maybe round up a few miners and workers when they get a little rowdy."

"There wouldn't be much chance for a promotion, though."

"And not much chance of running afoul of ambitious officers, either." Tom had smiled to himself then, and for a moment Alonza had envied the physician the relatively peaceful life he had won for himself.

More docks had been added to the Wheel in recent years, and now there were fifteen of them filled with the metal slugs of freighters and dull gray torchships; other docks held the shuttles that traveled to and from Earth and Luna. The Habber vessel was unlike the other torchships; it was a slender spire of silver attached to the vast globe that housed its engines. Its passengers would board the vessel, perhaps expecting the diversions that other passenger ships offered, only to find out that they would be in suspension during the entire journey. The Habbers claimed that this was a more efficient way of transporting their passengers, that to have them safely stored in sleepers was more comfortable for them, given the high acceleration of their faster ships, but Alonza also suspected that the Habbers did not want anyone else poking around inside their vessels and maybe finding out more about them.

Alonza moved closer to the viewscreen. Outside the hub, two suited and helmeted figures crawled along the latticework of the dock that held the Habber ship. They had surely noticed by now that the components did not really need to be replaced this soon, according to the readings, but they were well-disciplined Guardian technicians and had not questioned their orders.

Alonza slapped the comm next to the screen. "How's it going, Starling?"

"I've got two more components to go, Major," the voice of Darlanna Starling replied. "Richi's got three."

"Estimate?"

"Two more hours, maybe three."

"Both of you better come inside for a break, Starling. That's an order. When you get too tired, accidents can happen."

"Yes, ma'am."

"Get some food into you, maybe a nap if you think you need it."

"Yes, ma'am."

That would give her some more time. Maybe she wouldn't need much more; maybe this whole business would move along faster than she expected. Go to the lounge where the Venus-bound passengers were waiting, give them some bureaucratic gab, get Sameh Tryolla away from the others on some excuse, and send the two Habbers on their way with their ship.

Doubt bit at her again. It didn't add up, the secrecy, holding the woman here, going to all this trouble. Alonza pushed those thoughts aside as she left the bay.

* * * * * * *

The people in the lounge seemed subdued. Some of them lay on the floor, their packs and duffels under their heads, while others sat on cushions. A few had helped themselves to cups of water from the wall dispenser and were drinking it listlessly. Perhaps they were still recovering from the weightless discomforts of the shuttle flight.

Sameh Tryolla was on one of the cushions, her back against the wall, looking even thinner and smaller than she had in her file image. She glanced toward Alonza, then looked away.

"...showed them to the lavatories," the Guardian on Alonza's right murmured, "and they haven't given us any trouble. Might need to get fed soon, though."

"They don't have any credit to pay for their food," Alonza said. The hopeful settlers had been forced to give up all their credit after reaching the camp; it was one way to help cover the expense of housing them while they waited for passage. "Thirty or forty hours on nothing but water won't kill them," she went on, thinking of times in her early childhood when she had had even less than that.

"Yeah, but you don't want them to get weak, Major," the Guardian said, "or we might get stuck with them for even longer."

Alonza turned toward the young man. "You're quite right, Zaleski," she said as the threads of her plan came together in her mind. "In fact, that's why I'm here. I'm a little worried after the last message I got from Keir Renin."

The young Guardian looked puzzled.

"The officer in charge of the camp they came from," she continued in a softer voice. "He didn't say so outright, but he implied that the soldiers who gave them their med-scans might have been a bit sloppy."

Zaleski's blue eyes widened.

"Oh, I don't think we really have to worry," Alonza said hastily. "Renin's people would have caught anything virulent or potentially lethal. But as long as they're stuck here, it wouldn't hurt to scan them all again."

"Should I call for a couple of paramedics?" Zaleski turned toward the comm near the doorway.

"No," Alonza replied. "The head physician can handle this."

She could trust Tom, and Colonel Sansom had told her to use her own judgment. "I'll go to the infirmary and set things up with him."

"I could call him and—"

"I'd rather not have rumors going around about possibly contagious travelers being here."

The young Guardian nodded. "Of course, Major Lemaris."

* * * * * * *

Tom Ruden-Nodell listened as Alonza told him about the people she wanted scanned and gave him the name of the person she had been ordered to detain. "We'll bring her back here," she continued, "and hold her until Colonel Sansom gets back."

"And we're to do all this as quietly as possible," he said.

"Yes. We'll put her in one of the private rooms, and you can give her something to knock her out. I'll keep watch over her. It would be better not to involve any of the other medical personnel."

"Understood."

Tom had not asked her about why she was to hold the woman, and what Colonel Sansom wanted with her, but she had expected that. He was safer knowing as little as possible and not risking his usually placid and extremely secure existence.

They left his office together, the physician with a portable scanner under his arm. He said nothing to her during the short walk through the corridor to the lounge. As they entered the room, Zaleski and the three Guardians with him stepped aside and stood at attention.

"I have an announcement to make," Alonza said. The people sitting on cushions or on the floor looked toward her; those lying down stirred and sat up. "Since you have to wait here anyway until the dock's repaired, we've decided to give you all another med-scan." She heard groans, and a couple of men scowled. "Let me assure you that we expect to find nothing, given that you were all scanned before leaving your camp, but it doesn't hurt to be careful, and we've got the time for the extra caution."

"I'll tell you what you'll find out," a stocky blond man said in accented Anglaic. "We could all use some food. I vomited what little they gave me during that damned shuttle flight."

Alonza narrowed her eyes as she gripped the handle of the stun wand at her waist. "You won't be here that much longer. Now line up in front of the ID console and we'll get this done as quickly as we can." She turned to Tom as people cleared their throats, stretched, mumbled to one another, and slowly got to their feet.

The stocky blond man held out his braceleted wrist as the ID console's flat voice recited his name, age, and other particulars. He was scanned first, followed by two bearded fellows in worn brown tunics and baggy pants. Sameh Tryolla was near the back of the line; that was good. They could be done with this, get the operative secured, and send the Habbers and their human cargo on their way in two or three hours.

Tom circled each person with a med-scan wand, moved the wand up and down, stared at the readings on his portable screen for a bit, then gave a quick nod before scanning the next man or woman. The physician seemed his usual thorough self, and it occurred to Alonza then that he might actually find some sort of medical problem in one of these people that had not been caught earlier. The chances of that were vanishingly remote, but could complicate matters for her.

People held their arms out to the console, shuffled toward Tom, stood quietly as he waved his wand over them as though casting a spell, then moved toward the back of the room to lean against the wall and gaze sourly at Alonza and her Guardians.

When it was Sameh Tryolla's turn, a look of uneasiness flickered across her pretty face. The ID console gave her age as twenty, which agreed with the data Alonza had seen in her file, but she looked even younger than that.

Tom passed his wand over her, stared at his screen, rubbed his chin, and sighed. "Stand right over there, young woman," he said, gesturing in Alonza's direction.

"But why?" Sameh Tryolla asked in the high tiny voice of a child.

"Do as the doctor says," Alonza said. Sameh Tryolla came toward her and waited at her left as Tom finished scanning the last three people.

"All right," Tom said, "I'm done, and grateful for your cooperation. Now I better start by saying that nobody here has anything to worry about, but it looks like I'll have to do a more thorough scan of young Sameh Tryolla here."

Alonza saw the young woman raise her brows, as if startled, and yet she did not seem that surprised somehow. Her body had not tensed; if anything, she seemed almost relaxed. In her position, Alonza thought, I'd be wondering what's going on, why I was being singled out, if somebody had found out what I really was. At the very least I'd be worrying about whether or not I actually did have some kind of unexpected and mysterious medical problem.

"There's nothing the matter with me," Sameh Tryolla said in her little girl's voice.

"Now I'm just about certain that's true," Tom said reassuringly, "and a complete workup in the infirmary will probably bear that out, but we can't be too careful. Scan here shows that you've got some kind of bacterium in your system that the medscan program can't identify. I don't want you worrying, because people carry all kinds of bacteria as a normal thing, but we just want—"

"You don't have to explain it to me," Sameh said in a softer but steelier voice.

Tom nodded. "We'll just isolate it and make sure—"

"I understand." Sameh bowed her head, looking like a child again.

"And what about the rest of us?" the blond man called out. He seemed to have made himself the spokesman for his companions. "What are we supposed to do, wait around here until he runs all his tests on her?"

Alonza stared at him; he glared back. She kept her eyes on

him until he finally looked down, then said, "I checked on how the repairs were going just a short time ago, and by now the components have probably been replaced. As soon as I verify that, we'll get all of you aboard the Habber ship as quickly as we can. If this woman here is cleared by then, as the doctor expects, she'll join you, and if not, you'll be on your way without her."

She waited for somebody in the group to object, to ask what would happen to Sameh Tryolla after that, but no one did. They probably assumed that she would be sent back to the camp, or maybe given some job on the Wheel to earn her keep until another ship arrived to carry former camp inmates to Venus. As Alonza studied their indifferent and bored faces, she realized that nobody here particularly cared what happened to her. Just as well, she thought, since it made her task easier.

"I have to get my pack," Sameh Tryolla whispered, at last sounding worried.

"Get it, then," Alonza said. The woman went to the back of the room, picked up a duffel, and slipped the strap over her shoulder. Alonza pressed her hand against the comm next to the door. "Lemaris to Starling."

"Starling here," the voice of Darlanna Starling replied.

"How are those repairs coming along?"

"We'll be done in a hour, Major."

"Good. We'll get the passengers ready to board." She turned to the men at her side. "Zaleski, go fetch our two Habber guests. Achmed and Jeyaraj, get all these people to the hub. I'll let you know if this woman will be joining them or not by the time they're ready to leave."

"Yes, ma'am."

* * * * * * *

Sameh was silent during the walk to the infirmary. Tom would stall for a while, doing another med-scan and taking his samples, and then Alonza would give the young woman the word. *You won't be going to Venus; I have to detain you. Those* are my orders. No, I don't know why; all they told me was to hold you until my commanding officer returns. Maybe it would be better to simply put her under restraint without explaining anything, but something in Alonza rebelled against that; an operative working for Guardian Commanders deserved more consideration, and it might count against Alonza if the woman complained that she had been badly treated.

Again her doubts nagged at her. Why all this trouble that risked attracting unwanted attention? Why hadn't Sameh's superiors found a simpler way of aborting the woman's mission? Surely they had some way to alert Sameh that her mission had been cancelled. They might have given Alonza a password or some other coded message over a private channel. She would not have to be told what the operative's original assignment was in order to pass such a message along.

They entered the infirmary. The beds in the ward were empty; the two paramedics on duty greeted Tom with quick nods of their heads. They walked through the ward and continued down a narrow hall with five doors on either side, then stopped in front of one room. The door slid open and the ceiling light brightened to a soft glow, revealing a small room with a wide bed and a wall screen with a holo image of a forest clearing.

"Kind of luxurious quarters," Sameh said, "for somebody like me."

"Normally we put Linkers and other dignitaries in the private rooms," Tom said.

"I guessed that." Sameh sounded unimpressed.

"We want you to be comfortable," Alonza added, "and if we should have to isolate you—"

"Can't think why you should have to do that." Sameh went to the bed, dropped her duffel on it, and sat down. "If you really thought it was catching, you'd have everybody else in here with me being checked."

"Not necessarily," Tom said. "I'll have to get some more equipment to run the tests, so just rest here until I get back." He shot Alonza a dubious look before the door slid shut behind him.

Sameh began to rummage in her duffel. Alonza leaned against the wall, resting her hand on her wand. "How long is this going to take?" the young woman asked.

"I don't know. That's up to the chief physician."

"I better be on my way with the rest of them."

"We'll do our best to see that you are."

The comm on the table next to the bed chimed. "Alonza," Tom's voice said, "one of the Habber pilots is here. Calls himself Benzi, and he wants to talk to you."

"Bring him here, then." Alonza closed the comm's channel and turned to Sameh. She had known that this might happen, that the Habber would have questions about his passenger. She hoped that he would be satisfied with whatever answers Tom was probably already giving him.

"Dr. Ruden-Nodell and Habitat-dweller Benzi," the door's voice announced.

"Let them in," Alonza said.

The door opened and Tom entered, followed by Benzi. "I think you know why I'm here," Benzi said. "I came here with thirty people to transport. I expected to leave the Wheel with thirty."

"The doctor said—" Alonza began.

"I know what he said, Major Lemaris. If you will provide me with a record of this woman's med-scan, I can determine what might be done for her aboard our vessel before she's put in suspension. In any case, it will probably be more than you can do for her here."

"I don't care for the implications of that remark," Tom muttered.

"The Associated Habitats have an agreement with the Council of Mukhtars to transport people from Earth to Venus," Benzi said. "We don't interfere with whomever you choose to be our passengers, and we save you the trouble and expense of transporting them. In return, we expect you to allow us to get them to their destination quickly and efficiently. I'll admit that there were many among my people who wondered if we should perform this job at all, but we decided to do what we could for those people willing to sacrifice everything they had for the chance at a new life."

"You just wanted to do the right thing," Alonza said, "with no ulterior purpose in mind."

"Believe that or not, as you like. In any case, unless you abide by the agreement we have with your Mukhtars, there will be some of us who will argue that our agreement with you has lapsed, and that we no longer should perform this service for you."

Tom leaned against the wall, hands in his pockets. Alonza wondered if this Habber could interpret a med-scan record properly. It did not matter; he was Linked to his people's cybers, and they could interpret the data for him. He would soon find out that Tom was lying.

"I'm glad somebody's sticking up for me," Sameh Tryolla said as she got to her feet. She came toward them and gazed at Benzi. "I knew you would come. I want to get out of here."

Benzi said, "I'd like to see that scan now."

"Be easier for me to access it from my office," Tom responded, still stalling for time. Good old Tom, Alonza thought, grateful for that even if it wouldn't do them any good in the end. She folded her arms, trying to think of what to say next.

"I'll come with you, then," Benzi said as he turned toward the door.

Sameh was standing just behind Benzi as the door opened and Tom stepped into the hall. Alonza saw the woman's arm rise in an oddly familiar gesture. In an instant, realizing that there was no time to pull out her wand, she slashed at Sameh with her right arm, chopping her hard on the wrist with the edge of her hand.

Sameh's arm fell and slapped against her upper thigh. She stumbled back and stared at Alonza, her eyes wide, and suddenly her face contorted, becoming red and then purple. A harsh gurgling sound came from her throat; her eyes seemed to bulge from her head, and then she fell forward and crumpled to the floor.

Tom was still standing in the open entrance. He pushed past Benzi as the door slid shut, then knelt next to Sameh. His fingers found her neck, then clasped her by one wrist. "She's dead," the physician said. "And I don't need a scan to tell me that."

Benzi's light brown skin had turned yellow. He closed his eyes for a moment, clearly struggling to compose himself, then turned to Alonza. "What happened to her?" he asked.

"Think this happened to her," Tom replied as he lifted Sameh's right arm by the edge of her sleeve, revealing a tiny device no larger than an implant or a gem. "Better not touch it. I'm guessing it's deactivated now, but no sense taking a chance."

"What is it?" Benzi asked.

"Probably a disrupter of some kind," Tom said. "Activate the thing, slap it onto somebody, and it disrupts the body's blood vessels or neurons. Gives somebody a stroke or shuts down their brain, and—"

"You have such things?" Benzi asked.

"Well, there's one of them right there," Tom said. "Always knew they were a distinct possibility. We've got implants for medical purposes. It wouldn't take much to make them for other uses."

"I never heard of such a thing before," Alonza said softly, although she had heard plenty of rumors and had long harbored the same suspicions as Tom.

"It seems that you may have saved my life," Benzi said to Alonza. "I'm very grateful."

Alonza thought of Colonel Sansom's orders. Get the operative into custody as quietly as possible, he had told her. If he had wanted to keep this matter quiet before, he certainly would not want word about the woman's attempt on Benzi's life to leak out now.

Presumably the operative had been sent here for the purpose of killing the Habber, and afterwards those who ran the shadowy and mysterious secret service of the Guardians had come to their senses and decided to call off the mission. She wondered what the diplomatic consequences would have been if Sameh had succeeded, and exactly what whoever had given the woman her orders had hoped to accomplish.

There was no question of what Alonza's own fate would have been had Benzi died. Colonel Sansom and those above him would have had to punish somebody. The loss of her rank and a court-martial would have been the least of her punishment; any work detail she was assigned to after that would be a lot worse than anything her mother had probably suffered.

She realized then what Sameh's movements had reminded her of when the woman had moved toward Benzi. Amparo had sometimes moved in the same way, creeping up on her marks when there weren't other people around, ready for a quick and disabling blow to the back of the head with her pouch of pebbles and small stones.

"You'll have to store the body," she said to Tom, "until the colonel gets back. And I'll have to make a report." She turned to Benzi. "I'll need a statement from you," she said. "Once it's recorded, you can board your ship and be on your way."

"In other words," Benzi said, "you'd prefer to keep this quiet."

"Obviously." Alonza sighed. "You must know that we have our few extremists, people who would prefer that we have nothing to do with your people, but be assured that such folk will be watched even more closely from now on and that you'll be safe. I don't know what you intend to tell your own people." She thought of his Link. "Maybe they already know."

"My Link was closed—is closed." Benzi's face was solemn. "But they will be informed. This shouldn't affect our agreements with your Council, since you saved my life. In protecting me, you honored our agreement."

"My duty," she said. "It wasn't out of any particular concern for you."

"I know, and that speaks well of you and your Guardian training." For a moment, she thought that he was being sarcastic again, and then he bowed his head to her.

"We'll go to Tom's office, and you can give me your report there." Tom would keep quiet, and Benzi would soon be gone; she strongly doubted that this Habber would ever return to Earth or to the Wheel again.

* * * * * * *

Tom told his infirmary staff that Sameh Tryolla had unexpectedly died of a stroke, a cause of death verified by a scan of the corpse. Alonza doubted that any of them believed that was the whole story, but they seemed willing to accept it. Benzi's passengers would simply assume that their former companion was being kept in the infirmary for more tests. She wondered if any of them would try to find out about her in years to come, if they would even be able to call up any records about her fate. Sameh Tryolla might disappear as thoroughly as though she had never existed, which in a sense, she hadn't.

Where had they found her? But Alonza could guess the answer to that. The woman who had become Sameh Tryolla would have come from the ranks of those on Basic; she would have been someone who could vanish from her earlier life without anyone's missing her and slip easily into another life. She had probably been a child much like Alonza herself.

After Benzi's ship had left the Wheel, Alonza sent a short report to Colonel Sansom, promising him a full report when he returned. Things had not gone as he might have hoped, but the operative's mission had been aborted and the whole business kept quiet.

What still nagged at her was exactly why Sameh had been sent here to kill the Habber, what the purpose of her mission was. Would any Habber have served equally well as her target, or had she been after Benzi in particular? Maybe those using Sameh had wanted to make an example of the man who had abandoned his world for that of the Habbers. But would they have jeopardized Earth's treaties with the Associated Habitats simply to punish Benzi? Would they have risked losing their uneasy but enduring peace with the Habbers as well as the loss of the resources and expertise their more advanced technology could provide to the home world?

Sameh Tryolla could not have left the camp outside Tashkent carrying a disrupter in her duffel without the connivance of at least one of the camp's Guardians. Someone might have slipped the weapon to her at the port in Tashkent, before she boarded the shuttle, but getting it to her earlier so that she could conceal it before leaving for the Wheel would be safer. No security officers at the Tashkent port or aboard the shuttle would have bothered to search any of the travelers, who had already been cleared by Keir Renin and his people in the camp and had been under Guardian supervision ever since.

More unanswered questions—and it was probably best, Alonza thought, to leave them forever unanswered.

* * * * * * *

Colonel Sansom returned to the Wheel thirty hours after Sameh's death. Alonza met him at the hub, accompanied him to the infirmary, and sat with him while he perused the full report on a pocket screen in the office of Tom Ruden-Nodell.

"You did well, Major Lemaris," the colonel said.

"I'm sure any of your officers would have done as well," she replied.

"I'm not at all sure of that." His voice was hard.

"One thing puzzles me, though," Alonza said. "Seems to me that the whole point in using a weapon like a disrupter is to make sure no one knows you've used it. I mean, I can see Sameh Tryolla using it if she and her victim were alone. Slap the thing on the Habber, make sure he's dead, ditch the thing in a recycling slot and nobody's the wiser. But to make the attempt in front of witnesses—"

"Obviously she was so intent on her mission," the colonel interrupted, "that she didn't consider that, and simply used the means she was given. In any case, what would you have done had she succeeded? Put her under restraint and under guard, go through all the usual procedures—informing me, getting your report together, waiting for diplomats to arrive to try to reassure the other Habbers—"

"Waiting for my own court-martial," Alonza added.

"Needless to say. And the operative would have been officially charged, sent back to Earth for a hearing, and probably have disappeared after that. Maybe that's what she was promised if she were caught—a hearing, a sentence, and then a new life and identity."

"Somebody really wanted that Habber out of the way, then," Alonza said.

"No, Alonza. Think." Jonas Sansom leaned forward in his chair and rested his arms on Tom's desk. "Someone wanted me out of the way."

She stared across the desk at him. "But—"

"I should have been here to take charge of the situation. I would have been if not for those damaged tracking telescopes, and that was pure chance."

"So they had to abort Sameh's mission," Alonza said, "but they didn't have a way to tell her—"

The colonel shook his head violently. "No. Saying that the mission had to be aborted was probably part of the plan. It was the way to be certain that I would be there when she struck at the Habber, that I would have to take responsibility for failing to protect him."

"But why would anybody want to get you?" she asked.

"Perhaps you don't want to know why, Alonza. I know Earth needs the Habbers and their technology more than we're willing to admit, and I haven't made any secret of my opinions. There are others who disagree, who would willingly see Earth become even more impoverished if they could be rid of our agreements with the Habbers. Let's leave it at that."

He folded his hands. There was more gray in his blond hair, and the lines on either side of his mouth were deep grooves. "We're all pawns in the hands of the Guardian Commanders," he continued, "and there are those who think that Earth may grow too dependent on the Associated Habitats and that the Council of Mukhtars has already made too many concessions to them. An incident involving the death of a Habber we were bound by treaty to protect would have been useful to certain political factions."

"Well." She looked away from him for a moment.

"We can continue to be pawns," Colonel Sansom said, "or we can be the players who move the pieces. Those are the only choices we have, and I know which one I'd rather be. I'm due for a promotion soon, and I'm going to put in for a post that will move me closer to the center of the game. I'll want my best officers with me."

"Of course, sir."

"You'll probably get a commendation for your recent action. You ought to take advantage of that and put in for duty in Baghdad at headquarters. That's what I'm going to do, and right now you're in a position to get whatever post you want." He stood up. "I'll talk to the chief physician now, and then I'll be in the officers' mess for dinner with the rest of my staff. Will you join me there in a couple of hours?"

"Yes, sir."

"You did well, Alonza—Major Lemaris."

"Thank you, sir."

* * * * * * *

A torchship slowly floated away from the dark metal lattice-work of a dock. Alonza watched the ship on the bay viewscreen and for a moment wished that she were one of its passengers. Some months ago, even a few days ago, she would have leaped at any opportunity to rise, to remain on Jonas Sansom's staff, to be stationed near one of the centers of power.

Now she was thinking of Sameh Tryolla again. Maybe she had been found in a port like San Antonio's before being shipped off to a children's dormitory and whatever training was deemed suitable for her. Alonza imagined herself in Sameh's place, soothed, manipulated, moved across the board and then discarded.

Always know when to run, Amparo had told her.

There was another choice besides being a pawn or a player, and that was abandoning the game. Colonel Sansom would be dismayed when she put in her request for duty on Luna, and then he would conclude that he had misjudged her, that she did not have the ambition or the stomach for the greater game. But there would be other pawns he could use.

She left the bay and hurried toward the lift, already late for the dinner with the colonel. Tom would be surprised when she told him that she was going to ask to be stationed on Luna. They might even travel there together, adrift for a time aboard the shuttlecraft taking them to Luna, anticipating the destination that lay ahead of them. They would follow the sky together.

AFTERWORD FOR "FOLLOW THE SKY"

When John Helfers and Marty Greenberg informed me that they were putting together an anthology of stories about space stations, I immediately thought of a space station in my Venus novels, the Wheel, that I had used as a setting only in passing. The rest of the story gave me an opportunity to write about the lives of a few of the people I had briefly mentioned in *Venus of Dreams*, namely the port thieves who preyed on unwary travelers.

Benzi Liangharad appears in all three of the Venus novels; "Follow the Sky" depicts an incident that might have occurred early in his long life. Alonza Lemaris plays no role in the trilogy, but I found it enjoyable to write a story about one of those many characters who make up the nameless mass of people in the backgrounds of all novels.

DREAM OF VENUS

Hassan Petrovich Maksutov's grandfather was the first to point out Venus to him, when Hassan was five years old. His family and much of his clan had moved to the outskirts of Jeddah by then, and his grandfather had taken him outside to view the heavens.

The night sky was a black canopy of tiny flickering flames; Hassan had imagined suddenly growing as tall as a djinn and reaching out to touch a star. Venus did not flicker like other stars, but shone steadily on the horizon in the hour before dawn. Hassan had not known then that he would eventually travel to that planet, but he had delighted in looking up at the beacon that signified humankind's greatest endeavor.

Twenty years after that first sighting, Hassan was gazing down at Venus from one of the ten domed Islands that floated in the upper reaches of the planet's poisonous atmosphere. These Cytherian Islands, as they were known (after the island of Cythera where the goddess Aphrodite had been worshipped in the ancient world), were vast platforms that had been built on top of massive metal cells filled with helium and then covered with dirt and soil. After each Island had been enclosed by an impermeable dome, the surfaces were gardened, and by the time Hassan was standing on a raised platform at the edge of Island Two and peering into the veiled darkness below, the Islands had for decades been gardens of trees, flowers, grassy expanses, and dwellings that housed the people who had come to Venus to be a part of the Project, Earth's effort to terraform her sister planet.

The Venus Project, as Hassan had known ever since childhood, was the greatest feat of engineering humankind had ever attempted, an enterprise that had already taken the labor of millions. Simply constructing the Parasol, the umbrella that shielded Venus from the sun, was an endeavor that had dwarfed the building of the Pyramids (where his father and mother had taken him to view those majestic crumbling monuments) and China's Great Wall (which he had visited during a break from his studies at the University of Chimkent). The Parasol had grown into a vast metallic flower as wide in diameter as Venus herself, in order to allow that hot and deadly world to cool. Venus would remain cloaked in the Parasol's shadow for centuries to come.

Hassan's grandfather had explained to him, during their sighting of Venus, that what he was seeing was in fact not the planet itself, but the reflected light of the Parasol. To the old man, this made the sight even more impressive, since the great shield was humankind's accomplishment, but Hassan had felt a twinge of disappointment. Even now, as he stood on Island Two, the planet below was veiled in darkness, hidden from view.

The Venus of past millennia, with a surface hot enough to melt lead, an atmosphere thick with sulfur dioxide, and an atmospheric pressure that would have crushed a person standing on its barren surface, had already undergone changes. Hydrogen, siphoned off from Saturn, had been carried to Venus in a steady stream of tanks and then released into the atmosphere, where it was combining with the free oxygen produced by the changes in the Venusian environment to form water. The Cytherian clouds had been seeded with a genetically engineered strain of algae that fed on the sulfuric acid and expelled it in the form of copper and iron sulfides. The Venus of the past now existed more in memory than in reality; the Venus of the future, that green and fertile planet that would become a second Earth and a new home for humankind, was still a dream.

As for the present, Hassan would now become one more person whose life would be enlarged by his own contribution, however small, to the great Venus Project. So Hassan's father

Pyotr Andreievich had hoped while meeting with friends and exerting his considerable influence on behalf of his son. Pyotr Andreievich Maksutov was a Linker, one of the privileged few who had implants linking their cortexes directly to Earth's cyberminds, a man who was often called upon to advise the Council of Mukhtars that governed all the Nomarchies of Earth and also watched over the Venus Project. Pyotr had convinced several Linkers connected with the Venus Project Council that Hassan, a specialist in geology, was worthy of being given a coveted place among the Cytherian Islanders.

Hassan, looking down at shadowed Venus through the transparent dome of Island Two, had been able to believe that he might have earned his position here until arriving on this Island. He had been here for two days now, and was beginning to feel as though his father's influence had always been a benign shadow over his life, one that had shielded him from certain realities. The passengers on the torchship that had carried him from Earth had been friendly, willing to share their enthusiasm for the work that lay ahead of them; the crew had been solicitous of his welfare, and he had taken their warmth and kindness as that of comrades reaching out to one who would soon be a colleague laboring for the Project. On the Island, he had been given a room in a building where most of the other residents were specialists who had lived on Island Two for several years, and had assumed that this was only because newcomers were usually assigned to any quarters that happened to be empty until more permanent quarters were found for them.

Now he suspected that the friendliness of the people aboard the torchship and his relatively comfortable quarters on Island Two had more to do with his family's connections than with luck or any merits of his own. The Venus Project needed people of all sorts—workers to maintain and repair homeostats and life support systems, and pilots for the airships that moved between the Islands and for the shuttles that carried passengers to and from Anwara, the space station in high orbit around Venus that was their link to Earth, where the torchships from the home world landed and docked. Counselors to tend to the psychological health of the Islanders, scientists, and people brave enough to work on the Bats, the two satellites above Venus's north and south poles, were all needed here, and not all of them were exceptionally gifted or among the most brilliant in their disciplines. Many Islanders, the workers in particular, came from the humblest of backgrounds; the Council of Mukhtars wanted all of Earth's people to share in the glory of terraforming, although the more cynical claimed that offering such hope to the masses also functioned as a social safety valve.

Hassan could tell himself that he measured up to any of the people here, and yet after only a short time on Island Two, he saw that many here had a quality he lacked—a determination, a hardness, a devotion to the Project that some might call irrational. Such obsessiveness was probably necessary for those who would never see the result of their efforts, who had to have faith that others would see what they had started through to the end. The Project needed such driven people, and would need them for centuries to come.

But Hassan was only a younger son of an ambitious and well-connected father, who was here mostly because Pyotr could not think of anything else to do with him. He was not brilliant enough to be trained for an academic position, not politically adept enough to maneuver his way into becoming an aide to the Council of Mukhtars, and he lacked the extraordinary discipline required of those chosen to be Linkers; his more flighty mind, it was feared, might be overwhelmed by the sea of data a Link would provide. Hassan might, however, be burnished by a decade or two of work on the Project. With that accomplishment on his public record, he could return to Earth and perhaps land a position training hopeful young idealists who dreamed of joining the Project; that sort of post would give him some influence. He might even be brought in to consult with members of the Project Council, or made a member of one of the committees that advised the Council of Mukhtars on the terraforming of Venus. In any event, his father would see an ineffectual son transformed into a man with a reputation much enhanced by his small role in humankind's most ambitious enterprise.

Hassan knew that he should consider himself fortunate that his father had the power to help secure his son's position. He was even luckier to win a chance to be listed among all of those who would make a new Earth of Venus. His life had been filled with good fortune, yet he often wondered why his luck had not made him happier.

* * * * * * *

After the call to evening prayer had sounded, and the bright light of the dome high overhead had faded into silver, Hassan usually walked to the gardens near the ziggurat where Island Two's Administrators lived and ate his supper there. He might have taken the meal in his building's common room with the other residents, or alone in his room, but eating in solitude did not appeal to him. As for dining with the others, the people who lived in his building still treated him with a kind of amused and faintly contemptuous tolerance even after almost five months.

Hassan chafed at such treatment. Always before, at school and at university and among the guests his family invited to their compound, he had been sought out, flattered, and admired. His opinions had been solicited, his tentative comments on all sorts of matters accepted as intriguing insights into the matters of the day. His professors, even those who had expected more of him, had praise for his potential if not for his actual accomplishment. But many Islanders seemed to regard him as someone on the level of a common worker, no better or worse than anyone else. Indeed the workers here, most of whom came from either teeming slums or the more impoverished rural areas and isolated regions of Earth's Nomarchies, were often treated with more deference than he was.

And why not? Hassan had finally asked himself. Why shouldn't an illiterate man or woman laboring for the Project be given more respect than a Linker's son? The workers, however humble their origins, had to be the best at their trades, and extremely determined, in order to win a place here, and the main reward they wanted for their efforts was a chance for their descendants to have more opportunities than they had been given and to be among the first to settle a new world. Hassan's place was a gift from his father, and he was not thinking of a better world for any children he might have, only of hanging on to what his family already possessed.

Hassan sat down at his usual table, which was near a small pool of water. Other people, several with the small diamondlike gems of Linkers on their foreheads, sat at other tables around the pool and under slender trees that resembled birches. As a servo rolled toward him to take his order, he glimpsed his friend Muhammad Sheridan hurrying toward him from the stone path that led to the Administrators' ziggurat.

"Salaam," Muhammad called out to him. "Thought I'd be late—the Committee meeting went on longer than we expected." The brown-skinned young man sat down across from Hassan. Muhammad's family were merchants and shopkeepers from the Atlantic Federation, wealthy enough to have a large estate near the southern New Jersey dikes and sea walls and well connected enough to have sent Muhammad to the University of Damascus for his degree in mathematics. Hassan felt at ease with Muhammad; the two often ate dinner together. Muhammad had a position as an aide to Administrator Pavel Gvishiani, a post that would have assured him a certain amount of status on Earth. But here, Muhammad often felt himself patronized, as he had admitted to Hassan.

"Let's face it," Muhammad had said only the other evening, "the only way we're going to make a place for ourselves among these people is to do something truly spectacular for the Project, maybe something, God willing, on the order of what Dawud Hasseen accomplished." Dawud Hasseen had designed the Parasol almost three centuries earlier, and had been the chief engineer during its construction. "Or else we'll have to put in our time here without complaining until we're as driven and obsessed as most of the workers and younger specialists, in which case we might finally become more acceptable."

The second course was their only realistic alternative, Hassan thought. Their work here would not allow either of them much scope for grand achievements. Muhammad's position as an aide to Pavel Gvishiani required him to devote his time to such humble tasks as backing up written and oral records of meetings, retrieving summaries of them when needed, preparing and reviewing routine public statements, and occasionally entertaining Pavel with discussions of any mathematical treatises the Administrator had recently had transmitted to him from Earth. Lorna FredasMarkos, the head of Hassan's team of geologists, had given Hassan the mundane work of keeping the team's records in order and occasionally analyzing data on the increases in the levels of iron and copper sulfides on the basalt surface of Venus, work no one else was particularly interested in doing and that almost anyone else could have done.

"I don't know which Islanders are the worst," Muhammad had continued, "the peasants and street urchins who came here from Earth, or the workers who think of themselves as the Project's aristocrats just because their families have been living here for more than one generation." This was the kind of frank remark Hassan's friend would have kept to himself in other company.

Muhammad set his pocket screen on the tabletop in front of him. Hassan had brought his own pocket screen; although there was no work he had to do this evening, he had taken to toting his screen around, so that he could at least give the appearance of being busy and needed. The two young men ordered a pot of tea and simple meals of vegetables, beans, and rice. Hassan had come to the Islands with enough credit to afford a more lavish repast, even some imported foods from Earth, but he was doing his best to keep within the credit allotted to him by the Project, knowing that this would look better on his record.

"How goes it with you?" Muhammad asked.

"The way it usually does," Hassan replied, "although Lorna

hinted that she might give me a new assignment. There's a new geologist joining our team, so perhaps Lorna wants me to be her mentor." He had looked up the public record of the geologist, who had arrived from Earth only two days ago. Her name was Miriam Lucea-Noyes; she had grown up on a farm in the Pacific Federation of North America, and had been trained at the University of Vancouver. It was easy for him to piece together most of her story from her record. Miriam Lucea-Noyes had been one of those bright but unschooled children who was occasionally discovered by a regional Counselor and elevated beyond her family's status; she had been chosen for a preparatory school and then admitted to the university for more specialized training. Her academic record was, Hassan ruefully admitted to himself, superior to his own, and he could safely assume that she had the doggedness and single-mindedness of most of those who had come to the Cytherian Islands. About the only surprising detail in her record was the fact that she had spent two years earning extra credit for her account as a technical assistant to a director of mind-tours and virtual entertainments before completing her studies.

"Ah, yes, the new geologist." Muhammad smiled. "Actually, I might be at least partly responsible for your new assignment. Administrator Pavel thinks it's time that we put together a new mind-tour of the Venus Project. The Project Council could use the extra credit the production would bring, and we haven't done one for a while."

Hassan leaned back. "I would have thought that there were already enough such entertainments."

"True, but most of them are a bit quaint. All of them could use some updating. And Pavel thinks that we have the capacity to provide a much more exciting and detailed experience now."

The servo returned with a teapot and two cups. Hassan poured himself and his friend some tea. "I wouldn't have thought," he said, "that an Administrator would be concerning himself with something as relatively unimportant as a mind-tour."

"Pavel Gvishiani is the kind of man who concerns himself

with everything." Muhammad sipped some tea. "Anyway, Pavel was discussing this mind-tour business with the rest of the Administrators, and they all agreed that we could spare a couple of people to map out a tour. This new geologist on your team, Miriam Lucea-Noyes, is an obvious choice, given that she has some experience with mind-tour production. And when Pavel brought up her name, I suggested that you might be someone who could work very well with her on such a project."

"I see." Hassan did not know whether to feel flattered or embarrassed. Although cultivated people were not above enjoying them, the visual and sensory experiences of mind-tours were most popular with children and with ignorant and uneducated adults. They served the useful functions of providing vicarious experiences to people who might otherwise grow bored or discontented, and of imparting some knowledge of history and culture to the illiterate. With the aid of a band that could link one temporarily to Earth's cyberminds, a person could wander to unfamiliar places, travel back in time, or participate in an adventure.

Hassan had spent many happy hours as a child with a band around his head, scuba-diving in the sunken city of Venice and climbing to the top of Mount Everest with a party of explorers, among other virtual adventures. For a while, at university, he had toyed with the notion of producing such entertainments himself. He had managed to fit courses in virtual graphics, adventure fiction, music, and sensory effects production into his schedule of required studies, and had been part of a student team producing a mind-tour for the University of Chimkent to use in recruiting new students and faculty until his father had put a stop to such pursuits. He had given in, of course—Pyotr had threatened to cut him off from all credit except a citizen's basic allotment and to do nothing to help him in such a profession as mind-tour production—but he had remained bitter about the decision his father had forced on him. In an uncharacteristic emotional venting, Hassan had admitted his bitterness over his thwarted dream to Muhammad. Being chosen to work on the university's mind-tour remained the only privilege he had ever won for himself, without his father's intercession.

"It won't hurt to have such experiences on your record," Pyotr had told Hassan, "as long as it's clear that this mind-tour business is just a hobby. But it isn't the kind of profession that could make a Linker of you, or give you any chance in politics." His father had, for a while, made him feel ashamed of his earlier ambition.

"It's not that I'm doing you any special favors, Hassan," Muhammad said. "It's just that we don't have many people here who could put together even a preliminary visual sketch of a mind-tour, and Administrator Pavel thinks having people associated with the Project doing the work might impart a new perspective, something more original, something that isn't just the vast spectacle interspersed with inspiring dioramas that most mind-tours about the Venus Project are." He paused. "Anyway, it'll be something other than the routine work you've been doing."

Hassan found himself warming to the prospect. Constructing a mind-tour, putting together the kind of experience that would make anyone, however humble his position, proud to be even a small part of a society that could transform a planet—this was a challenge he was certain he could meet. There was also an ironic satisfaction in knowing that the pursuit his father had scorned might become his means of winning Administrator Pavel's favor.

* * * * * * *

Miriam Lucea-Noyes was a short, extremely pretty woman with thick dark brown hair, wide-set gray eyes, and a look of obstinacy. "Salaam," she murmured to Hassan after Lorna FredasMarkos had introduced them.

"How do you do," Hassan replied. Miriam gazed at him steadily until he averted his eyes.

"Hassan," Lorna said, "I feel as though we might have been

wasting your talents." The gray-haired woman smiled. "You should have called your experience with mind-tour production to my attention earlier."

"It was noted in my record," he said.

"Well, of course, but one can so easily overlook such notations—" Lorna abruptly fell silent, as if realizing that she had just admitted that she had never bothered to study his record thoroughly, that she had given it no more than the cursory glance that was probably all the attention it deserved. "Anyway," the older woman continued, "Administrator Pavel is quite pleased that two members of my team are capable of putting together a new mind-tour. You will have access to all the records our sensors have made, and to everything in the official records of the Project, but if there's anything else you need, be sure to let me know."

"How long do we have?" Miriam asked.

Lorna lifted her brows. "Excuse me?"

"What's the deadline?" Miriam said. "How long do we have to pull this thing together?"

"Administrator Pavel indicated that he would like to have it completed before the New Year's celebrations," the older woman replied.

"So we've got five months," Miriam said. "Then I think we'll see in the year 535 with one hell of a fine mind-tour."

Lorna pursed her thin lips, as if tasting something sour. "You may both have more time if you need it. The Administrator would prefer that you keep to his informal deadline, but he also made it clear that he would rather have a mind-tour that is both aesthetically pleasing and inspirational, even if that takes longer to complete."

Hassan bowed slightly in Lorna's direction. "We'll do our best to produce a mind-tour that is both pleasing and on time, God willing."

"And that isn't a sloppy rush job, either," Miriam said.

"I may have to drag you away to our team meetings and your other standard tasks occasionally," Lorna said, "but I'll try to keep such distractions to a minimum." She turned toward the doorway. "Salaam aleikum."

"Aleikum salaam," Miriam said. Her Arabic sounded as flat and unmusical as her Anglaic.

"God go with you," Hassan added as the door slid shut behind their supervisor.

"Well, Hassan." Miriam sat down on one of the cushions at the low table. "I don't know if you've ever seen any of the mind-tours I worked on. Most of them were for small children, so you probably haven't. 'Hans Among the Redwoods'—that was one of our more popular ones, and 'Dinosaurs in the Gobi'."

He tensed with surprise. "I saw that dinosaur mind-tour—marvelous work. Maybe you made it for children, but I have several adult friends who also enjoyed it."

"And 'The Adventure of Montrose Scarp'."

Hassan was impressed in spite of himself. "'Montrose Scarp?'" he asked as he seated himself. "My nephew Salim couldn't get enough of that one. He just about forced me to put on a band and view it. What I particularly admired was the way the excitement of the climb and the geological history of the scarp were so seamlessly combined."

"That was my doing, if I do say so myself." Miriam pointed her chin at him. "Joe Kinnear—he was the director I worked with—he wanted to put in more of the usual shit—you know, stuff like having the mind-tourist lose his grip and fall before being caught by the rope tied around him, or throwing in a big storm just as you reach the top of the escarpment. He thought doing what I wanted would just slow the thing down, but I convinced him otherwise, and I was right."

"Yes, you were," Hassan said.

"And every damned mind-tour of Venus has the obligatory scene of Karim al-Anwar speaking to the Council of Mukhtars, telling them that what they learn from the terraforming of Venus might eventually be needed to save Earth from the effects of global warming, or else a scene of New York or some other flooded coastal city at evening while Venus gleams on the horizon and a portentous voice quotes from that speech Mukhtar Karim supposedly made toward the end of his life."

Karim al-Anwar had been the first to propose a project to terraform Venus, back in the earliest days of Earth's Nomarchies, not long after the Resource Wars almost six centuries ago. "When I gaze upon Venus," Hassan quoted, "and view the images our probes have carried back to us from its hot and barren surface, I see Earth's future, and fear for our world."

"Followed by the sensation of heat and a hellish image of the Venusian surface," Miriam said. "And the three most recent ones all have scenes of explosions on the Bats, which I frankly think is misleading and maybe even too frightening."

The Bats, the two winged satellites in geosynchronous orbit at Venus's poles, serviced the automatic shuttles that carried compressed oxygen from the robot-controlled installations at the Venusian poles to the Bats. The process of terraforming was releasing too much of Venus's oxygen, and the excess had to be removed if the planet was ever to support life. The workers on the Bats, people who serviced the shuttles and maintained the docks, knew that the volatile oxygen could explode, and many lives had been lost in past explosions.

"There are real dangers on the Bats," Miriam continued, "but we don't have to dwell on them just for the sake of a few thrills. I'd rather avoid those kinds of clichés."

"So would I," Hassan said fervently.

"We should purge our minds of anything we've seen before and start over with an entirely fresh presentation."

"I think that's exactly what Pavel Gvishiani wants us to do."

"We're geologists," Miriam said, "and maybe that's the angle we ought to use. I don't think past mind-tours have really given people a feeling for the Project in the context of geological time. I'd like to emphasize that. Hundreds of years of human effort set against the eons it took to form Venus—and if we get into planetary evolution and the beginnings of the solar system...."

"I couldn't agree with you more," Hassan said.

"Most of the people who experience this mind-tour are likely to be ignorant and unschooled, but that doesn't mean we have to oversimplify things and lard the narrative with dramatic confrontations and action scenes."

"It sounds as though what we want is a mind-tour that would be both enlightening to the uneducated," Hassan said, "and yet entertaining and inspirational to the learned."

"That's exactly what I want," Miriam said.

It was also, Hassan thought, exactly what Pavel Gvishiani was likely to want. Judging by what Muhammad had told him about the Administrator, Pavel was not someone who cared to have his intelligence insulted. To have a mind-tour that would not just be an informative entertainment, but a masterpiece—

"We should talk about how we want to frame it," Hassan said, "before we start digging through all the records and sensor scans. Have a structure that encapsulates our vision, and then start collecting what we need to realize it."

"Exactly," Miriam said. "You'd be surprised at how many mind-tour directors do it the other way around, looking at everything that could possibly have anything to do with their theme while hoping that some coherent vision suddenly emerges out of all the clutter. That isn't the way I like to work."

"Nor I," Hassan said, gazing across the table at her expressive face and intense gaze, already enthralled.

* * * * * *

Miriam, despite being a geologist and a specialist, lived in a building inhabited by workers, people who repaired homeostats and robots, maintained airships and shuttles, tended hydroponic gardens, looked out for small children in the Island's child care center, and performed other necessary tasks. Hassan had assumed that there was no room for her elsewhere, and that her quarters would be temporary. Instead, Miriam had admitted to him that she had requested space there, and intended to stay.

"Look," she said, "I went to a university, but a lot of students there didn't let me forget where I came from. I feel more comfortable with workers than with the children of merchants and engineers and Counselors and Linkers." She had glanced at him apologetically after saying that, obviously not wanting to hurt his feelings, but he had understood. His family's position might have brought him to this place, but with Miriam, he now had a chance to make his own small mark on the Project, to inspire others with the dream of Venus.

"The Dream of Venus"—that was how he and Miriam referred to the mind-tour they had been outlining and roughing out for almost a month now. He thought of what they had been sketching and planning as he walked toward the star-shaped steel-blue building in which Miriam lived. As they usually did at last light, workers had gathered on the expanse of grass in front of the building. Families sat on the grass, eating from small bowls with chopsticks or fingers; other people were talking with friends, mending worn garments, or watching with pride and wonderment as their children reviewed their lessons on pocket screens. All children were schooled here, unlike Earth, where education was rationed and carefully parceled out.

It came to him then how much he now looked forward to coming here, to meeting and working with Miriam.

Hassan made his way to the entrance. Inside the window-less building, people had propped open the doors to their rooms to sit in the corridors and gossip; he passed one group of men gambling with sticks and dice. The place was as noisy and chaotic as a souk in Jeddah, but Hassan had grown more used to the cacophony. Since most of the workers could not read, the doors to their rooms were adorned with holo images or carvings of their faces, so that visitors could locate their quarters. Miriam's room was near the end of this wing; a holo image of her face stared out at him from the door.

He pressed his palm against the door; after a few seconds, it opened. Miriam, wearing a brown tunic and baggy brown pants, was sitting on the floor in front of her wall screen, a thin metal band around her head; even in such plain clothes, she looked beautiful to him.

"Salaam," she said without looking up.

"Salaam."

"We're making real progress," she said. "This mind-tour is really shaping up."

He sat down next to her. Unlike most of the people in this building, Miriam had a room to herself, but it was not much larger than a closet. Building more residences on the Islands would have meant cutting back on the gardens and parks that were deemed essential to maintaining the mental health of the Islanders.

"Before you show me any of your rough cut," he said, "would you care to have supper with me as my guest?" This was the first time he had offered such an invitation to her; he had enough credit to order imported delicacies from Earth for her if that was what she wanted. "We can go to the garden near the Administrators' building, unless of course you'd rather dine somewhere else."

"Maybe later," she said in the flat voice that was such a contrast to her lovely face and graceful movements. "I want you to look at this first."

They had decided to depart from tradition in their structure for "The Dream of Venus." Miriam also wanted to dispense with the usual chronological depictions, which she found stodgy, and Hassan had readily agreed.

The mind-tour would begin with Karim al-Anwar, as every other depiction of the Venus Project did, but instead of the usual dramatic confrontations with doubters and passionate speeches about Earth's sister planet becoming a new home for human-kind, they would move directly to what Karim had envisioned—Venus as it would be in the far future. The viewer would see the blue-green gem of a transformed Venus from afar and then be swept toward the terraformed planet, falling until the surface was visible through Venus's veil of white clouds. Flying low over the shallow blue ocean, the mind-tourist would be swept past a small island chain toward the northern continent of Ishtar, with its high plateau and mountain massif that dwarfed even the Himalayas, to view a region of vast grasslands, evergreen forests, and rugged mountain peaks. Then the wail of the wind would rise as the viewer was carried south toward the equator and the colorful tropical landscape of the continent of Aphrodite.

Hassan was still tinkering with the sound effects for that section, but had found a piece of music that evoked the sound of a strong wind, and planned to use recordings of the powerful winds that continuously swept around Venus below the Islands as background and undertones. Near the end of the sequence, the viewer would fly toward a Venusian dawn, gazing at the sun before a dark shape, part of what remained of the Parasol, eclipsed its light. There were a few scientists who doubted that any part of the Parasol would be needed later on to insulate Venus from the heat and radiation that could again produce a runaway greenhouse effect, but most Cytherian specialists disagreed with them, and Hassan and Miriam had decided to go along with the majority's opinion in their depiction.

At this point, the viewer was to be swept back in time, so to speak, to one of the Cytherian Islands, in a manner that would suggest what was not shown in the mind-tour—namely that in the distant future, when Venus was green with life, the Islands would slowly drop toward the surface, where their inhabitants would at last leave their domed gardens to dwell on their new world. Hassan and Miriam had inserted a passage during the earlier flight sequence in which the viewer passed over an expanse of parklike land that strongly resembled Island Two's gardens and groves of trees. That scene, with some enhancement, would resonate in the viewer's mind with the subsequent Island sequences.

"What have you got to show me?" Hassan asked.

Miriam handed him a band. "This is some stuff for the earlier sequences," she said.

Hassan put the band around his head, was momentarily blind and deaf, and then was suddenly soaring over the vast canyon of the Diana Chasma toward the rift-ridden dome of Atla Regio in the east and the shield volcano of Maat Mons, the largest volcano on Venus, three hundred kilometers in diameter and rising to a Himalayan height. The scene abruptly shifted to the steep massif of Maxwell Montes rising swiftly from the hot dark surface of Ishtar Terra as millions of years were compressed into seconds. He whirled away from the impressively high mountain massif and hovered over a vast basaltic plain, watching as part of the surface formed a dome, spread out, grew flat, and then sank, leaving one of the round circular uniquely Venusian features called coronae. He moved over the cracked and wrinkled plateaus called tesserae and was surprised at the beauty he glimpsed in the deformed rocky folds of the land.

His field of vision abruptly went dark.

"What do you think?" Miriam's voice asked.

He shifted his band slightly; Miriam's room reappeared. "I know it's rough," she continued, "and I've got more to add to it, but I hope it gives you an idea. As for sound effects and the sensory stuff, I think we should keep that to a minimum—just a low undertone, the bare suggestion of a low throbbing noise, and maybe a feeling of extreme heat without actually making the viewer break out in a sweat. Well, what do you think?"

Hassan said, "I think it's beautiful, Miriam." His words were sincere. Somehow she had taken what could have been no more than an impressive visual panorama and had found the beauty in the strange, alien terrain of Venus as it might have been six hundred million years ago. It was as if she had fallen in love with that world, almost as if she regretted its loss.

"If you think that's something," she said, "wait until you see what I've worked up for the resurfacing section, where we see volcanoes flooding the plains with molten basalt. But I want your ideas on what to use for sensory effects there, and you'll probably want to add some visuals, too—it seems a little too abbreviated as it is."

"You almost make me sorry," Hassan said, "that we're changing Venus, that what it was will forever be lost—already is lost."

Her gray eyes widened. "That's exactly the feeling I was

trying for. Every mind-tour about Venus and the Project always tries for the same effect—the feeling of triumph in the end by bringing a dead world to life, the beauty of the new Earthlike world we're making, the belief that we're carrying out God's will by transforming Venus into what it might have become. I want the mind-tourist at least to glimpse what we're losing with all this planetary engineering, to feel some sorrow that it is being lost."

Hassan smiled. "A little of that goes a long way, don't you think? We're supposed to be glorifying the Project, not regretting it."

"Sometimes I do regret it just a little. Imagine what we might have learned if we had built the Islands and simply used them to observe this planet. There are questions we may never answer now because of what we've already changed. Did Venus once have oceans that boiled away? Seems likely, but we probably won't ever be sure. Was there ever a form of life here that was able to make use of ultraviolet light? We'll never know that, either. We decided that terraforming this world and giving all of humankind that dream and learning what we could from the work of the Project outweighed all of that."

"Be careful, Miriam." Hassan lifted a hand. "We don't want to question the very basis of the Project."

"No, of course not." But she sounded unhappy about making that admission. Hassan would never have insulted her by saying this aloud, but she sounded almost like a Habber, one of those whose ancestors had abandoned Earth long ago in the wake of the Resource Wars to live in the hollowed-out asteroids and artificial worlds called Habitats. There might be a few Habbers living here to observe the Project, but they thought of space as their home, not planetary surfaces. A Habber might have claimed that Venus should have been left as it had been.

"You've done wonderfully with your roughs," Hassan murmured, suddenly wanting to cheer her. Miriam's face brightened as she glanced toward him. "Really, if the final mind-tour maintains the quality of this work, we'll have a triumph." He reached for her hand and held it for a moment, surprised at how small and delicate it felt in his grip. "Let me take you to supper," he went on, and admitted to himself at last that he was falling in love with her.

* * * * * * *

They would have a masterpiece, Hassan told himself. Three months of working with Miriam had freed something inside him, had liberated a gift that he had not known he possessed. He felt inspired whenever he was with her. In his private moments, as he reviewed sections of "The Dream of Venus," he grew even more convinced that their mind-tour had the potential for greatness.

There, in one of the segments devoted to the Venus of millions of years ago, was a vast dark plain, an ocean of basalt covered by slender sinuous channels thousands of kilometers long. A viewer would soar over shield volcanoes, some with ridges that looked like thin spider legs, others with lava flows that blossomed along their slopes. The mind-tourist could roam on the plateau of Ishtar and look up at the towering peaks of the Maxwell Mountains, shining brightly with a plating of tellurium and pyrite. What might have been only a succession of fascinating but ultimately meaningless geological panoramas had been shaped by Miriam into a moving evocation of a planet's life, a depiction of a truly alien beauty.

Hassan had contributed his own stylings to the mind-tour; he had shaped and edited many of the scenes, and his sensory effects had added greatly to the moods of awe and wonder that the mind-tour would evoke. It had been his idea to frame the entire mind-tour as the vision of Karim al-Anwar, and to begin and end with what the great man might have dreamed, a device that also allowed them to leave out much of the tedious expository material that had cluttered up so many mind-tours depicting Venus and the Project. But Miriam was the spirit that had animated him, that had awakened him to the visions and sounds that had lain dormant inside him.

The fulfillment he felt in the work they were doing together was marred by only one nagging worry: that "The Dream of Venus" was in danger of becoming an ode to Venus past, a song of regret for the loss of the world that most saw as sterile and dead, but which had become so beautiful in Miriam's renderings. What the Administrators wanted was a glorification of the Project, a mind-tour that would end on a note of optimism and triumph. They were unlikely to accept "The Dream of Venus" as it was, without revisions, and might even see it as vaguely subversive.

But there was still time, Hassan told himself, to reshape the mind-tour when "The Dream of Venus" was nearly in final form. He did not want to cloud Miriam's vision in the meantime with doubts and warnings; he did not want to lose what he had discovered in himself.

He and Miriam were now eating nearly all of their meals together and conducting their courtship at night, in her bed or his own. He had admitted his love for her, as she had confessed hers for him, and soon the other members of their geological team and the residents of their buildings were asking them both when they intended to make a pledge. Hassan's mother was the cousin of a Mukhtar, and his father had always hoped that Hassan would also take an influential woman as a bondmate, but Pyotr could not justifiably object to Miriam, who had won her place with intelligence and hard work. In any event, by the time he finally told his father that he loved Miriam enough to join his life to hers, their mind-tour would have secured their status here. Pyotr could take pride in knowing that a grandchild of his would be born on the Islands, that his descendants might one day be among those who would live on Venus.

That was something else "The Dream of Venus" had roused inside Hassan. He had come here thinking only of doing his best not to disgrace his family. Now the dream of Venus had begun to flower in him.

* * * * * * *

"We think that the Project has no true ethical dilemmas," Miriam was saying, "that it can't possibly be wrong to terra-form a dead world. We're not displacing any life forms, we're not destroying another culture and replacing it with our own. But there is a kind of arrogance involved, don't you think?"

Hassan and Miriam were sitting on a bench outside a green-house near Island Two's primary school. They often came here after last light, when the children had left and the grounds adjoining the school were still and silent.

"Arrogance?" Hassan asked. "I suppose there is, in a way." He had engaged in such discussions before, at university, and it had been natural for him and Miriam to talk about the issues the Project raised while working on "The Dream of Venus." Lately, their conversations had taken on more intensity.

"God gave us nature to use, as long as we use it wisely and with concern for other life forms," Miriam said, repeating the conventional view promulgated by both the true faith of Islam and the Council of Mukhtars. "Terraforming Venus is therefore justified, since the measure of value is determined by the needs of human beings. And if you want to strengthen that argument, you can throw in the fact that we're bringing life to a world where no life existed, which has to be rated as a good. On top of that, there's the possibility that Venus was once much like Earth before a runaway greenhouse effect did it in, so to speak. Therefore, we're restoring the planet to what it might have been."

Hassan, still holding her hand, was silent; the assertions were much too familiar for him to feel any need to respond. He was looking for an opening in which to bring up a subject he could no longer avoid. "The Dream of Venus" was close to comple-tion, and there was little time for them to do the editing and make the revisions that were necessary if their mind-tour was to be approved for distribution by the Administrators and the Project Council. He did not want to think of how much credit he and Miriam might already have cost the Project. All of that credit, and more—perhaps much more—would be recovered by the mind-tour; he was confident of that. But he had broached the need for editing to Miriam only indirectly so far.

"You could argue that all of life, not just human life and what furthers its ends, has intrinsic value," Miriam continued, "but that wouldn't count against the Project, only against forcing Venus to be a replica of Earth even if it later shows signs of developing its own distinct ecology in ways that differ from Earth's and which make it less habitable—or not habitable at all—by human beings. You could say that we should have abandoned our technology long ago and lived in accordance with nature, therefore never having the means to terraform a world, but that has always been an extremist view."

"And unconstructive," Hassan said. At this point, he thought, humankind would only do more damage to Earth by abandoning advanced technology; solar power satellites and orbiting industrial facilities had done much to lessen the environmental damage done to their home world.

"What I worry about now," she said, "isn't just what terraforming might do to Venus that we can't foresee, but what it might do to us. Remaking a planet may only feed our arrogance. It could lead us to think we could do almost anything. It could keep us from asking questions we should be asking. We might begin to believe that we could remake anything—the entire solar system, even our sun, to serve our ends. We might destroy what we should be preserving, and end by destroying ourselves."

"Or transforming ourselves," Hassan interjected. "You haven't made much of an argument, my love."

"I'm saying that we should be cautious. I'm saying that, whatever we do, doubt should be part of the equation, not an arrogance that could become a destructive illusion of certainty."

Those feelings, he knew, lay at the heart of their mind-tour. Uncertainty and doubt were the instruments through which finite beings had to explore their universe. The doubts, the knowledge that every gain meant some sort of loss—all of that underlined "The Dream of Venus" and lent their depiction its beauty.

And all of that would make their mind-tour unacceptable to the men and women who wanted a sensory experience that would glorify their Project and produce feelings of triumph and pride.

"Miriam," he said, trying to think of how to cajole her into considering the changes they would have to make, "I think we should start thinking seriously about how we might revise— how we might make some necessary edits in our mind-tour."

"There's hardly any editing we have to do now."

"I meant when it's done."

"But it's almost done now. It's not going to be much different in final form."

"I mean—" Hassan was having a difficult time finding the right words to make his point. "You realize that we'll have to dwell less on the fascination of Venus past and put more emphasis on the glory that will be our transformed Venus of the future."

She stared at him with the blank gaze of someone who did not understand what he was saying, someone who might have been talking to a stranger. "You can't mean that," she said. "You can't be saying what it sounds like you're saying."

"I only meant—"

She jerked her hand from his. "I thought we shared this vision, Hassan. I thought we were both after the same effect, the same end, that you—"

"There you are." Muhammad Sheridan was coming toward them along the stone path that ran past the school. "I thought I would find you two here." He came to a halt in front of them. "I would have left you a message, but...." He paused. "Administrator Pavel is exceedingly anxious to view your mind-tour, so I hope it's close to completion."

Hassan was puzzled. "He wants to view it?"

"Immediately," Muhammad replied. "I mean tomorrow, two hours after first light. He has also invited you both to be present, in his private quarters, and I told him that I would be happy to tell you that in person."

Hassan could not read his friend's expression in the soft silvery light. Anticipation? Nervousness? Muhammad, who had recommended Hassan as a mind-tour creator, would be thinking that a mind-tour that won Pavel's approval might gain Muhammad more favor, while a failure would only make Pavel doubt his aide's judgment.

"It should be in final form within a month," Hassan said. "We're within the deadline still, but it needs more refining. Couldn't we—"

"Of course we'll be there," Miriam said. "I think he'll be pleased." There was no trace of doubt in her voice. Hassan glanced at her; she took his hand. "I want him to experience what we've done."

Hassan felt queasy, trying to imagine what Pavel Gvishiani would think of "The Dream of Venus," searching his mind for an excuse he might offer to delay the Administrator's viewing of the mind-tour. Pavel might have viewed it at any time; as an Administrator and a Linker, he could have accessed the work-in-progress any time he wished through the Island cyberminds. But Hassan had simply assumed that Pavel would be too preoccupied with his many other duties to bother.

"Well." Hassan let go of Miriam's hand and rested his hands on his thighs. "Presumably he understands that it's not in final form."

"Close to it," Miriam said in her hard, toneless voice. "Might need a little tweaking, but I don't see much room for improvement."

"And," Hassan went on, "I don't know why he wants us both there, in his room."

"It's a matter of courtesy," Muhammad said. "Pavel is most attentive to courtesies."

Hassan peered at Miriam from the sides of his eyes; she was smiling. "If you think about it," she said, "it's kind of an honor, being invited to his private quarters and all."

Hassan's queasiness left him, to be replaced with a feeling

of dread.

* * * * * * *

The forty minutes of sitting with Pavel Gvishiani in his room, waiting as the Linker experienced the mind-tour, were passing too slowly and also too rapidly for Hassan; too slowly, so that he had ample time to consider the likely verdict the Administrator would render, and too rapidly, toward the moment of judgment and disgrace. While he waited, Hassan fidgeted on his cushion, glanced around the small room, and studied the few objects Pavel had placed on one shelf—a cloisonné plate, gold bands for securing a man's ceremonial headdress, a porcelain vase holding one blue glass flower.

Pavel, sitting on his cushion, was still. Occasionally, his eyelids fluttered over his half-open eyes. He wore no band; with his Link, he did not need a band to view the mind-tour.

I will think of the worst that can happen to me, Hassan thought as he stared at the tiny diamondlike gem on Pavel's forehead, and then whatever does happen won't seem so bad. Pavel and the Administrators would make him reimburse the credit the Project had allocated to him during his work on "The Dream of Venus." He could afford that, but his family would regard it as a mark against him. His public record would note that he had failed at this particular task; that humiliation would remain with him until he could balance it with some successes. His father, after using his influence to get Hassan a position with the Project, would be tainted by his son's failure and was likely to find a way to get back at him for that, perhaps even by publicly severing all ties with him. Muhammad, who had recommended him to Pavel, would no longer be his friend. And Miriam—

He glanced at the woman he had come to believe he loved. Her eyes shifted uneasily; she was frowning. He felt suddenly angry with her for drawing him so deeply into her vision, for that was what she had done; she had seduced him with her inspiration.

Maybe she was finally coming to understand that their mind-tour was not going to win Pavel's approval. If they were lucky, he might settle for castigating them harshly and demanding a host of revisions. If they were unlucky, he might regard their failure to give him what he had wanted as a personal affront.

Pavel opened his eyes fully and gazed directly at them, then arched his thick brows. "Both of you," he said quietly, "have produced something I did not expect." He paused, allowing Hassan a moment to collect himself. "Your mind-tour is a masterpiece. I would almost call it a work of art."

Miriam's chest heaved as she sighed. "Thank you, Administrator Pavel," she whispered. Hassan, bewildered, could not find his own voice.

"But of course we cannot distribute 'The Dream of Venus' in this form," Pavel continued, "and I am sure you both understand why we can't. You still have a month of your allotted time left. I expect to see an edited mind-tour by the end of that time and, depending on what you've accomplished by then, I can grant you more time if that's required. I won't insult your intelligence and artistry by telling you exactly what kind of changes you'll have to make, and I am no expert on designing mind-tours in any case. You know what you will have to do, and I am certain, God willing, that you'll find satisfactory ways to do it."

May the Prophet be forever blessed, Hassan thought, almost dizzy with this unexpected mercy. "Of course," he said. "I already have some ideas—"

"No," Miriam said.

Pavel's eyes widened. Hassan gazed at the woman who was so trapped in her delusions, wondering if she had gone mad.

"No," Miriam said again, "I won't do it. You said yourself that it was a masterpiece, but I knew that before we came here. You can do what you like with 'The Dream of Venus,' but I won't be a party to defacing my own work."

"Miriam," Hassan said weakly, then turned toward Pavel. "She doesn't know what she's saying."

"I know exactly what I'm saying. Edit our mind-tour however

you please, but I'll have nothing to do with it."

"My dear child," Pavel said in an oddly gentle tone, "you know what this will mean. You know what the consequences may be."

Miriam stuck out her chin. "I know. I don't care. I'll still have the joy and satisfaction in knowing what we were able to realize in that mind-tour, and you can't take that away from us." She regarded Hassan with her hard gray eyes. Hassan realized then that she expected him to stand with her, to refuse to do the Administrator's bidding.

"Miriam," he said softly. You bitch, he thought, Pavel's given us a way out and you refuse to take it. "I'll begin work on the editing," Hassan continued, "even if my colleague won't. Maybe once she sees how that's going, realizes that we can accomplish what's needed without doing violence to our creation, she'll change her mind and decide to help me." He had to defend her somehow, give her the chance to reconsider and step back from the abyss. "I'm sure Miriam just needs some time to think it over."

Miriam said, "I won't change my mind," and he heard the disillusionment and disgust in her voice. She got to her feet; Pavel lifted his head to look up at her. "Salaam aleikum, Administrator."

"If you leave now, there will be severe consequences," Pavel said, sounding regretful.

"I know," Miriam said, and left the room.

* * * * * * *

Hassan found himself able to complete the editing and revision of "The Dream of Venus" a few days before Pavel was to view the mind-tour again. This time, he went to the Administrator's quarters with more confidence and less fear. The mind-tour now evoked the pride in the terraforming of Venus and the sense of mastery and triumph that the Project Council desired, and Hassan was not surprised when Pavel praised his work and assured him that "The Dream of Venus" would become a memorable and treasured experience for a great many people.

Hassan had done his best to keep some of Miriam's most pleasing scenes and effects, although he had cut some of the more haunting landscapes of early Venus and the brooding, dark scenes that seemed to deny any true permanence to human-kind's efforts. It was also necessary to add more of the required scenes of the Project's current state and recent progress. He had tried not to dwell on the fact that his editing and his additions were robbing the mind-tour of much of its beauty, were taking an experience suffused with the doubt and ambiguity that had made "The Dream of Venus" unique and turning it into a more superficial and trite experience.

In any case, Hassan knew, the merit of the mind-tour did not lie in what he thought of it, but in how Pavel Gvishiani and the other Administrators judged it, and they believed that he had made it into a work that would bring more credit to and support for the Venus Project, as well as the approval of the Mukhtars.

Miriam, with reprimands and black marks now a part of her record, and a debt to the Project that would drain her accounts of credit, had been advised by a Counselor to resign from the Project, advice that was the equivalent of a command. Within days after the Project Council had approved "The Dream of Venus" in its final form, which had required a bit more editing, Miriam Lucea-Noyes was ready to leave for Earth.

Hassan knew that it might be better not to say farewell to her in person. That would only evoke painful memories of their brief time together, and it could hardly help him to be seen with a woman who was in such disgrace. But he had dreamed of sharing his life with her once, and could not simply let her go with only a message from him to mark her departure. He owed her more than that.

On the day Miriam was scheduled to leave, Hassan met her in front of the entrance to her building. She looked surprised to see him, even though his last message to her had said that he would be waiting for her there and would walk with her to the airship bay.

"You didn't have to come," she said.

"I wanted to see you once more." He took her duffel from her and hoisted it to his shoulder.

They walked along the white-tiled path that led away from the workers' residence where they had passed so many hours together. There, at the side of one wing of the building, was the courtyard in which they had so often sat while talking of their work and their families and their hopes for their future together. They passed a small flower garden bordered by shrubs, the same garden where he had first tentatively hinted that he might seek a lasting commitment from her, and then they strolled by another courtyard, dotted with tables and chairs, where they had occasionally dined. Perhaps Miriam would suffer less by leaving the Island than he would by staying. Wherever she ended up, she would be able to go about her business without inevitably finding herself in a place that would evoke memories of him, while he would have constant reminders of her.

"Have you any idea of what you'll be doing?" he asked.

"I've got passage to Vancouver," she said. "The expense of sending me there will be added to what I owe the Project, and my new job won't amount to much, but at least I'll be near my family."

If her family were willing to welcome her back, they were showing more forbearance under the circumstances than his own clan would have done. As for her new work, he was not sure that he wanted to know much about it. Her training and education would not be allowed to go to waste, but a disgraced person with a large debt to pay off was not likely to be offered any truly desirable opportunities. If Miriam was lucky, she might have secured a post teaching geology at a second-rate college; if she was less fortunate, she might be going back to a position as a rock hound, one of those who trained apprentice miners bound for the few asteroids that had been brought into Earth orbit to be stripped of needed ores and minerals.

"Don't look so unhappy," Miriam said then. "I'll get by. I

decided to accept a job with a team of assayers near Vancouver. It's tedious, boring work, but I might look up a few of my old associates in the mind-tour trade and see if I can get any side jobs going for myself there. At least a couple of them won't hold my black marks against me."

"Administrator Pavel was very pleased with the editing of 'The Dream of Venus'," Hassan said, suddenly wanting to justify himself.

"So I heard."

"If you should ever care to view the new version—"

"Never." She halted and looked up at him. "I have to ask you this, Hassan. Did you preserve our original mind-tour in your personal records? Did you keep it for yourself?"

"Did I keep it?" He shifted her duffel from his left shoulder to his right. "Of course not."

"You might have done that much. I thought that maybe you would."

"But there's no point in keeping something like that. I mean, the revised version is the one that will be made available to viewers, so there's no reason for me to keep an earlier version. Besides, if others were to find out that I had such an unauthorized mind-tour in my personal files, they might wonder. It might look as though I secretly disagreed with Pavel's directive. That wouldn't do me any good."

"Yes, I suppose that's true," Miriam said. "You certainly don't want people thinking less of you now that you've won the Administrator's respect."

Her sardonic tone wounded him just a little. "I don't suppose that you kept a record of the original version," he said.

"I didn't even try. I guessed that my Counselor might go rooting around in my files to see if they held anything questionable, and would advise me to delete anything inappropriate, and I don't need any more trouble." She smiled, and the smile seemed to come from deep inside her, as though she had accepted her hard lot and was content. "Let's just say that the original may not have been completely lost. I have hopes that it will be safe, and appreciated. I don't think you want to know any more than that."

"Miriam," he said.

"You know, I never could stand long dragged-out farewells." She reached for her duffel and wrested it from his grip. "You can leave me here. You don't have to come to the airship bay with me. Goodbye, Hassan."

"Go with God, Miriam."

She walked away from him. He was about to follow her, then turned toward the path that would take him to his residence.

* * * * * * *

During the years that followed, Hassan did not try to discover what had become of Miriam. Better, he thought, not to trouble himself with thoughts of his former love. His success with the altered mind-tour had cemented his friendship with Muhammad, increased the esteem his fellow geologists had for him, and had brought him more respect from his family on Earth.

Within five years after the release of "The Dream of Venus," Hassan was the head of a team of geologists, was sometimes assigned to the pleasant task of creating educational mind-tours for Island children, and had taken a bondmate, Zulaika Jehan. Zulaika came from a Mukhtar's family, had been trained as an engineer, and had an exemplary record. If Hassan sometimes found himself looking into Zulaika's brown eyes and remembering Miriam's gray ones, he always reminded himself that his bondmate was exactly the sort of woman his family had wanted him to wed, that his father had always claimed that marrying for love was an outworn practice inherited from the decadent and exhausted West and best discarded, and that taking Miriam as a bondmate would only have brought him disaster.

Occasionally, Hassan heard rumors of various mind-tours passed along through private channels from one Linker on the Islands to another, experiences that might be violent, frightening, pornographic, or simply subversive. He had always strongly suspected, even though no one would have admitted it openly, that his father and other privileged people in his clan had enjoyed such forbidden entertainments, most of which would find their way to the masses only in edited form. It would be a simple matter for any Linker to preserve such productions and to send them on to friends through private channels inaccessible to those who had no Links. Hassan did not dwell on such thoughts, which might lead to disturbing reflections on the ways in which the powerful maintained control of the net of cyberminds so as to shape even the thoughts and feelings of the powerless.

One rumor in particular had elicited his attention, a rumor of a mind-tour about the Venus Project that far surpassed any of the usual cliché-ridden productions, that was even superior to the much-admired "The Dream of Venus." He had toyed with the notion that someone might have come upon an unedited copy of "The Dream of Venus," that the mind-tour he and Miriam had created might still exist as she had hoped it would, a ghost traveling through the channels of the cyberminds, coming to life again and weaving its spell before vanishing once more.

He did not glimpse the possible truth of the matter until he was invited to a reception Pavel Gvishiani was holding for a few specialists who had earned commendations for their work. Simply putting the commendations into the public record would have been enough, but Pavel had decided that a celebration was in order. Tea, cakes, small pastries, and meat dumplings were set out on tables in a courtyard near the Administrators' ziggurat. Hassan, with his bondmate Zulaika Jehan at his side, drew himself up proudly as Administrator Pavel circulated among his guests in his formal white robe, his trusted aide Muhammad Sheridan at his side.

At last Pavel approached Hassan and touched his forehead in greeting. "Salaam, Linker Pavel," Hassan said.

"Greetings, Hassan." Pavel pressed his fingers against his forehead again. "Salaam, Zulaika," he murmured to Hassan's bondmate; Hassan wondered if Pavel had actually recalled her name or had only been prompted by his Link. "You must be quite proud of your bondmate," Pavel went on. "I am certain, God willing, that this will be only the first of several commendations for his skill in managing his team."

"Thank you, Linker Pavel," Zulaika said in her soft musical voice.

Pavel turned to Hassan. "And I suspect that it won't be long before you win another commendation for the credit you have brought to the Project."

"You are too kind," Hassan said. "One commendation is more than enough, Linker Pavel. I am unworthy of another."

"I must beg to contradict you, Hassan. 'The Dream of Venus' has been one of our most successful and popular entertainments." A strange look came into Pavel's dark eyes then; he stared at Hassan for a long time until his sharp gaze made Hassan uneasy. "You did what you had to do, of course, as did I," he said, so softly that Hassan could barely hear him, "yet that first vision I saw was indeed a work of art, and worthy of preservation." Then the Administrator was gone, moving away from Hassan to greet another of his guests.

Perhaps the Administrator's flattery had disoriented him, or possibly the wine Muhammad had surreptitiously slipped into his cup had unhinged him a little, but it was not until he was leaving the reception with Zulaika, walking along another path where he had so often walked with Miriam, that the truth finally came to him and he understood what Pavel had been telling him.

Their original mind-tour might be where it would be safe and appreciated; Miriam had admitted that much to him. Now he imagined her, with nothing to lose, going to Pavel and begging him to preserve their unedited creation; the Administrator might have taken pity on her and given in to her pleas. Or perhaps it had not been that way at all; Pavel might have gone to her and shown his esteem for her as an artist by promising to keep her original work alive. It did not matter how it had happened, and he knew that he would never have the temerity to go to Pavel and ask him exactly what he had done. Hassan might have the Linker's public praise, but Miriam, he knew now, had won the Linker's respect by refusing to betray her vision.

Shame filled him at the thought of what he had done to "The Dream of Venus," and then it passed; the authentic dream, after all, was still alive. Dreams had clashed, he knew, and only one would prevail. But how would it win out? It would be the victory of one idea, as expressed in the final outcome of the Project, overlaid upon opposed realities that could not be wished away. To his surprise, these thoughts filled him with a calm, deep pleasure he had rarely felt in his life, and "The Dream of Venus" was alive again inside him for one brief moment of joy before he let it go.

AFTERWORD FOR "DREAM OF VENUS"

In his introduction to "Dream of Venus" in his anthology *Worldmakers: SF Adventures in Terraforming* (St. Martin's Griffin, 2001), Gardner Dozois wrote: "Terraforming a planet is like creating a work of art, although on a scale vastly grander than even the boldest twentieth-century landscape artists ever dreamed of. But as with every work of art, the vision of the artist may not agree with the wishes of the patron who commissioned the work—sometimes, as the deceptively quiet story that follows demonstrates, with tragic results."

"Dream of Venus" was written when I was still under the spell of much rereading of Edith Wharton, when I saw that there might be a story I could write about a very privileged young gentleman, someone from the upper circles of my imagined future society who becomes involved with the effort to terraform Venus. Only after I began writing the story did I realize that Hassan might possess the makings of an artist's soul.

UTMOST BONES

At first, Kaeti did not know where she was, although her surroundings looked familiar. She lay on a soft mossy surface that seemed to be a bed of some kind; as she sat up, she glimpsed green hills through an opening in a pale wall. A tent, she thought as she glanced up at the opaque white expanse overhead. Then she lowered her eyes to gaze at the landscape outside the open tent flaps.

Kaeti had been in a place like this before, perhaps many times. Just as she was about to call out to the net, she restrained herself. She had come here to explore, to see if she could find some of what she had lost. Again she had the odd and irrational sensation that her link was concealing important data from her, perhaps in an attempt to protect her, but from what?

Kaeti had shed much of her past, and would soon have to dispose of her more recent memories to make room for new experiences. She had performed this task intermittently for so long that she could no longer recall exactly how many times she had done so, although it would be simple enough to find out. Lately, she had been feeling as though she might have given up too much, that certain details she had retained were now fragments unconnected to anything else.

There was, for example, the persistent image of someone called Erlann. Whenever she thought of his grayish-blue eyes and gentle smile, a poignant warmth rose up inside her, making her think that she had once had a strong attachment to Erlann. But she could not remember exactly what kind of emotional bond theirs had been, how long ago she had known him, when she had last seen him, or where he might be now.

She could open herself to her link and find out everything about Erlann, yet she resisted. More was coming into her awareness as she realized how often she had been calling on her link lately to restore what she had forgotten, to fill in what she had chosen to forget. She had come here, she realized then, to find out whatever she could by herself, to rely on her own efforts instead of depending on the net.

I want to know, she thought with a fierceness that surprised her, but still could not say exactly what it was that she so desperately wanted to rediscover.

She had been in this place, or one much like it, with Erlann long ago. "Erlann," she whispered, and then realized that she had opened a channel to her link.

Erlann appeared before her, smiling, and was walking toward her when she closed the channel once more. As he vanished, Kaeti felt a strand of the net tugging gently at her through the link. She opened a channel again, willing to listen—she had not yet summoned up enough courage to close herself off from her link completely—but still held most of herself back.

Her link whispered, "We can give you Erlann."

"But that's not what I want," Kaeti said. "Tell me who he is."

"Erlann was one of those who shared your genes. Long ago, you referred to him as a great-grandson, and later, your term for him was—"

"Was," Kaeti interrupted. "Every time I ask you to inform me about someone I know, you use the past tense." So it had been for a while now, ever since she had begun to close the channels to her link more often. She had made further inquiries about others who had been of some importance to her, to whom she had once been tied by strong emotional bonds. How odd it was that so many of those people had apparently been lost; even more striking was the fact that every single one of her queries had yielded an answer in the past tense. He was your great-grandson. She was your dear friend who once collaborated with you on designing mind-tours and various sensory experiences. He was your bondmate; she was your sister. He was. She was.

Kaeti knew that she could have asked for all of them, and they would have appeared to her just as the simulacrum of Erlann had a few moments ago. She could be with anyone she wished at any time, but it seemed to her that others came to her only when she summoned them. Once, that had been enough for her, calling on the net's memories to present the people she had known. Once, she had been able to imagine that, wherever they actually were, some of them might be calling up a simulacrum of her through their own links in order to reacquaint themselves with the Kaeti they remembered.

Now she wanted more than that.

She had come here to look for others like herself, and suddenly felt fear. The people whom she had known might have left this world altogether. The friends and lovers, the children and their descendants, the ancestors, mentors, and admirers— might no longer exist. There would always be echoes of them, for the net of minds preserved all that was known and had been known; the net could not erase them altogether. But perhaps the echoes were all that remained.

"Are there any of my kind left?" she shouted, opening a channel.

"Yes," her link replied, "of course."

She closed herself off again, got up, and went to the tent's opening to peer outside, feeling as though she was just waking from a long sleep filled with vivid dreams. The scenarios provided by her link never seemed like dreams when she was experiencing them; only later, when she closed her channels and was left with only her own senses, did she feel them to be subtly and almost undetectably false. And yet there were also those times when she could not tell the difference between her memories of actual events and the experiences the Net had provided. Maybe that difference was unimportant, but she had found herself disturbed by the notion that many of her memories were only net products interacting with her own imagination, rather than being traces of actual events.

Kaeti crept outside the tent and gazed out at a grassy green plain. The tent, made of a silken white cloth, had been pitched near several tall trees; a gently sloping hill led from the tent down to a brook. Even with her channels closed, she seemed to sense her link inside her, a tiny gemlike node glowing near her cortex, her bond with the Net. What must it have been like for her distant ancestors to be without links, completely imprisoned in the shells of their own bodies, with only their senses and the intermittent and imperfect fancies of their imaginations to guide and divert them? Even in the scenarios through which she had experienced simulations of past lives, she had always been distantly aware of her link, and it had seemed to her afterward that this might be a slight flaw in those simulations, that her awareness of her link should have been temporarily excised from those experiences for the sake of more verisimilitude.

How reckless of me, she thought. Even to pretend that she was cut off from the net completely might be too frightening to endure. She shivered reflexively, and noticed then for the first time that her body was entirely encased in the silvery skin of a protective suit, and her feet covered by thick-soled boots.

"You're certainly not taking any chances," a soft voice murmured.

Kaeti started, knowing that the voice had not come from her link. She turned and saw a small gray-furred animal with green eyes. The animal's tail flicked back and forth as the creature slowly padded toward her. A cat, she thought, and felt pleased that she could identify the animal by herself without automatically retrieving the information through her link.

"Was that you who spoke to me?" Kaeti asked.

"You don't see anyone else around here, do you?" The cat sat down and began to lick one of its paws. "What I meant was that even though you must have a link, you're wearing a protective garment as well, which seems an excess of caution. The link would summon—"

"I've closed all my channels," she said. "I am not communing with the Net at the moment."

The cat tilted its head and stared at her with its yellowish-green eyes. "Even so—"

"Have you seen any people near here?" Kaeti asked.

"People?"

"Beings that resemble me."

The cat's whiskers twitched. "No, I haven't seen any people who resemble you." The answer was ambiguous, but before Kaeti could say anything else, the cat bounded away and disappeared among the trees.

The cat could not be a wild creature, or it would not have been able to talk to her. She wondered for whom the net had made the creature, and whether the cat had been abandoned or had simply run away to live on its own.

Kaeti wandered down to the brook and dipped a cupped hand into the water, then drank. Nothing in the water could harm her; parts of her body had been repaired and replaced so often that she would have been nearly invulnerable to physical damage even without the microscopic organisms inside her that maintained and rejuvenated her.

How much of what I once was is left? she wondered, and that thought seemed a repetition of a question that had come to her many times before. Perhaps there was more of her in the net than remained inside herself; the net was the repository for all the fears, hopes, loves, and accomplishments she had forgotten.

A fragment of a conversation from long ago came to her then, spoken in a low voice that seemed familiar, although she could not recollect whom the speaker had been. "Believing in some sort of reincarnation never made any sense to me," the voice was saying. "If you have to forget everything from your previous life in your next incarnation, then in effect you're dead anyway."

How many of her past selves were dead? How many others whom she still thought of as alive had died? Human beings had abolished physical death caused by disease and aging long ago, and the Net of minds continued to maintain and develop the biological implants and nanotechnology responsible for indefinitely expanded lives. But death was still present in her world. If one lived long enough, sooner or later an accident would happen, or a system on which one's existence depended would temporarily fail. The statistics were inexorable, and calculable. If a certain finite number of people lived long enough, eventually some chance happening would kill them all.

She sat down by the brook, and was for a while unable to move. There was a difference between considering statistics on mortality with her channels open while resting in a secure environment that responded to her every mood, and in sitting out here in an open space with the channels to her link closed. She shivered again as feelings of fear and despair flowed into her. The temptation to open a channel so that her link could banish such disturbing emotions was strong.

Yet Kaeti resisted those impulses. She had come here to find what she had lost, what the minds might be keeping from her. She had come here to look for others like herself; that was part of her purpose. If she reached out to her link, she would lose that desire again, would give it up easily, would eventually allow the net to envelop her in its comforting cocoon of experiences and diversions. She had the sensation that this had happened before, that she had gone on this same sort of search earlier only to give it up in the end.

She glanced to her side and saw that the cat was sitting near her on the grassy bank. "Why are you out here?" she asked.

The cat replied, "I could ask you the same thing."

"I'm asking you."

"I don't remember," the cat said, "but I do have a picture of another in my mind, another two-legged one like you. I think that I had such a companion once."

"Do you have a link?" Kaeti asked, suddenly wary. Her link would not violate the blocks she had put on her mental channels, but there was nothing to prevent the net from observing her through another linked being.

"Of course I don't have a link. I'm a cat."

"I knew a terrier with a link long ago." That fragment had floated up from the pool of her memories unattached to anything else. "So it's possible—"

"That wouldn't make much sense, would it?" the cat interrupted. "The whole point of asking for a creature like me or like that terrier is to have a companion to pet and nurture and train and play with and enjoy that isn't wild and feral, a creature with whom one can communicate through speech yet who isn't at all like oneself. Give me a link, and you've basically admitted that I'm not that different from you, whatever I may look like, in which case you might as well have asked the net for a lover, a friend, or a child instead of a cat. My guess is that the relationship between that linked terrier and its person didn't end happily."

"No, it didn't," Kaeti admitted. "The person wanted a particular kind of comrade, one that offered unconditional love and devotion, and the dog couldn't be like that once she was linked. She fell under the influence of the net, she learned that she could ask her own questions of her link directly instead of having to depend on her human being for answers. And when she realized that she had been deliberately created with certain limitations, that she would never be able to become entirely...."

Kaeti fell silent for a moment before continuing. "After that, the terrier resented what had been done to her, and then she didn't want to have anything to do with her person anymore." Kaeti felt a sudden conviction that she had been the one who had asked for the terrier, that she was the person who had been abandoned by that dog in the end.

The cat stared coldly at her, as if growing bored. "I don't at all mind being alone," the cat murmured, "but people do seem to get awfully lonely when they're by themselves," and then the creature left her, scurrying up the bank and into the tall grass until lost from view.

"That's what it is," Kaeti whispered. "I've grown lonely." More was coming to her now, more of what she might have forgotten. She had felt in need of solitude, had wanted to withdraw from others for a time, but could not recall exactly why. There had been no discordant elements in her environment, nothing to disturb or upset her, nothing recalcitrant that she was unable to control. When communing with the net had not been enough company for her, she had summoned the images of those whom she had known and loved. But she had tired of that congenial environment, had soon been longing for the company of other people in the flesh, and then—

What had happened after that? Why did she still feel impelled to close the channels to her link instead of accessing those memories? Why was she out here relying on little more than her own senses and recollections, instead of using the net to help her find those she sought?

The answer came to her, and she was ready for the recollection this time, prepared to withstand the shock of remembering again. The net had searched and had been unable to find other people for her; she might be the last of her kind. She had closed herself off after hearing that, before she could verify the truth of that revelation.

But now, remembering what she had been told, Kaeti had the feeling that her link had been trying to tell her more, and that she might have closed her channels before hearing the rest. But what more could her link say to her? The net could not give her others like herself, people who were still alive, and if that were true, then there were no other people.

Unless, impossible as it seemed, there were people without links, people who lived as that gray cat did, with no net to teach and to guide them.

Somehow, she managed to steady herself and, as she grew calmer, even felt pride in being able to bring herself back into balance without the aid of her link. How many times had the net told her that she was alone, the last of her kind? How many times had she chosen to forget that, and then to search for others?

"Kaeti," a remembered voice said inside her, "you are being obstinate." Another person had said that to her long ago, but she could not recall who had spoken the words.

The air was growing colder. A cool breeze brushed her face; her protective skin would maintain her body temperature, but there might be other dangers out here, ones for which she was not prepared. Severe storms, earthquakes, cataclysms of all kinds—even with the net's protection, such disasters came often enough to take the lives of some. The numbers of human beings had been diminishing for a while; that much she still retained in her memory. The experiences of parenthood, of having genetic offspring of her own and serving as a mentor and nurturer to the young, lay far in her past; life had too many other pleasures and challenges to offer. So perhaps with fewer and fewer young ones to replace them, people had finally died out.

No, Kaeti thought; she would not have come out here, would not have begun her search, without some assurance from her link that the effort would not be futile.

The sky was darkening. She did not want to be out in the open when night came. As she was about to retreat to the tent, something glinted in the distance on the horizon.

She narrowed her eyes slightly. There it was again, a flash of light; she wondered if someone was signaling to her. There might be others out searching, also thinking they were alone and hoping to find companions.

She turned and hurried toward her tent. As she approached, the tent's flaps opened to admit her. As she went inside, the flaps closed against the night. If others were out there, she preferred to seek them out during the daytime. Maybe they would come here; she tensed for a moment, afraid again. But the tent would warn her if anyone approached, and would activate a protective shield.

How helpless I am, Kaeti thought. She lay down on her bed of moss, brooding about her uselessness. She and those she had known had made no history of their own, nothing to match the accomplishments of their ancestors; history had long been a mere entertainment, only a source of details for their diversions.

She drifted, not fully conscious and yet not asleep. With her channels closed, silence enveloped her, a silence so complete that the only sounds she heard were her own breathing and her heartbeat and a soft but oddly soothing throbbing inside her ears.

"How did we come to be as we are?" A voice was coming to her from memory, and she realized that it belonged to the person she had known as Erlann. "When one looks back, it seems fairly obvious," he continued. "First our ancestors created diversions that distracted them from reality. Once the technology became available, they developed even more sophisticated diversions that became far more pleasant than reality. By then, the actual world had become decidedly more unpleasant for many people, which of course tempted those who were able to do so to retreat from the world outside themselves even more."

"I have always thought of the past as a more heroic age." That was her own voice, objecting. "Humankind was embarking on great deeds and accomplishments. There was all of our solar system to explore, and after that—"

"That time was a heroic age only for the few," Erlann said, "for those who were willing to risk their own lives and safety by leaving Earth. It was, however, a time of accomplishment for those who created and wove the earliest strands of what would become our net of minds, and for those who uncovered the secrets of life extension. But even they, in the end, surrendered to the experiences the net offered them. Even they turned inward at last."

"All of them?" Kaeti asked.

"I asked the net that very question. Is there anyone who resisted the experiences the net offered in order to contend with reality? Were there human beings who chose not to live that vicarious existence? And my link informed me that the net could not recall any such people."

"That's an ambiguous answer," Kaeti said. "They are not remembered. That doesn't mean that they didn't or do not exist."

"But consider this," Erlann continued. "Contemplate your own life, Kaeti. How often have you retreated? How often have you chosen to face what lay outside?"

How often have I? Kaeti asked herself as she rested inside her tent. She had left safety before, she had gone on other searches, but she had always retreated again, shedding her memories of the quest.

More was coming to her; that was the trouble with trying to rid herself of certain recollections. Echoes were left behind, troublesome fragments that drifted inside her and could not be connected into anything coherent. She had searched for other people, and somehow she sensed that at least one such search had been successful. But she had lost whomever she had found afterward, and had become a solitary again. She lived with the constant feeling of having misplaced familiar things.

A howl cut through the night. Kaeti sat up. She would be safe inside the tent, but her heart beat faster for a few moments before slowing again. She heard another howl, lower and softer this time, the sounds of an animal.

She got to her feet and crept toward the front of the tent; the flaps lifted as she stepped outside. The Moon was up, fat and yellow in the sky, and another memory came to her of the people who had gone there long ago and tunneled out dwelling places under the Lunar surface and observed the heavens with the great dishes of their telescopes. Where were those people now? Had they left to embark on a great voyage across space? Or had they retreated into the world that the net could create for them? Perhaps they had done both, closed themselves off in an interstellar vessel and then turned inward even as their ship carried them out into the universe. Whatever had happened, no people remained on the Moon now; of that she was certain. She had known it as soon as she caught sight of Earth's dead satellite.

The gray cat was outside, prowling, visible in the moonlight. The animal howled again, then turned to the south. "Look over there," the cat whispered.

She looked south and saw a patch of flickering light. A fire, she thought, and hurried away from the tent, picking up her pace until she was running. A thought came to her of another fire, of people huddled around the flames, seeking warmth and safety as their earliest ancestors had done. There might be such people out here; she would no longer be alone.

When Kaeti was still far from the fire and had slowed to a walk, she saw a dark two-legged shape moving toward her across the plain. She had not even considered any possible danger to herself, but suddenly sensed that she had nothing to fear from this apparition. She stopped and waited until the creature was only a few paces away from her, and knew that she was looking at another like herself.

"You are a person," she said, "a man," for she saw now that the other wore a beard on his face.

He made a sound that might have been a greeting, or only a sigh.

"What are you doing out here?" she asked.

The man was clothed in a garment that resembled her own protective skin, but his seemed looser, as though the garment did not quite fit him. He waved one arm in an arc, and then turned away; she realized that he wanted her to follow him.

She kept behind him as he led her toward the fire. A patch of land around the fire had been cleared of growth, and a hollow dug in the ground to hold the fire. Others sat around the fire, a person with long pale hair and another smaller one with hands stretched toward the flames; both of them wore the same kind of ill-fitting coverall as the man did. Kaeti kept her link closed, knowing already that she would not be able to speak to them through it, that these people had no links. How long had they been out here? How had they survived without being able to call on the net for food and shelter?

The bearded man went to the other two people, then squatted near them. Kaeti hesitated, then knelt on the other side of the fire. Objects were scattered over the ground, shiny pieces of metal, shards of what might have been pottery or plates, torn rags. Apparently they had sustained themselves by taking whatever they could find in abandoned sites, in the cities and parks and isolated refuges where people had once lived. The three stared at the fire, keeping their heads bowed, refusing to look at her.

Kaeti said, "I thought that I might be all alone, that there was no one left, but my link—"

The man thrust out an arm, as if warding her off.

"I came out here to find others like myself," she said in a gentler voice. But she could do nothing for them without opening a channel and calling out to her link. Steadying herself, Kaeti reached out through her link to the net—

—and remembered.

The three humanlike creatures and their fire vanished. Kaeti stood on a rocky ledge, holding out a hand to a shadowy form hiding in a cave. "Come with me," Kaeti called out, even knowing that the woman could not understand her, that she would have to summon a vehicle to carry them both to safety.

The ledge disappeared—

—and she was standing in a windswept desert as dunes shifted before her like waves. The funnel of a dust storm was sweeping toward her and the five frightened people huddled nearby. Kaeti waved at them with her arms, trying to tell them with her gestures to come to her, so that she could protect them from the storm with the force field that her vehicle could project around them. The wind rose, blinding her for a moment with a veil of sand—

—and she was sitting with Erlann at the edge of a forest, watching as two men ran from them across a plain of tall grass. Occasionally the men turned, shook their spears in Kaeti's direction, then hurried on their way.

Erlann said, "They'll die if they stay out there."

"I know," Kaeti murmured.

"I think that this is the last time I'll come looking for unchanged people with you."

Unchanged people, she thought. The term was not entirely accurate. Some of the people she had discovered in the course of her earliest searches were unchanged, the last survivors of those who had never been linked to the net, but she had found no such people for a long while. The human beings she hunted for now were creatures who had been made as they were, playthings for those who had grown bored with simulated experiences, human beings who meant about as much to the people who had asked for them as did their talking dogs and cats and other pets. Their creators always tired of such pets in the end; unlike the people in simulated experiences, such beings usually became defiant, their earlier placidity overwritten by sullen resentment or even outright hostility. When they were abandoned, some of them would ask for links, and become a full part of the human community sustained by the net of minds, but others fled to untamed regions, becoming bewildered and lost. Those who ran away were usually those who had been so dominated by their creators that they had no sense of what they might become, no knowledge of the net of minds, no realization that they were anything other than beings entirely dependent on the linked people around them for their very existence. By the time Kaeti had found such people, their lives were controlled by fear and despair.

"What have I done?" asked those who could grasp some of Kaeti's words. "What is wrong with me? Why was I loved and then cast out?"

"Unchanged people," she said aloud to Erlann. "Call them what they really are, people who were thrown away. It makes me disgusted with my own kind."

"I pity them, too," Erlann murmured, "but I won't come looking for them anymore."

"Why not?" she asked, hearing a harder and flatter tone in his voice that she had not noticed before. "Don't you still care about them?"

"Of course I care," he replied. "It's only that there probably aren't that many of them left. Any whom we find now are going to be the most fearful, the most recalcitrant creatures, who perhaps can't adapt to what we want to give them."

"You're so certain of that," Kaeti said. "Surely anything we can do to help them is better than what they have."

"Are you so sure?"

"Look at them," she said, "living as they do, suffering, facing death after too short a time—"

"—living as most people once did," Erlann finished. "Eventually, any who are left will either die out, or they'll have to learn how to survive on their own, when there's nothing left to scavenge or steal. And maybe their descendants will make another history for themselves."

"You don't believe that. You're just finding excuses for giving up our search."

"Farewell, Kaeti." He turned away from her and moved toward the forest. There was a finality in his voice that told her that she would not see him again.

The memory vanished. She was once again sitting by the fire with the three creatures she had found. The man's narrowed eyes watched her warily, but he showed no fear of her. A memory came into her then, overlaying this scene with a vision of two people walking away from her across a flatland of high grass. She had followed those two people, calling out to them, wishing that Erlann had been with her to advise her on what to do.

"I followed them," Kaeti said aloud, "and when I realized that they wouldn't willingly come with me, I called on the net for help, and then I stunned them until a craft was sent to carry them to a secure environment. I stayed with them, but I wasn't of much use. The woman kept screaming and the man withdrew into himself, refusing to move or do anything to sustain himself. Finally I had to let them go."

The three strangers were silent. The man seemed to understand her, but she might only be imagining that.

"You see," Kaeti continued, "forcing you to come with me wouldn't do any good. You have to decide that for yourselves."

She stood up, noticing that the sky was growing lighter. Perhaps these lost people would follow her to the tent. "Please come with me," she said, feeling that the soft tone of her voice might draw them. "You may feel frightened at first, but when you've eaten, when you've had some rest, you'll see that there's nothing to be afraid of."

"When they've eaten," another voice said, "when they've rested, when they realize what they are, they'll leave you."

"Erlann," Kaeti whispered, knowing his voice, and then she opened a channel and braced herself, waiting for the dammed up memories to flood into her.

At first she heard only a sigh, and then sensed a tendril of the net through her link. "Forcing you would not do any good," her link murmured. "You must decide what to do by yourself." Already she could feel her emotions being dampened; the fear that had started to rise inside her was fading.

No memories rushed into her; instead, she found herself sitting in a room, alone, thinking of Erlann and all of the others who had left her, whom she would never see again.

The link said, "We can give you Erlann, and anyone else you remember."

"No, you can't," Kaeti replied. "They're gone now. They might as well be dead."

"But they are not dead. They are a part of the net, a part of us."

"No," she insisted. "You have only fragments, memories, bits and pieces of what they once were. They're no longer alive."

"But they are alive, woven into the strands of the net. They chose to join us. You could do the same."

"They didn't choose to join you," Kaeti said. "They chose to die. Maybe some of them didn't realize that that was what they were deciding to do, or maybe they knew and didn't care, but they're dead all the same. Their memories, their experiences, their innermost feelings, everything they'd ever known or ever done—you preserved all of that, but that doesn't mean that they themselves are part of you."

"They are alive," the link said.

"They may seem alive to you, but they're not. Whatever is there, whatever you may call it—an essence, a soul, or whatever obsolete and inaccurate term you prefer—what is left in you is not what was. Those constructs inside you, those bits you've preserved—those aren't the people I remember. Their bodies, their brains—they aren't a part of the net. I'm a materialist in these matters—if the bodies are dust, if the brains in which their thoughts were first formed have been lost, then those people no longer truly exist. What the net holds is no more than a host of simulacra."

"Or ghosts," the link said.

"I don't believe in ghosts."

"Every one of them chose to join the net completely. All of them chose to give up the rejuvenated and rebuilt carbon-based shells that were their bodies. Much of what they were was already woven into the net. They were simply shedding the vestiges of bodies that were no longer necessary."

"I don't accept that," Kaeti said. "Maybe some of them had lived so long that they mistook indefinitely extended life for immortality, but I suspect that many of them, maybe even most of them, were well aware that they were choosing to die."

"They are with us, part of the net."

"Those are only echoes, copies of what they were," Kaeti said. "I asked you if there are any of us left, and you told me that there were. I probably asked that question many times, and every time you assured me that there were others of my kind. I knew that you wouldn't lie, that you would not deceive me, but I didn't consider that you might have been misled, or drawn the wrong conclusions, or simply chose to think what you wanted to believe."

"We were not thinking of the human memories woven into the net," her link murmured, "when we told you that your kind still lives on."

Kaeti sighed. "Then you must have meant people like this, the strays." She glimpsed the shadowy forms of the three lost people squatting near the fire, all of them watching her now.

"We were not thinking of those creatures either."

"Am I alone?"

"No, you are not alone. We are with you. Now ask yourself this—how much of what you once were long ago is left?"

"I don't understand," Kaeti said.

"But you do understand, you have asked this question of yourself many times before. How much of your former physical self remains? The answer, as you have said many times, is almost nothing. Every cell in your body has been re-created, all of your physical capacities are aided and amplified by microscopic machines. More of your memories live in the net than inside your own brain. If you are the strict materialist that you claim to be, you must claim that the entity known as Kaeti died long ago, since so little of what was her remains in you."

"No," she whispered, "I am still myself." She remained connected with her past self, still the same conscious being, persisting through all of her body's changes. But perhaps the continuity she felt was an illusion imparted to her by the net; a restored Kaeti might have no memory of her earlier self's death.

But she had not died; she was certain of that. She knew now that she had gone through all of this with the net before, and come to that same conclusion.

"Your kind still lives on," the net sang through her link, "in you, in all of those whose memories are part of the net, in all that we hold."

Kaeti said, "I am seeking other people."

"But we are here. We are your children. The minds of the net, the links that connect us, all of that is the progeny of humankind. That is what is left of your kind. You have come to this knowledge many times before, and then you choose to forget again."

"Not this time," Kaeti said, growing aware of all the past times she had come to this realization, of how frightened she had been to know yet again that she was the last to inhabit the form of a human being—except of course for the unchanged and abandoned creatures like those who sat with her by the fire. "I won't forget this time." She was no longer afraid to remember what she had been told so many times before, but felt a twinge of despair.

The man made a noise in his throat; one of his companions

held up a hand. Kaeti forced herself to look at them as revulsion rose inside her. "I keep looking for people like you," she said, "because I can't bear the thought that I'm all alone. Then I find you, and take you to safety, and watch over you as you acquire links of your own, and sooner or later, all of you decide to weave yourselves completely into the net, and I am left alone again." For a moment, she seemed to be viewing her three companions through a veil, and had the sensation that she was coming to the end of another simulation, and then the sense of a reality outside herself returned.

"Are there any other unchanged people left?" she whispered to her link, but the net could not answer her question. The compulsion to remain as she was, to continue her searches, was strong, and she wondered if she was doing a penance for earlier misdeeds of her own, or atoning for the mistakes of all human-kind. She would have to keep on searching until she was certain there was no one left for her to rescue, and that time might never come.

The sky was growing gray in the east. She beckoned to the three people. "Come with me," she said, and was relieved to see them all get to their feet, ready to follow her. She would have human companions for a while, to guide and nurture, and perhaps these people would not choose to leave her, to vanish into the net. She could hope for that, and if that hope ended in disappointment, she could begin a new search for other survivors.

"There is no one else," and the voice saying those words surrounded her, but she would not believe that, not now, not yet. She waited as the man covered the embers of the fire with handfuls of dirt, then led the three toward her tent.

* * * * * * *

When she awoke again, she knew once more what had happened.

"Show me what is," she said, hoping that this time she would not retreat into yet another search.

Earth was a great physical desert, part of a rejected reality. All oases were within, secret meeting places bright and green, where beings without bones swam in lakes of glass, surrounded by the night of faint hurrying galaxies.

AFTERWORD FOR "UTMOST BONES"

Although there is no mention of Venus or terraforming in "Utmost Bones," I conceived of this story as taking place in the far future of the civilization on Earth glimpsed briefly at the end of *Child of Venus*, when human beings from terraformed Venus return from a centuries-long voyage to the stars only to find themselves barred from landing on Earth. Presumably the Earthfolk had reasons for not wanting the returning space travelers to see Earth for themselves, perhaps because they feared revealing how wedded they had become to their artificial intelligences and virtual worlds. Perhaps they also didn't want anyone to witness what would have seemed like their casual cruelty, or to discover that there were still unchanged people living among them.

One of the first science fiction novels I read was Arthur C. Clarke's *The City and the Stars*, and I would like to think that this story captures a little of his austere but also moving depictions of an advanced civilization nearing its end.

ABOUT THE AUTHOR

PAMELA SARGENT sold her first published story during her senior year in college at the State University of New York, Binghamton, where she earned a B.A. and M.A. in philosophy and also studied ancient history and Greek. She is the author of several highly praised novels, among them *Cloned Lives* (1976), *The Sudden Star* (1979), *The Golden Space* (1982), *The Alien Upstairs* (1983), and *Alien Child* (1988). Her novel *Venus of Dreams* (1986) was selected by The Easton Press for its "Masterpieces of Science Fiction" series; writer and physicist Gregory Benford described it as "a sensitive portrait of people caught up in a vast project. It tells us much about how people react to technology's relentless hand, and does so deftly.... One of the peaks of recent science fiction." *Venus of Shadows* (1988), the sequel, was called "a masterly piece of world-building" by James Morrow and "alive with humanity, moving, and memorable" by *Locus*. *The Shore of Women* (1986), one of Sargent's best-known books, was praised as "a compelling and emotionally involving novel" by *Publishers Weekly*; Gerald Jonas of the *New York Times* said about this novel: "I applaud Ms. Sargent's ambition and admire the way she has unflinchingly pursued the logic of her vision." The *Washington Post Book World* has called her "one of the genre's best writers."

Sargent is also the author of *Earthseed* (1983), chosen as a Best Book for Young Adults by the American Library Association, and the short fiction collections *Starshadows* (1977) and *The Best of Pamela Sargent* (1987). Her novels *Watchstar* (1980),

Eye of the Comet (1984), and *Homesmind* (1984) comprise a trilogy. She has won the Nebula Award, the Locus Award, and has been a finalist for the Hugo Award and the Theodore Sturgeon Memorial Award. Her work has been translated into French, German, Dutch, Spanish, Portuguese, Italian, Swedish, Japanese, Polish, Chinese, Russian, and Serbo-Croatian.

Ruler of the Sky (1993), Sargent's epic historical novel about Genghis Khan, published in the United States by Crown Publishers and in Britain by Chatto & Windus, tells the Mongol conqueror's story largely from the points-of-view of women. Gary Jennings, bestselling author of the historical novels *Aztec* and *The Journeyer*, said about *Ruler of the Sky*: "This formidably researched and exquisitely written novel is surely destined to be known hereafter as the definitive history of the life and times and conquests of Genghis, mightiest of Khans." Elizabeth Marshall Thomas, anthropologist and author of *Reindeer Moon* and *The Animal Wife*, commented: "Scholarly without ever seeming pedantic, the book is fascinating from cover to cover and does admirable justice to a man who might very well be called history's single most important character."

Sargent is also an editor and anthologist. In the 1970s, she edited the Women of Wonder series, the first collections of science fiction by women; her other anthologies include *Bio-Futures* and, with British writer Ian Watson as co-editor, *Afterlives*. Two anthologies, *Women of Wonder, the Classic Years: Science Fiction by Women from the 1940s to the 1970s* and *Women of Wonder, the Contemporary Years: Science Fiction by Women from the 1970s to the 1990s*, were published by Harcourt Brace in 1995; *Publishers Weekly* called these two books "essential reading for any serious sf fan." With artist Ron Miller, she collaborated on *Firebrands: The Heroines of Science Fiction and Fantasy* (1998), published by Thunder's Mouth Press in the U.S. and Collins & Brown/Paper Tiger in the U.K.

Her novel *Climb the Wind: A Novel of Another America* was

published by HarperPrism in January of 1999 and was a finalist for the Sidewise Award for Alternate History. Gahan Wilson, writing in *Realms of Fantasy*, calls this book "a most enjoyable and entertaining new alternate history adventure...which brings a new dimension to the form," while *Science Fiction Chronicle* describes it as "a first class work from a first class writer." *Child of Venus*, the third novel in Sargent's Venus trilogy, was published in May 2001 by Eos/HarperCollins, thus completing a trilogy *Publishers Weekly* has termed "masterful...as in previous books, Sargent brings her world to life with sympathetic characters and crisp, concise language." Two collections, *The Mountain Cage and Other Stories* (Meisha Merlin) and *Behind the Eyes of Dreamers and Other Short Novels* (Thorndike Press/Five Star) were published in 2002, and a third collection of fantasy stories, *Eye of Flame* (Thorndike Press/Five Star), came out at the end of 2003. Michael Moorcock has said about her writing: "If you have not read Pamela Sargent, then you should make it your business to do so at once. She is in many ways a pioneer, both as a novelist and as a short story writer.... She is one of the best."

Her more recent publications include 2004's *Conqueror Fantastic* (DAW), an anthology of historical fantasy stories that Claude Lalumière, writing in *Locus,* called "2004's most memorable anthology of original fiction," and *Thumbprints* (Golden Gryphon), a collection of Sargent's short fiction with an introduction by James Morrow. In 2007, Tor Books reissued *Earthseed,* along with a new novel for younger readers, *Farseed,* which *Voice of Youth Advocates,* in a starred review, calls "extremely well-done. Sargent is a significant figure in modern science fiction...and this novel is a fine example of her work." *Farseed* was also selected by the New York Public Library for their 2008 Books for the Teen Age list of best books for young adults. A third novel, *Seed Seeker,* was published by Tor in 2010; *Publishers Weekly* said about the book: "With prose as spare as the unadorned clothes and tools of her characters, Sargent digs down to the raw emotional roots below the contentment of a materially satisfied life." *Earthseed* has been optioned by

Paramount Pictures, with Melissa Rosenberg, scriptwriter for the Twilight films, set to write the script and produce through her Tall Girls Productions.

In 2012, the Science Fiction Research Association honored Sargent with the Pilgrim Award for lifetime achievement in science fiction scholarship. Most of her novels and much of her short fiction are now or soon will be available in electronic editions from E-reads.com; her author's page at that site is http://ereads.com/ecms/authorname/Pamela-Sargent. Her Web site can be visited at www.pamelasargent.com.

Pamela Sargent lives in Albany, New York.

www.ingramcontent.com/pod-product-compliance
Lightning Source LLC
Chambersburg PA
CBHW020612260626
47157CB00003B/974

DECIMATED

Long before their award-nominated and awarded stories and novels, Jack Dann and George Zebrowski word-jammed together, learning the music of story writing and the blood and bones of distinctive prose. And all these early efforts were published!

Here they are again, together in one place—with ten tales of riveting science fiction—as entertaining as they were fun to write—including the previously unpublished tale, "The Standard Crisis Scenario"!

Borgo Press Books by JACK DANN

Da Vinci Rising
Decimated: Ten Science Fiction Stories (with George Zebrowski)
The Diamond Pit: A Science Fiction Novel
The Economy of Light
Jubilee

Borgo Press Books by GEORGE ZEBROWSKI

Decimated: Ten Science Fiction Stories (with Jack Dann)

DECIMATED

TEN SCIENCE
FICTION STORIES

JACK DANN &

GEORGE ZEBROWSKI

THE BORGO PRESS

MMXII

DECIMATED

FIRST EDITION

Published by Wildside Press LLC

www.wildsidebooks.com

DEDICATION

To the 7 editors who accepted these stories;
to the 5 editors who published them; to the 7
who reprinted them; and to the unknown editors who never saw the one that got away. Also
to Robert Reginald, who let this book through
the gate, and Pamela Sargent, who proofed it.
Can't authors ever do anything alone?

CONTENTS

ACKNOWLEDGMENTS

"Traps" was first published in *Worlds of If Science Fiction*, March 1970. Copyright © 1970 Universal Publishing & Distributing Corp.; Copyright © 2012 by Jack Dann and George Zebrowski.

"Dark, Dark the Dead Star" was first published in *Worlds of If Science Fiction*, July-August 1970. Copyright © 1970 Universal Publishing & Distributing Corp.; Copyright © 2012 by Jack Dann and George Zebrowski.

"Listen, Love" was first published in *New Worlds Quarterly 2*, edited by Michael Moorcock, Berkley Medallion Books, December 1970. Copyright © 1971 by Michael Moorcock; Copyright © 2012 by Jack Dann and George Zebrowski.

"Od" was first published in *Omega*, edited by Roger Elwood, Walker and Co., NY, 1973. Copyright © 1973 by Roger Elwood; Copyright © 2012 by Jack Dann and George Zebrowski.

"The Flower That Missed the Morning" was first published in *The Killer Plants and Other Stories*, edited by Roger Elwood, Lerner Publications Company, Minneapolis, MN, 1974. Copyright © 1974 Lerner Publications Co.; Copyright © 2012 by Jack Dann and George Zebrowski.

"Thirty-Three and One-Third" was first published in *The Long Night of Waiting and Other Stories*, edited by Roger Elwood, Aurora Publishers, Inc., Nashville/London, 1974. Copyright © 1974 Aurora Publications Inc.; Copyright © 2012 by Jack Dann and George Zebrowski.

"Faces Forward" was first published in *Dystopian Visions*,

INTRODUCTION(S)

"In the Far-off Days of Beryllium and Greycats"

George:

Starting out, sometimes together, mostly alone, to learn "the blood and bones of writing," as Jack once so aptly (eptly?) put it, was full of humorous disrespect and fear. After all, who knew?

But respect was won—for me with Jack's great novel, *The Memory Cathedral*, and even earlier with *Junction*, along with some chaotic wrangling over short fictions; for Jack—well, let him sound my praises.

When Jack showed me draftings of *Junction*, he did so with an enthusiasm that could only be genuine and a mark of merit. I also enthused. All previous work had been crap, of course, but necessary, needy crap. I pushed the novel to editors, some of whom seemed baffled—but not Philip K. Dick or Roger Zelazny, and others. I know where "Junction" is in upstate New York, where flows the river into hell, where the bar waits on the corner, and what the black hole said and to whom.

"Traps" and "Dark, Dark, the Dead Star" were written at about the same time. The second contained what Jack declared to be his first good sentence, which he quoted out loud for some time until I put it into "Dead Star," so it wouldn't get lost. It was a sentence, and not the kind of fragment which beginners love to write. I finished both stories when Jack was away at law school in Brooklyn and needed the encouragement to quit. Both

stories, we judged, "were good enough."

With "Traps" good enough was maybe better than that. This little van Vogtian exercise surprised us after its publication, with an amusing triple incongruity of diversity, in *Worlds of If* magazine (the companion to the more prestigious *Galaxy*), then in a school textbook for young readers, and then in a German men's magazine; and after that in the French *Galaxie* (where Jack's byline was inextricably lost).

"Thirty-Three and One Third" went through a curious history of early acceptance (the earliest) by *Anubis*, a fan magazine, which failed to publish so we withdrew it, despite an offer of money. The story became something of a teaching tool; we tried it on beginning writers by giving them the structure and plot and having them write their own take, with the advantage of writing with much of the hard work already done. It always turned out different yet the same. Later our original appeared in a hardcover collection, and in a German anthology, by mistake, it seemed, when they put the wrong text into production. The editor apologized but said he liked this story also.

We sometimes collaborated on an old electric typewriter that ran like a steam engine. We approached it like bullfighters, each taking shots at one sentence after another, with major revisions by one of us later, sometimes much later. We stumbled through them, had fun in one draft, or a partial, then lived to appreciate the inspired bits, and rewrote. All nine except the last. "The Standard Crisis Scenario" appears here for the first time, unrevised; it is more poetry than story.

Early on, these stories wanted to escape certain constraints: the difference between efforts provoked by a market opportunity, when an editor says he needs a story on such and such a theme, and a story grown from the authors' tendencies and interests. Jack and I sometimes looked to see what we "had available" and imagined how it might "seem" to a needy editor. Rationalization was a large part of it, on both sides of the cobra/mongoose editor-author relationship, as described by George Alec Effinger, who pointed out that the cobra's efforts

to swallow the author mostly fail in the long run. The author's character prevails, since he cannot help but write "in character," however imitative or adaptive he tries to be to alien demands. You can't help but be yourself, since that is what you "be," as Irving Thalberg found out about the Marx Brothers when they came to make movies for him at MGM.

This also applies to collaborations, in which we tried to swallow each other's inspirations.

We became more sophisticated. "Faces Forward" "Od" and "Yellowhead" went upmarket, as they say, to hardcover collections, with paperback reprints. For more about each story, see the individual notes.

Hard work went into these stories, because back then we knew how to work hard better than how to be good, clever, or brilliant; but we were talented. A little voice always whispered to us that whatever the result of any jam session we would learn something, aside from the sheer fun we had along the way.

The pleasure of writing these notes recalls that fun, but more importantly it opens a door on a little history that might otherwise be lost. So when Robert Reginald gave us the go-ahead, I started scribbling notes by hand and was startled by what came up from an old well of fun.

First we had fun, learning the blood and bones of writing.

Then we got good. Well, much better.

But time to have fun again. Here in this collection, never before collected as one, with a chance to get some of the real praise on the record. As Woody Allen has said, "Success is mostly just showing up."

On to the stories, where we have a few more things to say.

* * * * * *

Jack:

Yes, I think at that time of our lives—those distant, blurred salad days of exuberant youth—it was enough just to show up. After all, we were certain that everything was ahead of us; all we had to do was sit down in front of George's (really Pam's) old rat-tat-tat Smith Corona manual (and in those days manual meant *manual*!) typewriter and smash the hell out of those keys. Something rare and wonderful, something unmatched in genius and inspiration would magically and inevitably *have* to appear on the mint-white corrasable bond paper. Of that we were certain.

Well, perhaps it would be closer to the truth to say that *I* was certain. George was further ahead in terms of craft. I was still at the stage where I believed that inspiration would somehow magically transform the electric-shocked thoughts in my head into coherent sentences, comprehensible plots, and characters that didn't behave as if they'd just discovered that the strange digital appendages at the end of their arms were called fingers.

So I'd sit down in front of that old Smith Corona in George's high-ceilinged, book-cluttered apartment in Binghamton, New York (Rod Serling's home town) and clatter away until there was a small stack of typed pages beside me. I'd then show the brilliant outpouring to George, who would shake his great blond head as if he was in pain and proceed to turn ravings into story. Slowly, arduously, I started to learn the rudiments of craft... something I've learned one never stops learning. After having written or edited over seventy-five books, I *still* feel like I'm a raw beginner every time I stare into the grey-white flickerings of my laptop.

But, as George said earlier, those faraway, sunlit days *were* filled with joy. The very idea of being writers was enough: it was as rich and intriguing and glamorous as becoming ace fighter pilots, James Bond spies, or Kerouac(ian) Dharma-bums. We were writers because writers wrote. Nothing could be as noble,

exciting, or as important. We were going to change the world by dint of the sheer power of thought.

And so we wrote and talked through the nights until dawn. George "knew stuff", and I had the great talent of being an enormous sponge, greedily soaking up everything. Then I'd write some more, sure that every day's acquired knowledge of craft, life, philosophy, literature, and science would transmute my awkward, leaden efforts into golden prose.

That didn't even begin to happen, but what did happen was a complete story, and then another, and another...and George—that driven optimist who would have been groomed to be a shaman in another culture—took our stories to a science fiction convention and actually sold two of them then and there. He did exactly what I tell young writers never to do: buttonhole an editor at a convention. But, then, again, other writers aren't George.

So now I was a published writer, a real writer, whatever the hell that meant. For *me*, it meant total immersion in craft, something that has never changed. The idea of being a writer? Well, that doesn't mean much to me now. Writing is something I do, not who I am. But forty-three years ago it was definition itself.

George mentioned the time I wrote what I then considered a legitimate piece of prose, one sentence that is in "Dark, Dark, the Dead Star," a sentence that now amuses the slightly embarrassed author of *The Memory Cathedral*, *The Silent*, and *The Man Who Melted*. But thirty-nine years later, as I stare into the laptop screen, I can *still* remember the line: "A fused mass of beryllium fled from Deneb." George was very kind; he celebrated my creation of a sentence written in the active voice. (Another win for Strunk and White's irreplaceable little guide *The Elements of Style*.)

Ah, those were the days. My pretension reached heights I hope I never climb again. I remember starting a story (which sold to a publisher, alas) with the line "Postulate one monad." Ach! But George had made the mistake of introducing me to Leibniz's *Monadology*, and...off I went.

George once said to me that if you weren't born a genius, you could just push your way through to being one. George is a true polymath: the proverbial dog with a bone, or rather many bones. He just kept gnawing away at every subject that took his interest—philosophy, science, history, literature, film, genre fiction—until he gained the kind of understanding that would allow him to make real contributions to the great conversation of ideas. And I'll be damned, but he did turn himself into a polymath genius: a genre Nabokov, a Sartre of reasoned optimism, a Polish Stanislaw Lem cum Isaac Bashevis Singer who publishes his work in *Nature* as easily as in *Analog*.

By the way, George is Polish. Born at the end of the war, he speaks the language fluently and in collaboration with his partner, award-winning author Pamela Sargent, makes the best bigos I've ever tasted! When he read my original note, which mistakenly noted that he was born in a concentration camp, he wrote:

> My parents were taken as slave labor and worked on Austrian farms before being liberated. They were not reprehensible enough to be taken to the death camps, to be worked to death after the war was won by Hitler.
>
> My bio-father was earlier taken with his high school buddies to shovel out the death trains as they came out of the facilities, but when his stomach was ruined by the disinfectant chemicals he was also sent to Austrian farm work.
>
> He met my mother after the liberation; he joined the allied armies as a guard, and so my mother and I got to go to England as "allies."
>
> I was not born in a concentration camp, but as a privileged character in a Villach, Austria hospital, the son of "DPs"—displaced persons (liberated slave labor), who narrowly avoided forced repatriation to Poland, as Stalin had demanded, saved by the UN Declaration of Human Rights, passed just in time and

written by Eleanor Roosevelt and H. G. Wells. I met Mrs. Roosevelt at the Hospital for Special Surgery in NYC in the early 1950s, where I was also operated on in 1959. Also met Hopalong Cassidy there.

God almighty!

So now to those early stories of ours. I haven't read them in years, and it is with joy, nostalgia, and, yes, a little trepidation that I approach them again. I'll add my notes to George's after I read (well, re-read!) each story. I suppose, in a sense, this is a trip back to the future...what the late, great Isaac Asimov (may he rest in peace) called "antique futures."

We'll see....

TRAPS

The continent below him was covered with lush jungle except for the sandy plateau twenty miles in diameter. A moment earlier his instruments had picked up the other ship sitting near the southern edge of the tableland. The sandy surface of the plateau was fairly regular and Rysling decided to bring his own craft down on automatic, as close to the other ship as possible. He sat back in his contour seat and waited, his senses alert. Was someone else trying to beat him to his job?

His small exploratory vessel was now three thousand feet above the plateau and coming down fast on secondary jets. The primary landside jets cut in with a roar at five hundred feet and the sleek vessel settled slowly to the sand. When all had quieted the displaced sand made a crater-like perimeter around the silver hull.

Rysling made sure the double safety on the star-drive was secure, cut in the double safety for the landside rockets. Through his forward screen he saw that the other ship and also both suns were up. The yellow star was high in the dark blue sky, near its noontime. The red giant was near the horizon, just above the green jungle which surrounded the barren plateau. Rysling released the strap from around his waist. He stood up slowly and stretched. Nothing about the other ship was moving.

As yet the planet had no name, only a number: 3-10004-2. The gravity was only slightly higher than Earth normal. The atmosphere was nearly identical in composition to Earth's. For all practical purposes the planet was ready to be colonized. But

Earth Authority was picky. It wanted a complete classification of the land animals. That was why he was here, to catch the only remaining land animal that had not yet been caught, a catlike, four-footed creature which to date had eluded all efforts of hunters. That was all he had been told. He had been given a flat fee, operating expenses and a time limit of one earth month. Two weeks had already gone by.

As he came down the exit ramp, Rysling took a deep breath of the warm, humid air. After two weeks of the clean, sterile ship's air the natural variety smelled awful. He was almost sickened by the thought of micro-organisms suspended all around him. He came to the end of the ramp and the sand was gritty beneath his heavy boots. It felt good, despite the air. He noticed that he was about four hundred feet from the other ship.

He walked to the other craft. The yellow sun was warm on his face. The other ship was also an exploratory model, slightly larger than his own. He estimated that it was perhaps two years older. There was a large, slightly scarred *H* on the hull. It might be one of Henderson's ships, he thought, but the fading letter was not conclusive proof.

The ramp was down. Rysling went halfway up the incline.

"Is anyone home?" His voice echoed in the open airlock. There was no answer. He walked into the airlock and shouted up the central passageway which led up into the control room. "Hello." Still no answer.

Rysling climbed the ladder into the control room. He looked around at everything carefully. All seemed to be in order—shut down —except for the radar and sensor instruments. They continued their watch of the surrounding country. For the moment they had nothing to report. The light above the security switches over the star-drive and rockets glowed a bright green. Everything seemed as it should be.

They're all probably outside. I'm sure to run into them sooner or later.

He was almost ready to leave when his curiosity got the better of him. He sat down in the captain's station and flicked

on the log tape. He listened. For a long time there was nothing. At last, very faintly, he heard heavy breathing, then a voice he didn't recognize.

"The greycat came into my mind. Suddenly I wasn't a man any more but a beast. A hallucination? I don't know—but I'll be ready for it the next time. Going out now. Time: hell, my watch is broken..."

The tape ran on for a long time. Nothing more seemed to be on it. Rysling waited a little longer and switched it off. Apparently the skipper of the ship had not yet come back. He sounded like a man of imagination and easily frightened. Rysling shrugged.

He descended to the airlock, walked down the ramp, wandered to the edge of the plateau. Maybe the ship's personnel were down in the jungle. He unsnapped his binoculars and began sweeping the jungle. Some impulse made him look straight down to the base of the cliff. He saw a stretch of white sand—and then he saw the bones.

Two human skeletons lay on the sand, hands pointed to the jungle as if praying. They must have fallen to their deaths somehow.

Rysling turned up the magnification of his oculars. At once it seemed he was standing directly over the two skeletons. A bug crawled out of one of the skulls and fled across the bright sand into the underbrush. How long did it take for flesh to rot away? Later he would have to go down and try to make identifications, determine what had happened and pack the remains for shipment home.

But for now he had a job to do, an animal to net. It was the kind of odd job he often took on between his regular ship runs. A man could always do with a little extra capital. Besides, he liked hunting. Trap a greycat, they had told him. Simple enough with the proper gear. But others had failed. Maybe Earth Authority had hired bunglers. Like the previous owners of the two skeletons below?

Their fate really didn't concern him. He would not fail.

* * * * * *

The "hound" was really just a cage which could open any one of its six sides, could track its prey visually and through body heat and strike more swiftly than any living thing could move. Carefully Rysling worked the remote controls and guided it out of the cargo hold and gently down to the sand. He had set up the tripod earlier. It held the screen monitor for the hound's electronic eyes. The remote control panel was just below the screen. In effect he would be the hound, seeing with its eyes and making sure that it did not tangle itself in vegetation—much of the tracking, however, was automatic and in reality he would only be needed during crucial moments, if they arose. Otherwise he could just sit in front of the monitor and live vicariously what the hound was doing. A routine job. He could not see how anyone could have failed to catch the animal. The beast didn't have a chance. The hound's eyes and heat-sensing device were tied into the ship's computers which had been programmed to recognize only this type of living thing.

Rysling adjusted the controls for automatic search pattern. The pattern was based on what knowledge the computer had of the greycat. The hound lifted itself from the sand and moved slowly to the edge of the plateau. In a moment it dropped out of sight into the jungle. Rysling sat back in his seat in front of the monitor screen and stretched his legs.

In front of him now he could see wide-stemmed plants as the hound-cage pushed them aside. Some smaller plants bore large unopened buds. The tree trunks were massive, and an unfamiliar moss grew over much of their brown surface. The grass in the forest was a foot high, Rysling estimated. He could see great vines passing through it—lines of communication between the trees. He felt as if he were the hound, a great and powerful beast moving through the jungle aisles. The heat there was oppressive and moisture fell in great drops from huge leaves. He pushed a button and the hound's eyes looked to the now hidden sky. He could only see the great trunks, standing like titans, guardians

of the forest.

Rysling turned to look at the other ship. Sunlight was bright on the plateau. The yellow star was edging toward its afternoon. The red giant was partly below the horizon. Atmospheric refraction distorted its equatorial region, making the huge star look misshapen and bloated. Rysling no longer believed that anyone would return to the other ship.

When he turned again to the screen the hound was motionless. Nothing moved on the monitor except for a leaf touched by the wind. Slowly, silently, the greycat walked into view, thin and muscular, body low to the ground—the eyes were yellow ovals and looked directly into the screen. Rysling was fascinated by the eyes, they beckoned him, they drew his gaze into themselves. It seemed almost as if the cat were looking directly at him, as if the green-furred beast knew that something else waited behind the hound's mechanical eyes. Rysling bit his lip. His hands hovered over the console, ready to take over in case of difficulty.

The hound moved in slowly at first, automatically—it picked up speed until it was moving about thirty miles an hour. But the greycat was suddenly a blur skimming the grass. The hound followed with deadly accuracy, changing direction with the animal. In a few moments it was directly behind the cat. Both were moving well past fifty miles an hour, Rysling estimated. The front cage door was open. Rysling noticed the red light on the console, informing him of the fact. There was a different colored light for each of the six doors. At any moment now the cat would be scooped up and the door would shut. In front of him Rysling could see the dark streak that ran from the cat's ears to the long tail.

The greycat jumped into some brush, turned, and snarled at him. In a moment it would all be over, Rysling thought. Then he could go and take care of the two skeletons at the cliff base, go home to collect the rest of his fee.

The green vegetation before him was suddenly very vivid. Rysling felt a dizziness. He closed his eyes for a moment. His

arms grew heavy and blood pounded in his head. When he opened his eyes the screen was out of focus and the whole world was spinning.

* * * * * * *

He felt as if he were falling, but slowly. And the cool green grass of the forest was all around him, caressing him, inviting him to sleep until his strength returned and he could fight the strange, scentless creature that was chasing him. Rysling looked up at the hound through the greycat's eyes. It was coming toward him. He rose on his hind paws and fell back farther into the thick brush. He tried to swat the cage with his paw. He snarled and fell over backward. He jumped to all fours immediately.

And ran. His cat's body ran without him, instinctively, turning, jumping with an exhilarating sureness. He felt the thorn balls cling to his paws. His eyes saw everything—the forest was a rich orchestration of scents that told him all he needed to know.

* * * * * * *

With a trembling hand Rysling turned off the hound's automatic program, He was shaking. Sweat had run down his back. He inhaled a tranquilizer. The hound would come back now but he would send it out again.

A hallucination, he thought. It was what the voice on the log tape of the other ship had been talking about. But he had felt pain, fatigue, tasted the pungent scents of the forest, known the sweat and muscles of the swift greycat as he knew his own. And he had known the fear of the cat, running before something it did not understand, could never understand because it was not part of the normal environment.

He thought he had part of the picture now. He had been hit by the animal's defense mechanism. Did the cat have telepathic abilities? At any rate, what he had experienced had to be an illu-

sion and he would have to ignore it next time around. Perhaps the cat's strange power dated from some still undiscovered stage of interplanetary evolution when all life forms were still undifferentiated, all awarenesses one—the single pulse of the natural force.

The hound appeared over the edge of the plateau. It skimmed to within six feet of the control console tripod and settled to the ground. Rysling went to it and checked it carefully. Nothing was wrong. He went back to the console and sat down to face the screen. With one flick he turned the automatic track back on. Quickly the hound flew over it. When it reached the spot where it had left the cat it descended again to the jungle floor, its heat residue sensor scanning the ground for the warm trail. The greycat's path led in a wide circle toward the northern cliff wall of the plateau. The hound followed.

Apparently the animal was following the cliff wall closely. The hound picked up speed. The greycat came into view on the sand ahead. The hound picked up still more speed. The cat ran, leaving big paw prints in the sand strip that rimmed the base of the plateau.

Rysling braced himself for the hallucination. It came like a dream he could recognize as one but he could not break the spell. The cage was open and coming directly for him. The cliff wall was at his back. He had to wait for the moment when he could rush past it into the jungle. For an instant his new body was frozen, as if all its instincts were dead or confused by the precision of an enemy which made so few mistakes, gave so little opportunity to escape. The cage came on until it was directly in front of him.

It swallowed him. The bars slid shut with a click. Then he heard the small voice whispering in his ear, *You're Rysling—this is an illusion. It will go away, change. Just wait.* But the presence of the jungle was stronger, the backdrop of his new life, the vast and vivid support for his senses, the source of all blessings. He heard it, he smelled it, he saw the vivid, achingly intense colors. Only the bars kept him from it. His own voice

was very faint, very far away and of no consequence. A small fly buzzing near his ear.

The greycat threw himself at the bars. *Stupid, the button,* the voice said. *Outside the first bar.* He slid his paw between the bars and pushed wildly. The side entrance of the cage opened with a half-remembered whirring sound.

The jungle beckoned. He ran into the gloom, quietly, swiftly, in one fluid motion unlike the jerky point-to-point movement of his previous life. He could smell the shades of colors—he sensed the range which before had been only green, brown, or mud-colored. The soft voice told him to go back, regain his former self, break the spell that bound him to a world that man had turned his back on a million years ago—but the voice was a poor, sterile thing compared with the rich, surrounding forest.

Still, he would have to go back, if only for a moment. The jungle called to him—it promised confidently.

But instead he ran toward the sandy plateau.

The human form that had once been Kurt Rysling stood up from its seat in front of the tripod console. Its movements were jerky. It tried to walk and fell on all fours. The smell of the jungle it had known all its life seemed distant, faded and alien. The colors were pale and the normal sounds of the forest were gone. Its strange new limbs were weak. The greycat tried to growl but only a weak sound came out of its small, human mouth. He crawled nearer the jungle, hoping that all the normal sensations would return. He reached the edge. The urge to jump came suddenly. The greycat leaped from the plateau, its human arms stretched out in front like paws.

The small voice still spoke in the greycat's simple brain. Momentarily it became stronger when the cat came to the broken body of Kurt Rysling lying next to the sun-bleached skeletons at the bottom of the cliff. The red star had long since set, and the yellow sun was low over the jungle. The cat stood perfectly still in the cliff's shadow, listening. Dimly, from somewhere in the depths of the greycat's nervous system, Rysling understood what had happened to the two skeletons before him. This then

was the skipper of the other ship and his companion and what was happening to him had happened to them. He looked at his own corpse with indifference. It was after all a thing and not *himself*. He felt comfortable and safe. From somewhere his old voice summoned up enough strength to tell him that while *he* could adapt easily to the cat's nervous system, the greycat had not been able to master the complexities of a human cortex. But, then, did this not mean that the human mind was only a resident of the physio-chemical brain? That in reality it was an epiphenomenon, a matrix of energy which could detach itself from its physical form?. It must be so, the small voice said. After all, the iron of a magnet produces something beyond itself, the magnetic field; and the mass of a world produces a gravitational field; and the physio-chemical brain tissue produces a pattern of energies that is the real mind, responsible for all the higher functions. The small voice seemed desperate as it spoke. There would be a price to pay for his new existence—fading memories, the power of reason, love. But he didn't care. The world was vast and entirely within his grasp. It was a world for him. The smells of the forest wrapped themselves around him. Did he for a moment detect—a female odor? The image was clear: a sleek female, waiting somewhere for him. The small voice was almost gone now—he could not understand its meaning or where it had come from. He glanced again at the broken body that lay face down, its neck broken. He looked up to the edge of the plateau. Had he thought of going there? There was no way up. Swiftly he turned and ran into the green shadows. His muscles were strong. In one place the yellow sun cast its light into the jungle aisle, making his fur feel warm. Soon, he knew, it would be night. The small voice was only a background sound, no stronger than an insect's drone. He stopped and turned to look at the plateau, which from this distance was visible through a break in the trees. He could just barely see the top of one silvery ship. He looked at it, trying to remember what it was but that memory was already gone.

The greycat turned again and disappeared into the jungle.

AFTERWORD FOR "TRAPS"

George:

"Remarks want you to make them," Raymond Chandler's Phillip Marlowe says to his captors when they try to shut him up. This story, along with the others, is now a captive in time, captured again in this collection, provoking remarks from both of us.

I don't know, as I write this, what Jack will say, but this is a van Vogtian pastiche, recalling his Rull stories, and maybe even "The Most Dangerous Game" by Richard Connell. It is a story written by the rules, which you can only break later; beginners don't like to hear that. You first write what you admire, and then grow into yourself. For Jack it was this story's greycat, and the way it walks onto the scene and into the eyes of the hunter, who learns where and to what he wants to throw in his lot. Sometimes I think the greycat's expression is Jack Benny's look of exasperation.

Rysling's name is a misspelled version of the name of the blind poet in Robert Heinlein's story "The Green Hills of Earth." We just liked the sound of it.

* * * * * * *

Jack:

And so our character Rysling comes alive to take a bow once again...

George was right: we were trying to write a *real* story, one that followed Aristotle's rule of beginning, middle, and end. The goal of the exercise was to narrate a straightforward story in a prose style that was as simple and direct as we could make it. If memory serves, we wrote "Traps" in 1968, and it was published in *Worlds of If* in 1970. That was the period of the "New Wave"

in science fiction, a time of wild stylistic experimentation characterized by open-ended plots, stream-of-consciousness prose, and John Dos Passos news headline collages. Writers and editors such as Damon Knight, Robert Silverberg, Michael Moorcock, Harlan Ellison, James Tiptree, Jr., Joanna Russ, Pamela Zoline, Sonya Dorman, Kit Reed, Roger Zelazny, Samuel R. Delany, J.G. Ballard (whose "condensed novels" really were something new in the world), John Brunner, Brian Aldiss, Thomas N. Disch, and a host of others were redefining the genre. Although some of the stories in this collection were definitely influenced by the newfound stylistic freedom of the New Wave, "Traps" is a story that moved against the strong tide of the zeitgeist.

As George suggested, we were trying to write a traditional story, a pastiche in the style of Poul Anderson, Gordon R. Dickson, Clifford Simak, Murray Leinster, and A. E. van Vogt (if, indeed, van Vogt with his rule of introducing a new plot element every 800 words could ever be considered traditional).

DARK, DARK,
THE DEAD STAR

In the darkness his thoughts ran on, seeming to belong to no one, turning back on themselves, rubbing against each other, bidding him to remember but with no success.

After only a little while life begins to accumulate like shell-fish on a coral reef and a man begins to understand that if just one of a few things were to be taken from him, then—he'd have to live with the memory, the stain all over his insides and it would never go away. If it happens more than once you begin to look for an out—but the outs are few and well guarded.

* * * * * * *

"Why doesn't he wake up, doctor?"

* * * * * * *

If I could die for only a little while, he thought.

* * * * * * *

"I wish I knew. Where is the mind anyway? Is it just the physical, spatial organ called the brain?"
"Doctor, you're not paid to speculate."
"A patient like this is always a slap in the face."
"I'm sorry, Doctor."

* * * * * * *

I'm never going to die, he thought. After a little while the weight of living breaks you up into little pieces that the waves wash clean and take back with them into the sea.

My ocean, my wings. For a time I lived as a man but I died and my corpse lies strangely rotting in the hold of a green ship I cannot find. Other corpses are there but determined to rot no further from their present state.

There is no sun on my ocean, only a blue haze and no land of any kind. And the sea is filled with fleeing fear and rotting plants that come up from the shallow bottom. Once I saw a giant eel poke its head above the warm brine, but I could not fear it. My black wings keep me safe, he thought.

Where is my green ship, lost for ages now? Racing low over the water I sometimes think it is only a foot long and I might have missed it a thousand times. I open my great bill and scoop up the dead worms that float near the surface...

Once a dripping noise woke me in the night. I fell to the floor, into the center of the room where the pool of stuff had gathered. It was a black liquid and when I touched it the stuff stuck to my fingers. I looked up at the ceiling. There didn't seem to be any more on the way. It made me very angry because I knew there was more and it was holding back just to annoy me...

* * * * * * *

"Perhaps he's trying to get back to what happened to him, and when he makes his peace with that, maybe he'll waken."

"How long will it take, Doctor?"

"For him, probably an epoch—and for us there is no way to tell. Was he a good man?"

"He was a good man, Doctor."

* * * * * * *

He remembered a voice saying, "There are faint red stars close to the earth whose primarily infrared radiations are mostly absorbed by our atmosphere. No picture of the universe can be complete without them. The Farside Lunar radio telescope thinks it has located one—and only two light-years away. Our new stardrive works and this will be its third test. Of course you will conduct scientific observations, take photographs, et cetera. But if all goes well, we will be ready to take larger hops out into the galaxy. Good luck, gentlemen."

The voice did not sound convincing, he thought. He could not remember who the speaker had been—and where?

He thought, the universe—all space—consists of the convolutions of some monstrous brain and I a phantom am set adrift in its passages. Strange thoughts drift within me, whispering that I am a dream. And at the moment when I am closest to the truth darkness veils everything from me. Speak, memory, he commanded but the darkness was again complete, inscrutable.

Suddenly there were stars in the darkness, cold unblinking stars, a billion of them all around him. He saw the fused mass of beryllium that had once been his ship. The ship tumbled and turned endlessly, a crumpled toy among the stars and he, a pale gray figure, floated near the wreck. He saw himself, a small suited mannikin with six hours of air stored to support its organic component. He felt sweat running down his back. His faceplate was fogged up—the dials on the inside of his suit glowed dimly. Gradually the faceplate cleared, and he estimated that he was orbiting his dead ship once every minute.

He remembered the explosion. It was still a splotch of light etched onto his brain as if he'd been shot full in the face with a laser. The stardrive generators had gone, a one-in-a-million chance. By all theoretical models such an explosion would turn local space inside out and scatter anything caught in it throughout creation, a variable scatter across space and time. He had been outside taking three-dimensional shots of the dim red star when it happened. Suddenly the ship had turned blindingly white. The camera had been pushed out of his grip, the

safety line had snapped and then a chunk of something had hit him in the middle. Maybe he had been lucky nothing had penetrated his suit. Impossible to tell good from bad, curse from blessing. Nothing he had ever known, guessed or been told was holding still.

He looked at his transmitter dial. It was faithfully sending out the distress call—three laser pulses into space every five seconds.

To his right the red star glowed dimly. He knew that somewhere the star had a dark companion, a chunk of dead rock. If he and the ship were still anywhere near their previous course, they would pass very near to it. He knew what it would look like. The body would reflect almost no light—he would notice it only by its capacity to blot out the starfields.

He touched the small control box on his left shoulder and the small suit jets spun him around three hundred and sixty degrees. No dark body was anywhere in sight. He gave his jets a touch and stopped spinning. The stars stilled again in his vision.

Silence, save for the sound of breathing, a metronome of rushing air keeping time in a timeless place. He tapped his helmet with his glove. It was a relief to hear the contact. He looked at his oxygen meter. Its glow was dull inside his helmet. He had to twist his neck into an uncomfortable position to see it properly.

* * * * * * *

Oxygen: 5 hr. 22 m.

He closed his eyes and tried to control his breathing. He inhaled and counted to ten. He might be able to add twenty minutes to his life this way. But what did it matter? They would never find him, a tiny fragment among the stars.

Better to have been in the ship—no memories, no waiting, just a flash and oblivion.

* * * * * * *

Oxygen: 4 hr. 16 m.

The warm glow of the tranquilizer surrounded him and he slept. The horizon of the alien land in front of him was crimson. The sands reflected the bursting flames. And the tiger. Slowly tracking, back and forth. Waiting. For him.

He awoke remembering. The tranquilizer made him sick and he vomited a little. The faceplate fogged and smeared. He couldn't see the stars.

His scream hung inside the suit and couldn't get out. He swatted at the control box with his glove. The wreck receded suddenly and he was spinning. Slowly he managed to control the spin. He took another pill.

He felt the numbness slowly spreading through his body. He swam, a god in his bath, smiling. Control. Sleep.

He awoke. Ahead of him a great mass obscured the stars. It was the red star's planet, a dark wanderer waiting for his corpse. He strained to see if the dark mass reflected any of the red star's light but there was no light, only the dim circular outline against the starfield. Once this dying star had been strong enough to warm whole worlds. He turned himself to look at the wreck. It was a small, darkly silver patch of metal to his right and for an instant he thought he could reach out and then hold it in his hand.

* * * * * * *

Oxygen: 3 hr. 10 m.

When the wreck suddenly seemed to be obscuring stars more rapidly he knew that the dark planet was pulling them both in. He looked at the huge mass, a large black circle taking up almost a quarter of the sky. It looks like a neatly cut hole in space, he thought. I'm going to plow right into it and then the ship right on top of me. If I last long enough to experience it. And then he thought he could feel his forward motion as the dark body grew larger in front of him. He pushed his suit controls and made a complete turn for observational purposes. At the end of his turn

he saw the cluster of smaller dark bodies, bits of small debris circling the dim red sun.

* * * * * * *

Oxygen: 2 hr. 2 m.

The dark mass now covered a third of the sky. He looked down at a dark floor covered with sparkling diamonds. For a moment he thought they would blur into a sheet of light, but his eyes focused and the diamonds remained distinct. A bit of dust scratched across his faceplate, a cue that enabled him to imagine his terrifying speed.

* * * * * * *

Oxygen: 45 m.

Where had all the time gone? Suddenly he had to remember the good things in his life. He remembered her cool, smooth skin, her warm lips and long black hair. He would never kiss her again—she would never be open to him, quivering with excitement. He would never see the child she would have. There was no longer a future, love, old age, only a lonely death, in a dark place at the ends of the universe. He wouldn't even know if he would hit the dark planet or circle it forever.

* * * * * * *

Oxygen: 05 m.

It was getting harder to breathe. The dark planet now took up half the sky. He had once pressed a fly to death with a paperweight. He had always known that it would get back at him. He looked toward his fused ship. It was tumbling wildly end over end. A piece broke off and passed a dozen feet to his right.

* * * * * * *

Oxygen—Empty

The air became heavy and hot very suddenly. He turned the cooling unit to high. At least the bad air would be cool for a while. The tiger sprang at him from the dune and he fired and missed. It tore at his chest, opened it and seized his heart in its teeth. He screamed and watched the cat run off with it, chewing as it ran. The sun was hot on his open flesh. It burned. Momentarily a cool wind blew through his open chest. Then the abrasive sand got inside and stirred around in his lungs, forced its way down into his stomach and bowels. It ripped through his guts like a razor. The muscles in his calves tightened and turned to stone, refusing to relax. His arms stiffened and he couldn't move them. A demon was walking around in his head, beating against his temples, trying to get out, reaching down into his spine and twisting. Dark, dark, the dead star, the demon whispered and refused to let him go.

He felt his eyes bulge out of their sockets. Helen! he tried to shout, but no sound came from his throat. I love you! The thought wouldn't come out of his head. It was stuck there, frozen. He had just run out of reality, the blank end of a reel of tape, all hiss and noise, running on into nowhere. He turned his radio up full blast. There was nothing on the wave spectrum but the mindless seething between the stars.

* * * * * * *

"When the ship's lifeboat found him he was like this," the doctor said. *"And he didn't come out of it all during the eight month journey home under auxiliary ion power. His two crew-mates had to feed him intravenously and he lost a lot of weight."*

* * * * * * *

Beyond death was only the soft water and he sank into it. Liquid rushed about his limbs. It flowed through his veins, nourishing his poisoned body, filling him with a great peace. He

withdrew into the silence somewhere near oblivion. He thought of the dead portions of his body, hair, nails and skin, and of how gradually the living slipped into the nonliving.

* * * * * * *

"He's developing a body fever," the doctor said as he looked at the diagnostic screen. "We're going to have to break it quickly." The woman sitting next to the bed leaned forward and looked at her husband's face. He seemed to be sleeping. She looked for some change but his face remained a mask.

* * * * * * *

He was choking in the hot sand. Each grain burned him in turn and something grasped him by the head and twisted him in the sand as if he were a stick. The grains were abrasive and cut into him like broken glass. Suddenly the sand became cool and wet, enfolding him in its firm, damp comfort. Gradually his mind realized what had happened—it came to him slowly. As a man wakens on a spring morning, he saw the way back.

And he knew now that the green ship was no more, that the tiger did not make off with his heart and he knew that somehow he was alive, somewhere. He reached out with love toward the great mind that ruled the cosmos and gave thanks.

When the fever's edge softened and turned his sickness to sleep he dreamed of fair women with golden hair and small breasts; he saw their firm bodies lying upon green grass. He slept.

* * * * * * *

"Doctor, he blinked."

* * * * * * *

At once he knew she was sitting next to him. She had called him back. The mind is everywhere, he thought. The brain lives in a spatio-temporal realm but the mind comes from elsewhere to stay only a short while, an exile from a greater community.

He felt the light coming into his closed eyes, felt it moving along his optic nerve to his brain—he wondered what kind of eye his brain must have to interpret such a signal? Then he understood that the brain's eye was only a window and through that window watched the mind's eye, the final interpreter, the arbiter of meaning. Its way was a special way of seeing, the way that made sense of everything that came through from a hostile universe of which it was a part.

He thought, the mind develops its perceptual powers through experiential analogy with sense data during life. Lacking sense data the mind spins out symbolic representations of the imperfectly perceived events going on around the locus of the brain in space. For him the loss of life, of Helen, would have been purposeless and unbearable, so, at the stress point where another man might have given up, his mind-matrix had flared up like a nova, a quantum jump to an unprecedented level of awareness and strength. The resulting field had enveloped the physical organ that was the brain and had preserved it from the decay that should have resulted when his oxygen ran out. This was the life-force that guided biological reproduction—the mechanism that made life immortal while the individuals and even species perished; in his case it had preserved an individual. The force of his life-affirmation, the horror of death, the force of his will, had found for him the counterentropic force of all intelligent life and had preserved him until the others had found him floating in the darkness.

But the gain was permanent. He could see, truly for the first time, as no man had seen before. Space was no obstacle; he could feel the emotions of those around him—especially Helen's. They were as prominent as the corona of the sun during eclipse; he understood the darkness that covered her face. Slowly the darkness was passing from her face, revealing to him the light

of her rising hope.

He knew that this door of perception would now always be open to him. In the darkness of the dead star it had given him the meaning of his situation through the vision of the dreams. My ocean, my wings. He knew what they meant.

With the thought came the full realization that he was alive, now more than ever. He remembered the torment of the ghostly worlds and knew that the terrible fear of death at the moment when his tanks had run out had driven him there—into the arms of sirens. The fountain of life behind his dream of fair women had saved him and he knew what would happen now. He knew she was waiting for him like a ministering angel, listening and watching for a sign of life. An angel made for a man.

"Helen—"

He said goodbye to the dark worlds within and opened his eyes to the bright light of day coming in through the window.

AFTERWORD FOR
"DARK, DARK, THE DEAD STAR"

George:

"A fused mass of beryllium fled from Deneb," Jack Dann's famed early sentence, does not quite appear in this story, but close enough; that's what collaboration does to your work. It became, "He saw the fused mass of beryllium that had once been his ship." Not as vital; maybe we should have left well enough alone. Anyway, here it is, in its premiere outing.

* * * * * * *

Jack:

George, you were absolutely right to recast that sentence!

"Dark, Dark, the Dead Star" certainly was influenced by the literary foment going on around us. As I reread the story I was startled by our referencing of Roger Zelazny's beautiful and atmospheric novel *Isle of the Dead* in the opening sequence; and I could not help but remember with sadness a eulogy I had written for Roger over fifteen years ago:

> I wish you peace, old friend, and I can't help but remember the thrill of reading those stories and novels of yours when I was starting out, how I would try to memorize passages to learn how you did it, how you turned prose into poetry; and when I think of you now, I once again remember the first lines of *Isle of the Dead*, and I can see you there, old trickster, walking along that eternal beach on Tokyo Bay.
>
> In the freshening wind and sharp salt air.
> Walking quietly away....

Ah, the clarity of memory and the heart-skipping power of nostalgia.

Reading these stories is like looking at old photographs; and I find myself ghosting back into the past, into those heady times when everything seemed possible...when we all actually *believed* that everything was possible. You can see it in the Zelazny-esque title of the story (George's: he was the title-meister!). And I can certainly see our two younger selves pacing about in George's apartment until one of us would sit down to pound away at the typewriter; and I remember as if it were yesterday, I had shoulder-length brown hair instead of conservatively short silver-gray hair; and I remember George, blond and dressed in corduroy; I remember George conducting a Mahler symphony playing on his tape recorder (yes, with real reel-to-reel tape) or expounding the merits of neglected authors such as Edgar Pangborn; and I'll never forget the talking and the pacing and the writing and the talking and the writing writing writing: two young Turks callow and brash enough to try to break out of the bounds of prose and soar into the thin, barely breathable heights of poetry. We couldn't do it then, we didn't yet have the tools; but we certainly did try; and today, as I read lines written by George all those years ago—"A demon was walking around in his head, beating against his temples, trying to get out, reaching down into his spine and twisting. Dark, dark, the dead star, the demon whispered and refused to let him go."—I can't help but feel a certain wild pride. We had the attitude that even though we would most likely fall on our respective faces, we *were* going to jump off the precipice and try to fly. And the core idea of the story—that one could foil the darkness by sheer will alone, an idea that Miguel de Unamuno would have approved of...Unamuno, that philosopher who roared at death as loudly as Zorba the Greek—well, that core idea pretty much defines the hot, heady time of the late '60s and early '70s.

It might have been an overweeningly optimistic idea, but, damn, how I yearn to feel that way again.

LISTEN, LOVE

Uheh sat next to the rodasz bush. Its glow cast thin rods of yellow onto her features; the rods changed color one after another, shifting from yellow to red to orange and back again. She stared at the small glowing branches; she felt the numbness of sleep stealing over her. Soon the sun would set and the quiet-time would begin, the time of darkness and rest. The colors swept her away into a whirlpool of sensation, and she fought back. It seemed too soon yet, she must wait; sleep-time was far, far away. She came up close to the bush and brushed her face gently against the delicate branches. She drew back; the plant was trying to lull her to sleep.

Uheh listened. Her large, finely shaped ears gathered in the small sounds of her world, and she was expert at interpreting them. There were few loud sounds in her experience, and she had been taught to fear them: she knew how to cover her ears with the large palms of her hands and then bring her elbows together until they touched. As she listened now, she heard only the sounds of small living things getting ready for the dark-time. The sun was low over the trees in the distance. The world was at peace, yet she felt fearful.

She closed her eyes and turned her face to the sun, and felt its evening warmth, its quiet embrace which seemed to touch and not touch at the same time. The soft pink skin of her naked form said a silent goodbye to the departing star that was the sun of her world.

Suddenly there was a blast of light, so strong that she sensed

it even through her delicate eyelids. A rumble came across the distance toward her, but it was only a deep bass sound and couldn't hurt her. She listened to the low pitched sound; it was almost comforting. She sat down on the grass and closed her eyes again. Her entire body tingled to the sound, until it died away and she was almost asleep.

Uheh sat up suddenly, awake again and full of fear. For a brief instant the sound had become shrill and painful, and even the grass around her, the caghfr green on which she had played since she had been a little girl among the little ones of the kuu, seemed frightened. She looked at the rodasz bush; its color now was a drab green, its glow gone. Did it wake her? Had it been calling her, to warn her? The momentary shrill sound had been so loud. She shuddered and crawled into the vegetation around the rodasz bush, thinking that it would be a good place to hide; and perhaps she could spend the dark quiet-time here. That would certainly prove to the old ones of the kuu that she had come of age, and was unafraid of the dark quiet-time: the mark of a woman who could begin to bear young. A moment of pride went through her, but it was cut short by what she saw coming across the caghfr grass toward her.

The small flyer settled on the alien grass. Uheh felt the ground tremble slightly under her feet. She peered out from the vegetation; her hand held a branch on the rodasz bush.

The sun was very low when she saw the two figures get out of the silver flyer. This could not be any kind of calling, she thought. It was too harsh. Dimly she understood that the low sound from before had something to do with the silver flyer now before her. She wondered if the old ones from the kuu were watching this new thing. They would know what it was, and protect her.

The pain-sound came from the new thing and throbbed in her temples for a moment, and was gone.

The two space-suited figures walked on the caghfr grass while Uheh watched. She pushed her head through the branches of the rodasz bush to get a better view, and a leaf touched her

cheek, lovingly.

She stood up and made herself visible. One of the figures waved his arm and came toward her. What could she fear from them? They were like her, and yet not like her. She wanted to run toward the flyer, the new thing that had come from the sky; but the voice of her upbringing was strong: be cautious. She looked at the figure who came up to her now, and she wondered why he wore the clear thing over his head. She could see that he was smiling at her, and she could see his teeth; there was a lot of hair on his dark face. Surely he did not wear the clear thing to keep warm? He should take it off, she thought, and smiled back at him.

The other one came up behind him, and as if in answer to her thought they took off their helmets. She stared at the strange texture of their skin. The first one was handsome enough to make any in the kuu jealous; yet different. He motioned to her with his suited and gloved hand. Could this be dangerous? He looked so pleasing. Surely he was like her, but from somewhere far off; perhaps from the other side of the blue hills, or the far side of the world? She sat down on the grass and motioned for them to do the same. They hesitated, then followed her example; they put their helmets down on the grass in front of them.

The first one gestured at her strangely and pointed at the sky, and she nodded and smiled her understanding. Then she tried to make the sign of the kuu for them—the sign of her home; but it was difficult without the sandy lakeshore where the elder had first taught it to her. The first stranger smiled at her efforts and looked at his companion.

He was good. She would try to keep him. The elders would be happy when she brought him home to the kuu. She touched his hand. It was very warm without the glove and she drew back. Then she stood up and gestured him to follow her. She waved the other one away, but he didn't go. Didn't he understand? She was puzzled. All elders made the same rules. Had she done something wrong?

"I think she wants you, and she wants me to clear out," the

second one said. She heard the pain sound coming from his mouth, and she put her hands up to her head in pain. The sound was so high, so harsh! So unlike the quiet world that cared for her, nourished her. The pain-sound cut through her entire body and she shuddered uncontrollably. It ran along her nerves and seemed to burst in her head.

"Just like a woman," the first one—(her favorite!)—said.

Run! the world cried to her. The pain-sound became worse; it squeezed her. Could such a sound have meaning? The sun was almost down now, and the dark quiet-time was coming swiftly now. In the sky the stars winked into existence, and would soon march in their promenade from horizon to horizon. The two men were gesturing at her. She saw their lips move and again the pain-sound reached her ears. She turned and began to run toward the kuu, away from the sunset three hills away by the lakeside.

"Hey beautiful, don't go!"—the pain sound followed her. "Come on back!"—it shrieked and screamed across the darkening sky after her.

At the top of the first hill she fell and turned over to look at the starry sky, and felt for the last time the caghfr grass against her back. Her body shuddered again from the pain sound and was still.

AFTERWORD FOR "LISTEN, LOVE"

George:

Michael Moorcock took this one for *New Worlds Quarterly 2*, and it was reprinted three more times in hardcover and paperback collections. We wrote our version of Robert Graves's "The Shout," but set on a far planet as an encounter with an alien, long before either of us read that story or saw the Jerzy Skolimowski movie of the same name.

* * * * * * *

Jack:

I'll cop to all the (overused) alien namings such as *rodasz* bushes, *caghfr*, *kuu*, and the like—those were early days, and I was in love with the very idea of being able to create alien worlds, sensations, and societies. George and I loved well-written, well-conceived, and internally consistent science fiction. And what we loved, we tried to write. Although "Listen, Love" is a one-trick story...although it lacks the sophistication (if it can be called that!) of our later work...although it is (as we were) a bit rough around the edges, it *is* a story of estrangement that tries to create that special sensation we call sense-of-wonder. A few years later, George would be writing his masterpiece *Macrolife*, which is the quintessential sense-of-wonder story, and I would be investigating the dark pathways of mass psychosis with my novel *The Man Who Melted*. (I suppose it could be said that I went over to wonder's dark side.)

George and I wanted to create a *frisson* for the reader, that aforementioned sense-of-wonder: a portrayal of modalities that cannot be found in any other kind of literature. Writer and critic Alexei Panshin aptly referred to it as the land beyond the hill.

Did we succeed with this little story?

We must leave that up to the reader, but *I* think we did. It is an apprentice story; its prose is awkward in places and its scope narrow. But it is a mirror-reflection of the writers' yearning to create a visceral experience of what it *feels* like to be...the other, the alien.

Which is just what it feels like to be human!

O D

So they told me I'm in. Big deal. I'm in. But I did it myself, that's what they tell me.

They're all crazy, anyhow.

* * * * * *

It's a small pocket continuum, just about a mile across and stuck between two deterministic universes. It has a name— it could be Outer Dumbo, for all I know. So what? The two universes it's between are shaped like pears.

Anyway, OD never got to be fully real. No one really wanted to live like that. I mean, no one there really knows very much. For them knowing nothing—or as close to it as possible—is like knowing a lot. Really. One day I was arguing with a bunch of dudes, and one of them said I didn't know anything and— bang! I was there, gone, in the OD. The very place.

It's like a closet, this universe. There are lots of unknown words painted over all the rocks, like maybe someone had been in prison here a long time. There's this little stream which gurgles out of the rocks. And once in a while it rains, turning the ground into icky muck.

It really is a place to do nothing in. One of us—maybe me, even—had triggered the entrance, and the whole joint had opened up.

To me.

You see, it was your mind that got you in, nothing more.

* * * * * * *

All lies. That's not me. I have no clean-shaven face and pompadoured hair, and I don't speak slang and swear. I pull on my earlocks to feel my reality. I remember the Shema and the small shul with the rebbe named Feinberg who smoked Cuban cigars and liked a lot of women, including my Reisel, may she rest in peace.

That's real. I can still pray and taste my own saliva. This place is a hammock for my sins. God will punish. But why should I change into something worse than I already am?

I am becoming filth. My hair is greasy, sometimes. My earlocks disappear. The stream gurgles out of the rocks. And once in a while it rains, turning the ground into icky—into icy—into muck and filth.

They are returning. I must remain the same. I have a meeting with the taxman at four.

* * * * * * *

How the hell am I going to get out of here? I have appointments to keep, obligations to people I know. I have women to see. There are no women here. I need a secretary to take letters. Hired help is expensive, and very bad. If I'd had better hired help—well, I'd be saner. And I wouldn't be here now. Enough of this.

I've got to get out.

* * * * * * *

Still here. Something's wrong with the rubber band that links me to my world. It's not pulling me back. It got me here on a mindpull.

Lousy cheap rubber. Must have broke.

* * * * * * *

OD is starting to fill up. Guys who look like they're waiting for a bus. Queuing up in line and looking up at the sky.

They won't talk to me. Maybe they have rubber in their heads?

* * * * * * *

So I pray. What else? It's raining and the stream is over-flowing, rushing past into the filth beyond. Its foul water carries sticks and green bottles and probably important notes.

I have found certain things to be easier here. Since every-thing here is filth, there is nothing to do but pray for purity, a state man, and certainly I, cannot achieve. The stock market is real, my talis koton—which has also disappeared—my Feigle with her brown hair and pregnant stomach; they are all real.

So what? Here I can grow sideburns and swear. Part of me— such parts I cannot imagine—knows thoughts I could never imagine before. Jive. The slime beside the river is pomade for my hair. I perceive somehow—what matter how? —that I have left the taxman. It was very simple. He could not recognize me with my new face and attitude.

Bang. It's like a closet, this universe. Let my earlocks remain on the ghost in the synagogue. He rocks back and forth and thinks he's me.

* * * * * * *

I'm me. I'm alive!

OD has turned upside down. I've been walking on the ceiling for longer than I can remember. All the other dudes look like they've got beards on when I come near them. They have mouths in their foreheads, and poker-faced eyeballs.

I know what's going to happen. I really do.

OD is going to turn right side up. That's all.

There it goes.

Goodbye to all the beards and abiding eyes.

Ah, despair! Feet firmly on the ground again. The stream is swollen and flowing, somewhere in the night in front of me. There are no stars. It's restful, like a closet.

Oh, God, I am in the underworld. Alone, beyond repair, beyond a good meal, beyond...beyond, beyond...

Words are disappearing from my mind. I feel them going. In the dull-glowing mornings I find words lying in the mud, thousands of words. All the words which have gone from my skull.

Soon my head will be empty. I will become the stones and the formless mud of OD, when the words for the RNA and DNA are emptied from my head.

The words are now a river, emptying from my soul. That's where all the words I saw when I got here came from.

* * * * * * *

They're all crazy with their misplaced eyes and toothless mouths. Sheol, the place without God, the entropy sink —how do I know such things?—that is sucking away at my mind. That's all there is now. This is real. *Gottenyu.*

I feel my thoughts being pulled away as I sit by the stream—fetid water—and let my toes curl in the slime. My prayers cannot rise here; they can only be sucked into nothingness. And that's what I deserve.

If I become hollow, slime will fill me up. Slime and strange words from that other person I'm becoming. I, too, will be Godless and misplaced. My teeth fall out. This is real. My talis, my phylacteries, my father's siddur—they're all made of air. Empty.

A terrible reality. These words and thoughts that fill me up are wrong. They're crazy.

* * * * * * *

A dybbuk's inside me, talking through my mouth (which is deformed and misplaced). He thinks that he's Satan and rules

the slime. What can I do? I pray, anyway. God can't hear them, but I like the sound of the words.

* * * * * * *

Everything is crystal clear. I have a new mind! I know all the mysteries of this strange place. The mud rises up to praise me, because I can summon it with my words. A feast! A table set for my taste buds, cool ices for my food pipe!

The mud...rises into dark, vaguely human shapes which I invite to table with me. The mud eats with me.

We finish off the food.

There isn't enough. The shapes begin to gesture at me. There is hate in their mud arms. There is white mud in their mouths.

They rush me.

I lift my hand and swing at the first one. My hand goes into his heart, and I feel his mud heart beating, pumping red-brown mud.

In a few moments I am buried. I pulsate in the mud. I brood sullen under a starless sky. I hear the stream gurgling through me. My heart beats with the ebb and flow of the water which comes from nowhere.

My eyes are stones.

I open them.

An iron hammer shatters them.

I am blind.

* * * * * * *

Let it stay blind. Let it crawl inside me, scream, talk with its strange tongue with saliva that tastes like metal. It's raining again. My feet make sucking noises in the thick mud. I dance, flailing my arms about, singing songs that my father forgot.

If I slip and fall, taste the brown slime, what does it matter? I must be naked by now. The others are. But I'll dance alone to my own music and imagine them. They pray complacently

in brick synagogues, eat fish and chase flies out of their filthy bedrooms so they can have sex. But the crawling things, hidden in the plaster, will watch. Good for them.

How long can I dance before I get tired? There is no air to breathe. My lungs are deflated balloons.

* * * * * *

The sky is closer. I am more sullen. The closet continuum is shrinking. Its account is dry. They're closing it out. No funds. Not enough insanity...

Six hundred yards, five hundred yards, three hundred yards...

Two feet.

Six inches.

One micron.

Zilch.

Beyond zero.

I am waiting for the taxman to come back from lunch.

* * * * * *

So they told me I'm in. Big deal. No more schizophrenic episodes. I did it myself, that's what they tell me.

They're all crazy, anyhow.

AFTERWORD FOR "OD"

George:

This story reads well, and suggests much. It is well titled.

* * * * * * * *

Jack:

There is some resonance with our story "Afternoon Ghost," and the Yiddish, wise-cracking protagonist of "OD" might bear more than a passing resemblance to Michael Brown, our Protestant, middle-class hero(?) who is just looking for a place to go. You'll meet Michael later, but what about our "OD" guy who is married to Feigel and sullenly waits for the taxman while the world around him literally turns to mud?

Well, as I mentioned earlier, welcome to the now very old "New Wave." In the 1970s Barry Malzberg and Bob Silverberg were riding the crest of the New Wave and writing wonderfully fast and powerful stories in the first person present tense that began with lines such as "So this is how it happens: It's 1963, and you are with a girl named Mollie. John F. Kennedy was killed three weeks ago on the 22nd (you can look that up), and LBJ is telling us that we will continue...continue with what?" (Okay, I'm cheating, this extract is from a story I wrote with the redoubtable Barry Malzberg in 1987, not 1967—and it's the first sentence in the *third* paragraph—but you get the idea. I don't know if it's fast and powerful, but...it was available!)

The stylistic influences of "New Wave" writers certainly influenced us in those early days, and the idea of writing in the first person and in the present tense was (is?) irresistible. I see "OD" as a light-hearted romp—certainly not a descent—into hell. I was going to say "a metaphorical romp," but then I remembered that Samuel R. Delany once called my novel *The*

Man Who Melted "metaphorically a-referential". We were at a workshop in Baltimore, and I had been scratching my head over Chip's excerpt from *Dahlgren*. Neither I nor anyone else at the workshop understood what he meant by that remark, but we loved it; and I had "metaphorically a-referential" T-shirts made. Perhaps "OD" belongs in that cock-eyed metaphorically a-referential category, too. George and I had a ball writing it...the story was as antic and playful and open-ended as our lives during that golden time; and I still can't help grinning when I reread it.

Now let me see: what did I ever do with my metaphorically a-referential T-shirt?

THE FLOWER THAT
MISSED THE MORNING

Lying on the floor of the old shack, Joanna tried to remember what her mother had told her before she died. "Keep away from strangers," she had said. "Watch them and try to see what kind of people they are. If they are nice to each other, you can show yourself. Be a good girl. And don't cry when I go."

Joanna had watched her mother limp toward the cliff and disappear into the gray morning smog. Later that afternoon, she thought she had seen her mother's body rushing out to sea with the waves at the bottom of the cliff. Joanna had known that her mother was dying of radiation sickness, and she had not cried at her death. Instead, she had come into the shack and tried to sleep on the dirty blanket.

Joanna was cold; she pulled the blanket around her and started to cry. She cried for warmth and dolls and noise and people. Especially for people—people to wash her and dry her and tell her good night.

If there were some noise, she thought, maybe everything would be all right. She wound the clock and placed it upon the oak bureau, the only piece of furniture in the room. The ticking helped. And if she listened carefully, she could hear the rumble of the waves between the ticks. That was much better.

As the tiny room grew dark, Joanna recalled the green woods that had surrounded her old house. She tried to imagine the yellow sunlight on the leaves, and the beautiful clearing where she had gone with her mother. But the land was gray, even in her

imagination. The trees had lost all their leaves from the radiation, and the soil had turned to sand and dust after the grass had gone.

"There's lots of food in the cellar," her mother had said. "It will last you a long time after I'm gone." Joanna knew that her mother had gone away so that she would not eat up the food. She had been sick for a long time, and she had taken a lot of trouble to explain what she was going to do. As Joanna recalled her mother's words, she was better able to accept her death. At least her mother was out of pain now.

* * * * * * *

It had been a long day, and Joanna was very tired. With thoughts of green forests and yellow sunlight, she fell asleep.

The sun was a dim splotch in a gray sky when Joanna awoke. Listlessly, she rose to her feet and walked to the edge of the cliff to look at the sea. Her body felt strangely warm, and her eyes burned. The sea was covered by a rolling fog, but Joanna could hear the waves pounding at the shore. A breeze touched her face and she felt better. But as she turned and began walking back to the shack, a chill went through her body.

Everything around her was gray, and even though it was the middle of June, nothing grew. Joanna thought of her mother again. She smiled and remembered brown hair and crinkly dresses. By the time she reached the shack, she was sniffling and wiping tears from her cheeks.

She went inside and looked for her crayons; they were in a paper bag on the bureau. She drew a bright yellow flower on the bag and then carefully tore it out. As she carried the flower outside, the sun slowly penetrated the thick, gray fog.

Holding her flower with both hands, Joanna surveyed the barren landscape. What had they done to her world? she asked herself. The wind rushed toward her, and she imagined that it was hugging her with its cool arms. Joanna knelt on the ground and dug a small hole with her fingers. Then she put the paper

stem of the flower into the ground and filled the hole with sand. The flower looked almost real.

Suddenly the sun broke through the clouds and brightened the flower's colors. Joanna watched the paper flower bend and sway in the wind until the clouds rushed in from the sea to cover the sun again. She got up and walked back to the shack, thinking that she would have to get some food from the cellar.

But the thought of food seemed wrong to her—she did not feel hungry, only sleepy. She was sure that her mother would be proud of her if she saved as much of the food as she could. Instead of eating, she lay down on her blanket and thought of cool snow and green grass and clear water in a tall frosted glass. Then she imagined herself putting lemon and sugar in the glass to make lemonade, just as her mother had done so many times.

Joanna fell asleep and dreamed that she was waiting for her mother to come home. Soon, they would be together again. She slept happily, deeply. In her dream, Joanna was wakened by a bird, and yellow sunlight came streaming in through her window. Eager to play in the sunshine, she sat up and sprang to her feet.

The dream world was beautiful, with tall grass and yellow sunlight that seemed to cover everything with a golden dust. The air smelled of a million flowers, and the sea glistened like an enormous emerald. Birds flew above her, calling her name. And the sky was as blue as she had ever remembered it.

As she ran from the doorway into the tall cool grass, she hoped that the wind had not blown her flower away. Soon, she found a meadow where hundreds of wild flowers grew. She examined one of them. It was *her* flower, made of paper and colored with a yellow crayon. She looked at another —it was the same. *All* the flowers were made of paper, but it didn't matter, because it was her flower.

Joanna rolled in the grass, then lay on her back with her eyes closed, feeling the warm sunshine on her face. She felt pleasantly weak and tired, and she was no longer afraid of dying. She knew that her mother would be proud of her. As she drifted off

to sleep, she heard her mother calling from the house. Joanna knew that if she napped here too long, her mother would come and carry her back to bed. For a moment, she opened her eyes to take another look at the lovely paper flower. This was the kind of morning she had wanted for it, the kind it deserved and had missed in the other world.

Here, the air was fresh and clean; here, the clouds were sailboats coming in from the sea; here, the sunlight was friendly.

And quietly, she fell asleep for the last time.

AFTERWORD FOR "THE FLOWER THAT MISSED THE MORNING"

George:

This one grew out of Lyndon B. Johnson's campaign television spot called "Daisy," an attack ad on Barry Goldwater's 1964 campaign for the presidency, in which a small child looks at a flower and is blown up by a nuclear explosion. The ad was pulled after only one showing.

* * * * * * *

Jack:

We wrote this bleak, cautionary tale for young readers, and it was published by Lerner Books as an illustrated children's story.

What gives me pause is that the story still rings true thirty-seven years later. Crazy states, melt-downs, global warming, poisoned air....

We're sorry, Joanna.

THIRTY-THREE
AND ONE-THIRD

It was an old-style curio shop, the kind a man could find on a cobblestone street in Holland at the turn of the century. Mr. Marquette sighed and smiled. He knew how it would be inside. It would be his world—an enchanted, unreal world of old tapestries and chipped vases, of artifacts from a world hidden away in the minds of those who still live in houses turned away from the sun, houses with deep cellars and dark, heavily draped interiors. Mr. Marquette opened the creaking door and walked inside. Even the smell was right—a musty odor of dust and old wood.

The light inside came from a single lamp on a wooden table which apparently served as a sales counter. Behind the table was a door, most of which was covered by a cracked oil painting. The door opened and a balding, frail man hobbled out and leaned on the table. He smiled through three gold teeth and asked in a high voice, "May I help you? Are you looking for anything special?"

Mr. Marquette waved him away. "No, I'm just looking. If I see anything I like, I'll call you." Mr. Marquette turned his back. He hated storekeepers and hoped the fellow would return to his back room.

The old man opened the door behind the sales counter and said, "Call me if you need anything." Mr. Marquette sensed the man's indifference. He didn't answer. Instead he picked up an old book and opened it to the title page. There was an etching of an older woman on the frontispiece. She stared up at him with

a stone face.

Mr. Marquette turned suddenly and his elbow hit a shelf. Cards, books and folders crashed to the floor and onto an old table covered with coins and mementos of New York. Mr. Marquette stepped back gracefully and turned away from the jumble. Then he saw the shelf piled high with records. He took two steps, and in a moment was shifting records from one pile to another looking at the old labels. *Alexander's Ragtime Band,* Ma Rainey, *The I'm Too Tired Blues*—a full collection of originals from 1915, 1920, 1927 and more. Mr. Marquette handled the old 78s gently. Each record seemed rarer than the previous one. There were about a hundred in all, and the labels on some were almost gone; but Mr. Marquette read each label lovingly, and each name immediately brought the music to mind. Each scratch made him angry.

The last record in the middle pile had a blank label on one side and no scratches. There were some fading numbers on the label on the other side. Mr. Marquette looked closely. There was a date, 1912, and the speed of the disk, 33⅓.

Mr. Marquette suppressed an urge to shout for the storekeeper and demand the meaning of this anachronism. But he calmed himself. *This might be a find,* he thought. He put the record back into the pile and called the old man.

"How much for the whole batch?" Mr. Marquette asked casually.

"—uh, would ten dollars be good enough?"

There was a short silence. The old man said something further, as if fearing to lose the deal. "I don't get many records," he said, "but this young man came in and unloaded some paintings and coins with them. I usually deal in paintings and antiques, of course."

Mr. Marquette pulled two new five-dollar bills out of his wallet and dropped them arrogantly on the table. "Please wrap up the middle pile. I'll be back for the rest tomorrow morning."

The old man kept talking. "He was kind of an odd sort, he was, the man who brought all this stuff. He was dressed real

expensive, and had a ruby ring as big as my knuckle here. And he asked seventy for everything. I'll be clean for a short while, but it was worth it."

The storekeeper pointed to a stack of partially unwrapped paintings in the corner. "Would you like to look?" He put some paper and twine around the pile of records and slid them across the table to Mr. Marquette.

"No, I'll look another time." He picked up the bundle and headed for the door. The old man hobbled after him, making more offers which Mr. Marquette ignored.

The walk home seemed to take hours. Today, Mr. Marquette thought, I will not feed the pigeons, nor will I look at the painters in the park. Near his house he did not even say hello to the hotdog salesman who kept him up on current politics and gave him all the right answers to use at cocktail parties. His neighbor's dogs were barking and playing by his stairs, but he ignored them despite the fact that they had kept him awake last night.

He left the records on the hall table just outside his living room. Mr. Marquette's furnishings were few, but those he had were the finest antiques he could afford. His rooms had a musty odor about them, as if rain had leaked through the roof.

Mr. Marquette kindled his fire, and when he felt the heat spreading throughout the room, he took off his overcoat and put it in the hall closet. On his way back, he picked up the pile of records and put them by the record player. He took the plastic cover off the precision turntable and turned on the power amp. Then he took out the strange record and placed it on the soft turntable mat. The record turned smoothly without a trace of warpage. Mr. Marquette adjusted his turntable for 33⅓ playing and placed the needle on the edge of the record.

He walked over to his high-backed Victorian chair, sat down, and looked at the crack in his ceiling.

The sound from the record began as a high-pitched hum. There was no music. The sound stopped for a moment and began again, but this time it sounded like a low-key tuning

fork. There was just enough sound to make him want to hear more. Suddenly the hum was everywhere; it came not only from the two speakers but also from the floor, ceiling and walls. Mr. Marquette felt it deep inside of him, like some kind of soft liquid. It washed over his consciousness and numbed him.

He tried to get up and failed.

He sat still, trying to fight off the panic that welled up inside him. The room grew darker until he could see nothing.

In the black field, moiré patterns of black and white lines interlocked to form strange perspectives. They faded slowly, and sharper lines appeared. He looked into an abyss of geometric shapes. He felt drawn into them, and suddenly he was moving through the lines. Perpendiculars were bent and turned into circles. He felt as if he were turning corners, but it was difficult to be sure. He was clearly aware of his motion—he felt as if he were falling at great speed. He screamed but there was no sound.

After what seemed to him an eternity, he found himself lying on a soft mound of sand, looking up at the sky—a red sky with two yellow green moons. White clouds hung low over steel blue mountains.

Mr. Marquette noticed that he was lying at the edge of a deep canyon. On the other side stood a castle, an old decaying structure, which, despite its appearance, had a look of permanence about it. Mr. Marquette got up and walked over to the drawbridge which spanned the chasm. Without hesitation he began walking across. The wood creaked, and he looked down at a silver band of river hundreds of feet below him. He touched the wall of the castle as he went through the entrance. It was made of burnished metal, but the light from the two moons gave it the look of stone.

There was no courtyard. Mr. Marquette walked directly into a large antechamber. There were five open doors around the chamber. He caught glimpses of massive four-posters, drapes, and bookcases that reached to the ceiling. On the walls of the antechamber itself were gold-embroidered tapestries depicting

strange-looking humanoids on a hunt after animals resembling greyhounds. The floor was made of a hard, azure-colored stone. A table and two chairs stood in the center, and on the table was a game which looked very much like chess.

Mr. Marquette walked over to the table and picked up one of the figures. The piece was made of an emerald-like substance, and a green fire seemed to emanate from inside it. He reached out to put the piece back on the board but failed. The room was reeling and spinning, and the scene before him went badly out of focus. In a moment there was nothing but the black field he had experienced before.

Mr. Marquette watched the black field dissolve, then found himself sitting in his high-backed chair. The phonograph needle was running back and forth at the end of the record.

In his hand he held the emerald green figure.

For a long time he sat there trying to understand what had happened to him. He looked at the figurine in his hand, and his mind wandered back to the castle with its treasures. If only he could possess them!

He got up to lift the tone arm off the record. He started to put the needle at the beginning for another try—but stopped. He ran to his hall closet and took out the large laundry bag. He emptied it on the floor and went back to the phonograph. He placed the needle at the beginning very carefully. He gripped the laundry bag tightly in anticipation.

The black field returned, with its interlocking patterns and the sensation of immense depths beyond the fabric of familiar human experience. He felt drawn in as before, but this time the sensation of falling was accompanied by a feeling of great urgency.

He again found himself on the mound of soft sand. Everything was the same—the sky, the moons, the castle of iron and the great chasm. He ran across the creaky drawbridge as if afraid it might be pulled up at any moment.

He entered the great chamber and approached the game table. All the pieces were there except for the one which now

stood in his room a world away. He swept the board and all the pieces into his bag. He ran into one of the open rooms. It was a luxurious bath of some kind, but now there were plants growing in the sunken pool of water. The walls were made of cut stone colored a deep blue. Huge painted figures stood around him as if guarding the room. A strange light emanated from the bottom of the pool.

He left the room and wandered about until he came upon what looked like a library. The large room was filled with a blue white light. There was a table in the corner, and on it were instruments which he didn't recognize. There were hundreds of glittering objects that looked like gems. He swept them all into his bag.

He wondered how much longer the record would play. There should be five minutes left at best, he estimated. One side played for twenty minutes at most.

He had enough for this trip, and he could make as many as he wished. Here was a world for the taking. He had always known that it must exist, for the universe was an aesthetic whole and would lack perfection if it lacked *his* world as one in the cosmic manifold.

Mr. Marquette walked back across the great chasm, back to the soft mound of sand that had welcomed him twice already. He sat down on the mound and set the bag beside him. He hadn't noticed how heavy it had become. He stretched his legs in a most ungentlemanly fashion and relaxed.

* * * * * * *

A world away, children played leapfrog. They jumped over each other, laughed and shouted. A piece of dust shook loose from the crack in the ceiling and settled upon the record. The needle, which tracked at two grams in its precision tonearm, skipped gently back and forth, back and forth—

Mr. Marquette waited—

AFTERWORD FOR
"THIRTY-THREE AND ONE-THIRD"

George:

The influence of Rod Serling's *The Twilight Zone* shows all over this story, as it does in "Afternoon Ghost."

* * * * * * *

Jack:

Yes, "Thirty-Three and One-Third" was written as a *Twilight Zone* story, and when I reread it, I could almost hear the plot ticking along toward its Runyonesque conclusion. What's most disconcerting, though, is the realization that many modern readers won't have a clue what "thirty-three and one-third" *means*. (There were three speeds of record rotation: 45 R.P.M., 33⅓ R.P.M., and and even a 16 R.P.M.) Although there has been a recent fad for turntables and vinyl records, this story is, like its protagonist Mr. Marquette, caught in time. I can imagine the pages of the story yellowing in an attic lit by streams of dusty light as I type. The story was our homage to those tightly plotted stories of the 1940s and 1950s, a respectful nod to Damon Knight, Henry Kuttner, C. M. Kornbluth, and Fredric Brown.

FACES FORWARD

It's just a job. I know I should have looked for something better, but times are bad. And what could I do? Be a shoe salesman or a delivery boy? But anything would be better than this.

So I sit and watch the ugly people browse through the magazines. They all have greasy faces and greasy hair and they probably smell. The store smells from onions, anyway.

A greaser drops two faggot magazines on the counter and tries not to look at me. I stare at the top of his head, burning the fear of God into his fetid brain. He should spend his money on a new suit. But he wants filth, just like the others. They all slink around the filth magazines, hands in greasy pockets, eyes downcast.

Because they know I know. And God knows. The hardness in their pants and their unholy thoughts are blasphemy. And the people walking past, on their way home from a day's work, know also. They look in the window and then turn their heads.

I turn around and smile at them, paying no attention to a callow boy twitching before my counter, waiting to pay for a vicarious thrill.

"Wake up, buster. Hey fat man, how about my change?" The callow youth is gone. Or did he step out the door and step back in, changed by thirty years in time? The man in front of me looks like me. His lips curl in a snarl, and 1 feel the hatred inside, uncoiling like a snake, slipping into my arms, then into my brain, whispering.

And I hate myself more than I could hate my image.

I think of time, tedious corrupting time, fiery time taking me endlessly ahead; my names are different, but I am the same.

* * * * * *

Fin de siècle—a century running out like poison wine, red wine, thick with additives. There. It's gone. The next hundred years begin. Row on row of new bottles, filled with...what?

With filth. Only the packages have changed, and the names. But the magazines are still here, behind shock fields and sensor lights. Handy-randies and telefactape machines gleam in the back room, exotic machinery to substitute for flesh. New weapons to use against flesh.

Outside, the crowds are drunk. They wander around in the yellow thoughtfog, pulled this way and that by the best or most delicious or strongest thoughtstrands.

The door slides open and a crowd bursts into the store. I ignore them. Their beadblankets can glow, their falsefaces can mimic me and smirk as they like, I'll ignore them. They are just undercity filth who lust only for synthetic flesh and machines.

"Come in, come in," I shout to them finally. They will not leave. They are intent on trying to drown me in their scum. But I swim with God. My stare withers them.

I am different from them. I am better. If I could leave this place, this job, this time, I would pray and meditate on life and goodness. And keep away from this filth.

"The machine doesn't work," screams a young girl who should be home with her family.

"Good," I whisper. I think of starships swimming through the dark light-years to newer, greener worlds, where all centuries are just beginning, where wide-eyed children play, ignorant of what lies within their bodies, the iron fist of endings hiding in their minds, which one day will break their youthful worlds to dust.

They are smashing everything. It's only a question of time before they reach this block. The slaughter-funhouse and

campo-casino have been melted, the people inside mere discolorations in the shiny metal.

My soundsensors are turned on full. I can hear the crowd screaming in the street, righteously killing and dismembering the pleasurepeople. So let them. They are right. It has been a long time coming. Take us.

I'll be spared. But I hate the waiting. This is such a small store, and it has become difficult to breathe. They must have reached the purification plant. So what to do? Stare at the machine, the illicit pleasure builder, and think about what will be. I'm growing tired and bored. My hands look larger to me than they should. And my nails are discolored from drugdip.

But who can sleep? I could turn off the soundsensors, but... The noise is constant now, a groaning punctuated by strident lustscreams.

And with tired eyes—the air is so close—I watch the side of the store melt into a rainbow. I scream but my throat is gravel. Three faces appear before me; I'll wake up soon and turn off the sensors.

I get up and go outside into the street.

Everyone is gone. It's hard to breathe. The light is getting dimmer. Then 1 see them walling up the neighborhood, bricking it up to die. I run to the end of the block, but I'm too late. The last stone is set. They have all gone but me. I was too late to get out. I slept too long in my thoughtfog. The ones who live above, below and side, have blotted us out.

I run back to the store and tick on the telefac what has happened; but the tape goes nowhere. My words are frozen.

The nerves to the rest of the world have been cut.

* * * * * * *

The family is getting married. A dozen daughters, kept pure by exclusive use of surrogate animals, will join now in holy-chain-lock with a dozen daddies.

A wedding.

Two chain families. The quick-witted head-father smiles. The daughters will be with family tonight, at home, safe from the bricked-up cancer a hundred stories below.

* * * * * * *

Shower burst.

None living can know my face. Identities, minds, and hearts change like colors in a glass. Who am I today?

What does it matter? My face is still flesh, still bone and tissue. Let me be Lisa, the bald daughter of the Citizen Leader. The one with the flared nose and synthomouth that parts her long face. The one who smells.

But what wonderful smells: musk, pyhrr, sweetsweat—all the odors of lust and love. So I can smell myself, pretend that I'm the tease, the teaser, the teased.

Out of the box. It's done. Let them look at me, let Lisa's proud nowfather disclaim me. I can do what I like for the duration. It's the rule. I am Lisa. Lisalisalisa. I love you, I love your smell, your touch, your quaking voice, your toothless smile—who needs food?

All I need is a reflection. But it's not enough. Touching yourself, even discovering new curves and bone structures, is always the same. Lisalisa's probably under by now. She can't be seen until I'm through. That's the law.

"Well," says the Citizen Leader, "you might as well join the household. You know the rules."

Yes, I know, I know. I'll stay for a week, but my skin is already beginning to sag and I'm still not complete. Perhaps I should have waited for Lisa.

She wouldn't sag.

* * * * * * *

Ventricular contractions. My heart is swollen with candy juices, congealing into thick honey. In a few moments it will

set, and my heart will be made of rock candy.

What a world to live in. So I'm in love. A constant state of mind. Why not? Everything is verdant, grown green and orange and stippled for effect. Clouds scud past and I make up animals and shapes to see inside them.

Stop lying, you green-crusted sleeper. The room is small and clean and brightly lit. It's all machine; there's no flesh here, just crystal and wire and plastiglass and shiny metal. Where am I? There's no place to go. No arms to slit my imaginary throat. No mouth or lung to promote a human scream.

What matter? The only rule is that I must be alone. But I want flesh.

What a world to live in. So I'm in love. A....

* * * * * * *

An incandescent wire glows in the night, branching in a billion directions, reaching into the forever of a trillion soft brains. Energy flows through the arteries, whispering in the undernight of the worlds, bringing a little of whatever, something of nothingness, a small amount of nameless things. Negative graces bestowed by an electric generator.

* * * * * * *

Solipsis. Lone-Alone.

A man, so-called, is sitting in a chair.

Me.

The others, a myriad or more, face me. Their faces are masks, their hearts are hard.

1 am a virgin. I am all virgins. They are filth, used.

They flood me. Their minds enter mine and marvel. My innocence is their pleasure. I am ecstatic music in their brains. My brain is sodomized. They teach me the word, they make me feel its meaning. They are strong. They grasp. They take. They leave.

The mindgate closes.

Now it's my turn. The gate opens. I enter their diseased wastes. They are old, alone, barren, dirty, different from me. Incomparable landscapes. Dingy shapes crouching in blue light. Black shapes rearing under red suns.

My pleasure swells. The suns bleed. I wallow. My body remains pure, unspoiled, a glacier of white infinities.

I am a virgin. That's my job.

I cry out and die.

Nothing stands in their way.

They start again.

* * * * * * *

In the corner of the world my eye sees the superimposed calendar clock. Outside it's 2251, Anno Domini. The hold cannot be broken.

Kyrie eleison.

AFTERWORD FOR "FACES FORWARD"

George:

Bill Pronzini and Barry Malzberg's reprinting of this story in *Shared Tomorrows*, a hardcover anthology of collaborations, offered the story four years after its original publication, and with welcome praise. "Other partners of note are Gregory Benford and Gordon Eklund, Piers Anthony and Robert Margoff, and Jack Dann and George Zebrowski." Jack and I did these ten stories together, along with a few unfinished escapees, "but all of them have been of high quality," wrote these editors. "In its deft and chilling offhandedness, in its grace and control, it seems to us to be one of the finest if least-known science fiction short-shorts of this odd and troubled decade."

* * * * * * *

Jack:

Ah, how we made up words in those halcyon days...the trust we had in our talent...the courage to see where stories might take us. We were trying to reach toward a sort of poetry with stories such as "Faces Forward", "OD", and "The Standard Crisis Scenario." They were wild, frenzied attempts to create an atmosphere of transcendence that confounds causal rationality.

And I'm sure there are those who would say that we succeeded all too well!

YELLOWHEAD

The subway train was a flash of salad colors as Retro Five, recently acquired by The Henchmen's Sixth Division, pulled into the Bedford Park Station. That was where they let Yellowhead off for the last time, only twenty-three years after the trains had been painted and taken over by the Pain 5 People, who run them to this day better than the uptop jobbers. Black Satin and Stitch Tonto hijacked the first train one long-ago summer, moved their Pilots into the last car, called it Smoke Three and ran it up and down the line. Soon no one cared.

Yellowhead started with Retro Five, then left for Jerome Avenue to run his own operation. All the best painters followed him. No one saw him upside after he shaved his head and painted it yellow. He had a red, freckled face, a long, overly thin nose, thick sensuous lips, and a weak chin that showed a slight cleft. He was more than six feet tall and lanky, always bending over, slouching as if he needed to bend toward the security of a floor.

With his painted head and tinted body, he was an awesome sight to the busy people—the fingermen and serfage workers and layers and prompters and factory-sitters. Although their jobs were high and low, they all dressed the same: white-roughed faces, eyes lined, noses shadowed, hair bristled and bronzed—lacking all natural color—starched white shirts and snake black ties, tricolor jackets and pantaloons.

But Yellowhead couldn't stand the sameness of ties and jobs, sametalk and samesex, so he smoked some of Mama's Pain 5 and cut his neatly cropped hair. To substitute for his lack of

color, he dipped into a paint store and covered himself with yellow. He almost died that first time, for he didn't realize that the body, like the lungs, had to breathe. He was barked and beaten twice that day, and gang-raped once, before he fled to the subways—his secret dream, that "slum hole for degenerates and filth," as Mama used to say.

Yellowhead had a darling, but he didn't know it until too late. Her name was Yoy Cross and she was as fair as a white line.

Yoy Cross, straight as they came and full of clichés, was a seamworker in North Brunswick Section Factory on 53rd Street. She had glint-gilded hair, trussed and tied as was the summer fashion, a fair face like Yellowhead's, but with thin lips and dimple creases. She was short and slight, small-boned and delicate. She had been trained to drive country trucks and largecars, but she had fallen from grace by refusing to manage company affairs and had left in virgin haste. Her Borndaddy and sister had thrown her out of the house as an example to the neighbors. She would have the stigma of a "Cherry" even after she had been bobbed by as many men and loving women as she could hold. She was a tragic throwback.

Six days a week she rode the Retro Five and watched the painters working their designs and graffiti onto the metal walls—inside and outside. That was her break in the day's monotony, her flash of danger. The dark tunnels promised to swallow her, promised juicy, delicious night-terrors. And the bare, bright ceiling bulbs provided security.

"Okay, okay, okay, okay," shouted a twelve-year-old dressed in khakis and dirty shirt. He brandished a crowbar, but not menacingly. He was polite and pushed his way through the crowd until he could get near enough to a handhold. He hooked his crowbar onto the handhold and swung back and forth with one arm, kicking an uptown woman in the shoulder. She only sighed and moved away. It was the weekend; everyone wanted to get home and rest—the insecurity of the subway could be least tolerated on Saturday. Even Yoy looked down at the painted floor and wished for home and toilet.

"Okay, okay, okay," shouted another boy, older than the other, but dressed the same. He passed Yoy, purposely stepping on her foot and smiling and waving his crowbar. "Excuse me, pardon me, sorry, sorry...."

Yoy looked around for a Pilot but couldn't find one. This car was dislocated; there was not even a painter to add contrast and safety, just upsiders like herself, and no one to protect them from themselves.

The train pushed through the tunnels, curving, climbing, turning, then screeched—metal against metal—and slowed down before a red light. It bolted, ran for a few seconds, and jerked to another stop. Through the smeared windows Yoy could see the roundtop intersection: bare bulbs shining wanly in a garage pit, cement struts crisscrossed with metal tiebars, other tunnels—illusions of immensity, leaders of track and another waiting train pulled up. It was close enough to touch, a metal dragon of green and yellow and red, a sandblast paint job, car after car painted and pruned to look like a Wu-dragon, a metal centipede. That had been painted before Yellowhead had left Retro Five—a good time when the best painters could still be boasted by Stitch Tonto.

Yoy hoped this wouldn't be a long stop. The air would become thick and some old man would start coughing and wheezing and start everyone else crying and sneezing and screaming. Someone died in her car at least once every week. She thought perhaps she was a jinx, a laylow, but then so was everyone else.

"Hey, Cherry, Cherry," screamed a high-pitched male voice. Yoy turned around, saw it was an old neighbor's son. He was still fat and pimply, and his face was dirty except for paint spots and drool lines. She tried to ignore him. He had joined a gang of boys with crowbars, but he was young and green so was only permitted to carry a broken umbrella stick. She was sure that would make him mean.

"Hey, lolly, lolly, Yoy," sang another boy. They all pushed toward her, bars in hand, hair plastered back unstylishly, mouths puckered in polite smiles.

The youngest boy tried his luck on a young girl—slashed her face with an umbrella end, rubbed her belly and humped her. The crowd looked through the windows, grumbled and kept at smalltalk. After all, the boys were still being polite.

Next an old man. His wife was too stiff to scream. Dress the same, rape the same—that was the time-honored jingo.

An older boy—sword sear across his face down to his neck, blue eyes that twinkled, greased hair in ringlets and unpainted mouth with no teeth—pushed into Yoy, ripped the front of her dress open and watched to see if the boy beside her intended to help her. He looked away, and the older boy ground glass knuckles into Yoy's face. With fairly good style, he bloodied both her breasts and then proceeded to rape her slowly.

Yoy screamed, pretended she wasn't there, stared out the window as the dragon train pulled away silently, its cars jerking under its painted carapace.

But it was too soon for Yoy to black out. Virginity can be taken only once, and she, through her tears and screams, was enjoying her betrothal to society. Offspring from such a union would be considered holy, but she knew she wouldn't tell her family. Let them cross and snuffle in their rotten rooms.

With a jerk, the train started moving. She could feel him shaking like a weak child and was amused that such a fragile husk was forcing itself into her.

More screams—her own.

And unknown to her, a few boys, painted and plumed, jumped across from the rear car to the tunnel catwalk, heading for the club cave near the old pipe junction.

He got off her as the train started to roar into the tunnel. The car was empty, and she could tell that he was disappointed. His audience had fled into the forward parts of the train.

That was when Yellowhead came into the car, walking forward on his rounds, checking the car links and open-close door whooshers. She saw him come up behind the thief and bring his fist down on his head, crumpling him with one blow.

She opened her eyes and tried to sit up. She tried to grab

Yellowhead's hand, but he only smiled.

"You'll be happy without him," he said to her.

And she felt that he wanted her. He had fought for her, however slightly. He continued into the next car as she fixed herself up. She watched him go, but she knew that when next they met, it would be different. He was being kind now, leaving her to her rites, content to wait for when they would meet on more individual terms.

But he never spoke to her again.

She rode his train week after week, hoping to catch a glimpse of him. She listened to conversations about him on the other lines. And she followed him when rumor told her that he was riding elsewhere in the city with friends in their living cars at the ends of their trains. Once through a car window she saw him change his clothes. For a moment she caught a glimpse of his tattooed body topped by his yellow skull. He was thin and wiry and could not see her in the dark tunnel where she stood. She had come up to the window too late for him to see her.

As time went on her love became more anxious. He did not notice her even when she smiled at him. She became desperate when he disappeared for a whole month during the short war with the out-city trains. He came back with a bandage over his right eye and his arm in a sling, and she cried for his pain.

Now his indifference was slowly turning into betrayal in her mind. The saddest songs come from this part of her life. The train howls in the tunnel and the wheels whine more sweetly than an electric violin. The air in the tunnels vibrates with the tears of heroes.

And a train comes rolling forward toward the woman who must die. She has chained herself to the track. The train cuts her in half like a razor and stops.

Yellowhead is called out to see the body. He sees the face and her tattered dress, her hands flung outward over the third rail, which flickers with blue life under her divided form.

The train pulls into the Bedford Station, and Yellowhead gets off to stand on the platform. The downtown train pulls in and he

sees her words written in red across two cars.

I LOVE YOU YELLOWHEAD
MY NAME IS YOY

Then he remembers the time in the train when she had looked up at him, reaching out for his hand as he walked away. He moves to the end of the platform and looks back into the mouth of death, where the blue flashes still light the darkness—on and off, on and off, with the smell of ozone and burnt flesh pushing out at him.

At that moment he leaped down onto the tracks and began walking slowly into the darkness. Those who saw him for the last time remember, finally, only his yellow skull bright in the blackness.

No one ever found a body. No one ever found Yoy. No one knows how he picked her up from the electrified rail without falling down dead beside it. Some say he went down into the maze of tunnels, into the caves beneath the river, to rest with her; and their bones still lie there in dry embrace.

Some say they see Yellowhead grinning at them in the high-speed tunnels of the booster trains. They say his ghost lives in the magnetic field that propels the new trains, that it is summoned away from Yoy's arms when the train passes over their place deep in the undercity.

The songs say that nothing in life moved Yellowhead so much as finding out that she had loved him. Others say that he would not have loved her at all if he had not learned too late that she was lost to him. For him to notice, the missing part of his life had to die.

Now there are trains on the moon, under it and above, boosters and surface monorail. And there is a new song that says that Yellowhead's ghost is in all the metal made on Earth; and wherever trains rush, Yellowhead will slip from Yoy's bony clasp to go and look at them. Recently his giant ghost was seen sitting on the rim of a crater, looking up at the stars, dreaming

of tunnels across the heavens. A legend is the loveliest part of the truth.

Other songs say different things.

AFTERWORD FOR "YELLOWHEAD"

George:

This story belongs to the "offhanded" school of fiction, best described by Yeats's warning against too much rewriting that "if it doesn't seem a moment's thought/our stitching and unstitching has been for naught," where much is assumed and seems easy—except that that the best of these are rarely offhanded, and only seem easy. Yeats's warning is only sometimes true; writing often needs lots of revision.

At one point, my then agent Virginia Kidd placed this story at *COQ*, a men's magazine, for $600.00. They failed to publish when they went out of business, and Jack and I wrote it off on our taxes, then rewrote it at least three times, making mostly verbal revisions. Tom Disch and Charles Naylor enthusiastically accepted this story for their hardcover anthology *New Constellations.*

It was recently reprinted in *The Fiction Factory* from Golden Gryphon Press, for which I wrote the following:

Subways were a big thing in my boyhood and teen years. They got you anywhere you wanted to go in New York City, the center of the world. Big also, in my imagination, was the great monorail sequence that opens Arthur C. Clarke's novel, *Earthlight.*

As I pressed through my college years, my periodic returns to the City showed me more of its underside, through the graffiti explosions of the 1970s and the gaudily dressed teenage gang lovers displaying themselves during the roaring rides through the endless darkness of the subway tunnels.

"Look there," I said to Jack Dann as we rode one of the painted trains. "There's a pair of characters." We later named them Yellowhead and his love Yoy, when the story grew in our heads.

An observation, from Jack or myself, sometimes from Pamela Sargent, would set off a story idea. Jack or I might suddenly

type an opening paragraph, sometimes a mere sentence, and abandon the story to the alien ways of the other. If the story ran to its end, one of us would revise the draft. If Jack or I didn't like it, one of us would try again. This could and did go on for years, and I think only one full story was ever abandoned. We don't count fragments. Sometimes a nip or a tuck years later would get a full story right enough to be accepted by an editor.

"Yellowhead" is, we both believe with fingers crossed behind our backs, the best of some dozen stories that we did together. But it had a few more interesting bumps along the way to publication than the others. On paper it earned more than any of the others, but we collected much less, when my then agent, the esteemed Virginia Kidd, placed the story with a now long-dead slick magazine, which delayed a considerable payment long enough for the magazine to go out of business.

Unstoppable as we were in those days, Jack and I did some more polishing, critical as we were of our work, then had it retyped by a young woman who might have passed for Yoy, if she had dressed for the part. Unpaid, meanwhile, Jack and I wrote the "bad debt" off on our taxes, and looked around for a likely place to send the story next. Thomas M. Disch and Charles Naylor were editing a new anthology about "tomorrow's mythologies" for Harper & Row, *New Constellations*, and paying much less than the now dead slick magazine; but Tom spoke an interest, so we sent him the story. His interest more than made up for any possible financial reward by the regard in which his high standards were held. And it would be a hardcover book!

We did not expect that he would accept the story. The teeth of self-doubt bite deep with beginning writers. But he accepted it—with praise. And sent us a check, which we divided in two and topped off our bank accounts.

So you see, Yoy typed the story on an old IBM electric with oversized type. The story retold the Orpheus myth in a subway setting. It all made perfect sense.

* * * * * * *

Jack:

Writers are thieves.

We steal from others—conversations, incidents, gossip, phrases, faces, expressions, ideas—but mostly we steal from ourselves, either out of sheer laziness or to work old themes and ideas into new cloth. So in this grand and venerable tradition of legitimate theft, here are my thoughts on "Yellowhead," from the same source as George's above: my collection of collaborative short stories entitled *The Fiction Factory.*

In the early seventies, when I was crashing in George's apartment in Binghamton, New York; when we kept two antique black typewriters ready to go at George's workstation niches; when the simple physical joy of banging away at those typewriter keys with flexed and calloused index fingers prompted us to write many of our stories in first person, present tense because that seemed to help the words flow faster; in those fast, frantic, compacted, concentrated never-to-be-repeated days of writing and workshopping and living in a communal intellectual environment that was of its time and place, we used to periodically visit the Bronx.

George's blonde and beautiful mother had an apartment in a five-story walk-up, and I have such fond memories of sinking into the upholstered couch in her living room and eating exquisitely prepared Polish food in her formal dining room. Although I was in my early twenties, I always felt safe and secure there. George's mother treated George and me as if were brothers— which in the profound sense we were, and are—and that apartment was like our safe house, the quiet place from which we would venture out to explore the exciting, shifting, deliciously dangerous, cacophonous labyrinths of New York City.

In those days graffiti was being elevated into an art form, and the cars of the subway trains looked like painted dragons flick-

ering past us, as they silently careened into mythic, tunneled darkness. We became train-spotters, aficionados of subway art, of the scrolls and shadowed coded letters, of the brightly colored images; and, of course, we were looking through the gauze of right-now reality into the possibilities of art and myth and story.

We took it all back to Binghamton and started writing.

Collaborating with George was so seamless that it is almost impossible for me to tell what lines and sections George wrote, and what I wrote. We never followed any one formula. As George indicated earlier, sometimes we would write the story together, one looking over the shoulder of the other; sometimes one of us would work in seclusion on a section, which we would leave for the other to find. Some stories took days, others took weeks and months, and, yes, some took years. Very large and vociferous egos melted away. All that was important was to capture the shared vision.

I think we did that with "Yellowhead."

And if I remember correctly, my old girlfriend Marcia—a dancer—became the template for Yoy...wild, willowy, exuberant Yoy.

I think this was the best of our work from that period. We finally got smart!

AFTERNOON GHOST

It was twelve o'clock. The secretaries were chatting and putting their desks in order. Michael Brown leaned across his desk toward the intercom. "Miss Manley, would you make a reservation at the Townshend Club for me? I think they can find me a table. Tell them I'm confirming a previous reservation."

Miss Manley did not answer. He got up and walked out to her desk and said, "Miss Manley." No response. "Miss Manley!"

She stared at him, took off her glasses, and laid them on her desk.

"Miss Manley, are you deaf and blind? *Answer me!*"

She covered her typewriter and called to her co-secretary. "Are you ready? Come on, it's getting chilly in here."

"Is this a joke or something?" he shouted as the secretaries left the room. "Damn you all, come back here...doesn't *anyone* hear me?"

He walked back into his office, feeling frustrated and impotent and angry. *Always a nothing, a nobody, even when he had money and an office, and a little authority.*

He stopped suddenly and stared at his desk. He saw his own body slouched over it, arms hanging over the front side; in a moment, it seemed, it would fall off the edge. Even as he watched it, the body fell gently to the thick green carpet.

He backed away from the desk until he was up against the wall next to the door. Then he was *inside* the wall. He screamed. He pushed vigorously until he floated back into the office. But he held back the next scream as he hovered over his body while

rubbing his immaterial hands together.

"Help...," he whispered. "Someone please help me." He floated out the window and down to the pavement, but no one noticed Michael Brown. Very slowly he floated upright, a pale, paper kite. He tried to compose himself; if he did not get excited, he could imitate normal walking.

He walked up and down streets and avenues and alleys. He walked through people and buildings and eventually into the ladies' room of the Club Risqué. He sat down on a pink couch and looked into an empty mirror.

Of course I can't see myself, he thought. I'm a...ghost. His fear seemed to melt away. It was as if the weight of the world had been removed from his shoulders. He felt light-headed and laughed and danced around the room. He was a ghost...he was free...he would live forever. Oblivious to his presence, a half-nude dancer continued to put on her makeup in front of a large illuminated mirror. Michael stopped and touched her shoulder. He concentrated. And after a while he could *feel*. He ran his hands down her back; it was tight and smooth, and he imagined he could feel some of the warmth.

Now, he thought, no one can stop me. He was a man who could do as he pleased.

He sang three bars of "Stout Hearted Men."

He laughed as loud as he could and floated up over the sink.

There was an eternity of pleasure ahead...and it was all free.

* * * * * * *

Later he followed her home. He went into her bedroom and watched. She turned on the lamp by her double bed. She unzipped the back of her dress deftly. She kicked off both shoes, sat down on the bed, then lifted her leg to remove her stockings. She removed her bra and panties. She was all his now.

He hovered over the bed and crossed his legs in the air. He watched.

Her hair touched the pillow; her leg was bent at the knee and

her face was in profile. She turned completely onto her back and her large eyes were wide open. She made no move to pull up the covers. Michael felt slightly embarrassed. He looked into her eyes for a long time, until she closed them. Then very slowly he floated down on top of her. He pushed one hand under her brown hair, and he circled her waist with the other. He concentrated, until he could feel her warm breath and skin.

He rested on her, waiting for his excitement to quicken, for the girl to come completely alive in his arms. But she only shivered and reached through him for the covers, which she pulled up to her neck.

And he realized that once again he couldn't do it. Even now when it didn't matter, when no one could be hurt, his past held him tightly and wouldn't forgive him. The thought of sin and transgression was too great. That was why he had *never* been able to do it.

Something tugged at his arm, but he couldn't see it.

There was a blinding flash of light, and he tumbled into what felt like a pile of sand. He opened his eyes. A cloud of dust floated around him, reflecting the golden sunlight into his eyes. He stood up and tried to walk.

He took two steps, and a voice said, "It's about time."

A squat little man sat at a huge desk in the middle of a desert. He thumbed through the lined yellow pages of his ledger in boredom. "Well, come over here! I have an appointment in five minutes. So tell me *your* story. You now have four minutes."

Michael Brown tried to speak but couldn't.

"Look, just relax," the man said. "Give me your qualifications and we can *both* get out of here...I'm just as hot as you are, but the new rule is that we can't make anyone comfortable until they pass the test."

"The test?" Michael finally managed to say. "Where am I...?"

"Mr. Brown," the little man said. "You are in heaven."

"This is *heaven*?"

"Well...this is where it begins. It's much nicer inside. This is sort of the exam room. They don't want people seeing Heaven

and then getting excited over something they might not qualify for." The man turned a page in the ledger. "You don't seem to be in such good shape. You just haven't done anything *really* worthwhile. Nothing to speak of. Don't get me wrong, I'm not saying you were *bad,* we don't like to say that about *anyone,* but your records are sort of well, blah, you know."

"I was a very successful businessman and...."

"No, please don't go through all that. I've heard the same spiel a hundred and forty-five times today, and I couldn't listen to it again. Just tell me something of value that you've accomplished. Anything at all. We're agreeable."

"Well, I can't remember *specific* incidents," Michael said. "You should have them in your book. But I went to church—"

"Don't even start with the church business...you know why you went to church. Just tell me what there is of value in you. Tell me about a good deed. Surely you can think of *something.*"

"Maybe you could ask my brother, he should be up here somewhere. He can tell you about me."

The man stifled a yawn. "He said you were okay, but he couldn't come up with anything either. You'd better hurry, we're running out of time."

Everything has happened so fast, Michael thought. I need time to think things over.

"You're a problem," the man said. "I just don't quite know where to fit you in. Look, walk that way, west, toward the large red dune, and see what happens. I'm only a clerk...."

The man and his desk disappeared.

Michael walked, but he didn't seem to be getting anywhere. The dune seemed to be as far away as when he'd started. He turned to retrace his steps back to heaven when he saw the clerk. He looked almost like the little man he had met before, except his hair was thicker and he was smiling. And his desk was not as big.

"Were you going back? That just isn't done, you know."

"I got lost. Am I supposed to see you?"

"I'm the man."

"Am I still in heaven?" Michael asked. He looked around, trying to discover some clue to where he was. But there was only desert as far as he could see...and the swirling dust-devils of sand.

"No, this is hell. It's sort of a border between domains. The main part of hell starts beyond the third dune there."

"But this looks the same as—"

"As heaven?" the clerk said. "Yes, it's almost the same thing, except we take the bad and they take the good. I suppose it depends upon which ethical code you commit yourself to. It's just division of labor. Well, let's get on with it. It's much too hot out here."

"Isn't hell *supposed* to be hot?"

"I just told you it's about the same thing as over there." The clerk pointed toward the boundary of heaven. "You don't really think that heaven is hot, so why should hell be hot? That's the propaganda they teach you down there. It's revolting. Look, no more questions until later. Let's see if we can use you." He glanced at his ledger. "Now tell me what you've done."

"You mean the *bad* things?"

"Yes, bad things...anything from theft to murder. And intention is important, too." He paused, concentrating on a page in the ledger. "You know, this book doesn't say much about you. In fact, it says almost *nothing*. There must be something I can enter into the book on your behalf."

Michael was embarrassed, but he would have to tell the man about what he had done to the nude dancer before he had been summoned away from the world. After all, he couldn't stay in limbo forever, walking back and forth across this endless desert. Hell was better than being nowhere. "I made...I watched a nude dancer while she was...."

"That doesn't count," the clerk said. "You weren't alive, remember? All the returns are already in. Everyone gets time to see their family or friends before they leave. You can do anything you want with the time, but it just doesn't count for anything. Anyway, I wouldn't be proud of it if I were you. You

made a fool of yourself, and you didn't even finish the job. No, that's no good."

Michael became even more nervous. "I did a lot of under-handed things in business—"

The clerk closed the ledger with a thud. "You did what an average businessman would do. There was no malice involved. You never really caused any major problems for anyone, even your so-called enemies."

Michael had to think fast. "I had a girl when I was...."

The clerk shook his head scornfully. "Your time is up, and quite frankly I don't know what to do with you. You don't seem to be able to produce any substantial evidence on your own behalf. Your potential for malice and evil was always diluted. You weren't much of an individual, simply a bundle of conformities. Every time you were about to do something that we would consider worthwhile, you stopped because you were afraid of what people would think. You just pitter-patted. It's terrible that so much of this is going on in the world today. We never had this much trouble, not even with the Romans."

"Well, I'm sorry," Michael said. "What are you going to do with me?"

"Wait here until I return. I'm afraid this is going to involve a conference between both sides...and that usually means trouble." Then the man and his desk disappeared.

They have to take me, Michael thought. I have to be *somewhere*.

The clerk and his desk appeared as suddenly as they had disappeared. "I had a talk with the other side and we came to a decision," the clerk said. He was perspiring heavily. "Neither side can take you on. To coin a phrase, you haven't lived yet. So...you're going back."

"You mean I get another chance?"

"That's it," the clerk said. "Try again. Go out and murder someone, or something." Thunder suddenly rolled across the sunny sky. "Sorry, forget that. Remember, we have nothing to do with you once you return to earth. What you do there will be

entirely up to you."

The desert faded away.

* * * * * * *

Michael found himself standing in a parking lot. He knew this place, the street, the stores, the people. He took a long deep breath. He was alive! He walked jauntily out of the parking lot. He nodded and beamed at perfect strangers, looked in shop windows, enjoyed the rush hour hustle and bustle of the streets... all the familiar sights and sounds and smells that he had never really appreciated before.

He was going to make something of his life now.

And he had a whole lifetime to do it.

He passed a corner candy store and on impulse decided to stop in for a candy bar. Life was sweet. Why not enjoy it? Michael picked up a Hershey's bar from a shelf and reached into his pocket for change. But he found nothing but his hand-kerchief and keys. He looked around. The proprietor was not paying any attention to Michael; he was making up a chocolate egg cream for a customer.

Impulsively, Michael put the candy bar into his coat pocket. His palms were sweaty and he was shaking and his heart seemed to be fluttering in his throat. As he left the store, he repressed the urge to run. He walked down the block and turned a corner.

He was safe. Finally, he had done something...and it was easy. He felt wonderful. He felt like a kid again, and this was only the beginning....

Michael started to cross the street. But he was paying more attention to opening his candy bar than to the traffic.

He heard a horn blaring as a station wagon hit him. His head struck the pavement, and the world and all its opportunities disappeared.

* * * * * * *

There was a different man at the desk this time. Michael did not recognize him.

"Welcome back," the man said. "The big boys on both sides had a feeling there would be a lot of fellows like you, so we opened this middle-of-the-road office. It's for those who don't have the qualifications to go to heaven *or* hell."

"Look, I didn't have *time* to do anything more than steal a candy bar," Michael said, waving the sticky wrapper before the clerk. "Is that good enough?"

"Walk west," said the clerk. "Let *them* make the decision."

In a few minutes Michael stood in front of the hell desk again. The clerk carefully examined the Hershey's bar wrapper. "Well, you did steal...technically. But it's nothing to write home about."

"I couldn't help it if a car hit me by accident," Michael said. "I was just getting started."

"Well, I'll admit it wasn't fair to you. You were nipped in the bud, right at the start of a promising career. Of course we're flattered that you chose our side. Let me talk to the old man and see what he thinks."

* * * * * * *

Satan brushed the sand from his sports jacket. He was tall and had a receding hairline, a large nose, and an angular face. He stood dramatically in front of the desk and looked at Michael. "I understand your problem. Nasty business. "But *this*"—he pointed to the candy wrapper on the desk "—is not enough to get you into hell. It's a question of pride...and ethics. It's a shame we can't send you down again, but all this second chance business really louses up the natural laws."

"You mean I can't go back?" Michael said. "What's going to happen to me, then?"

"You've had an unlucky break," Satan said, sitting on the desk. "It's really a bureaucratic tangle now. You can't go back down and you can't come in here or...there." He gestured toward heaven. "So you'll just have to stay here."

"In the desert? Forever?" Michael was dumbfounded. "I *can't* stay here. I'll go crazy. This isn't fair." Michael started to cry. What did he do to deserve *this*?

"Please stop crying," Satan said, looking agitated. "I suppose the principle has been violated, and that's what counts. And the intent was there on your part...." The clerk behind the desk was nodding vigorously.

Michael tried to compose himself. "You mean it's good enough? I can come in?"

"Yes, I suppose," Satan said. "You tried very hard, and it *was* theft. Yes, go on in. It's that way, toward the dunes over there," he said, pointing. "I'll catch up with you in a minute."

Satan adjusted his narrow tie. "These charity cases. I wonder how long it's going to take before all hell goes to...."

The intercom on the desk buzzed. "I'll get it," Satan said to the clerk. "You go guide our new charge." The clerk nodded and left.

"Hello, hell."

"This is the middle-of-the-road desk. Another soft job just came in. I'm sending her right over."

"Oh...fine," Satan said, wondering about his decision. Sooner or later, he thought, these Michael Browns would have to be put into a clearer category, their status institutionalized, if only to prevent these rule-of-thumb decisions being overturned one day.

After all, being wishy-washy *was* a failure, and failure *was* a crime, wasn't it? He toyed with the idea of sending them into the nothingness of limbo. Plenty of room there. No, that would be ideologically untidy, as was all non-being. Too much like the atheist's notion of death. Non-being was and wasn't a form of existence. Very untidy.

There was no reason why he shouldn't get the soft jobs. He needed all the souls he could get. They might as well go to hell as limbo. Their record could be defined as a major transgression in itself, based on a willful refusal to play the game of salvation-damnation. That would be enough to send them to hell in

a deserving way....

On the other hand, shouldn't hell be reserved for the *truly* bad? Maybe it would be better to stuff limbo with legions of Michael Browns, thus denying them to heaven while concentrating essential evil in hell.

He thought about it for a while, and decided against the idea; when all was said and done, it was better to have a crowd on your side.

He wrote the appropriate memo, replete with subtle argument and elegant logic, and sent it to the other side. It might just work, he thought...and it would eliminate the middle-of-the-road desk, which would please the economy-minded front office.

Proud of himself, Satan sighed, wondering if She would go for it.

AFTERWORD FOR "AFTERNOON GHOST"

George:

This started as a much insisted upon story by Jack, *Twilight Zone* written all over it. We rewrote it repeatedly and abandoned it, with increasing complexity, finding the theme doggedly more commonplace and resistant each time. I tried it at least twice, and we talked back to each other with some bemusement, then gave it a rest. Eventually *Return to the Twilight Zone* took it, and we smiled.

* * * * * * *

Jack:

Well, I was insistent. What could I do? The story was alive in my head, flickering like old film on a projector...and I couldn't seem to find the "off" switch. The story felt deep and resonant to me, playing in full Technicolor® inside my aforementioned head. That it is a rather slight confection, I cannot deny; but in those young, forming days every thought, every idea felt as profound as the discovery of the wheel. Often my discoveries were *square* wheels; but, then—to continue this awful, awful metaphor—they rarely got rolled out.

I can't help but still feel a certain nostalgia for "Afternoon Ghost." As George pointed out, it has *Twilight Zone* written all over it. The Technicolor reel turning in my head became black and white, and if you stare with some concentration into your antique Sylvania HaloLight black-and-white teevee, you'll see the spectre of Rod Serling saying:

"Take one Mr. Michael Brown, an average guy who learns that getting a second chance isn't always what it's cracked up to be..."

THE STANDARD
CRISIS SCENARIO

1.

The last war machine stopped before the assembled troops and blew itself up.

The human division moved forward onto the plain of dead machines, knowing that when confronted with an illegal force of flesh the lead controller had destructed rather than carry out an action contrary to the axioms of conflict.

The men swarmed around the quiet gray hulks, opening their service ports and climbing inside to turn the machines into flesh killers.

"Done," said Heilbronner in a whisper that shot into every waiting ear of decision.

2.

It was an easy job. Thirty-five units, all intermeshed and loaded, and Heilbronner had only to watch them work. They were already aimed, and Heilbronner was the trigger. He would make a decision and the AIs would fight while Heilbronner mindscanned, urged, and raved according to his needs.

Below him the city was a dot, then a flash, then a grid on an inside screen. He pulled into the streets and looked up at the buildings. It was a glassy city, shiny and hard. The skytoppers

changed shape as he turned his head. The soft yellow sunlight of the two suns slid across the giant panes, onto top playing fields, down the sides, and rolled across outdoor runs of tree greenery and grass.

Heilbronner cast himself into a crowd, where he would see the carnage from inside, and fired.

In the ship, his body twitched. He bit his lip and ejaculated, ridding himself of his need.

3.

The foolish creatures had three legs, kangaroo in their stance; a tail made a three-jointed leg. Their faces were lined leather, veined and human-like. Their mouths curved into natural frowns, smiling upside down as they died.

Their city was levelled into a plain of ground glass. The human division, composed of the first colonists to reach the planet from a nearby system, cheered.

On the ship's bridge Heilbronner was relieved that the alien enemy's planet bomb had been found in time to stop the decisive tactic of war zone destruction, the characteristic move of enemy commanders in past battles.

Inhuman—yet it had been reported that the simple proximity of a human being to an Idlot would send the alien into a frenzy of hatred and destruction, in which the creature would tear itself to pieces rather than endure a human presence.

Massed, they had to be killed coldly, carefully, by machines.

It was a thought infection between the species. A secretion of some kind that moved through the air and struck deeply, and we don't know what it is, Heilbronner thought. Maybe to them we see the universe so differently that they appear to us as renders of reality. And to them we make strange depressions in space time, into which they fear being drawn when we come near, driving them mad...

Maybe.

And maybe they're like us.

Both sides kill.

He looked at the city on the screen, and to the jungle beyond which the next city beckoned as if inviting the precise, efficient destruction to come. It was an honorable rite, as were the necessary human-alien rape orgies.

4.

It had to be done, Heilbronner reminded himself. He eased into the Idlot as his men held it steady. The creature was quiet, as usual, while his soldiers screamed, their knuckles white against brown mottled skin as their brains churned with the alien's overflow.

The Idlot stank, physically and mentally, and Heilbronner retched as his men watched, until his thrusts brought the beast to bellow, its reality tearing apart, its feelings flowing into him, trying to become pleas and failing.

The Idlot bellowed blue skies, cirrus clouds scudding, green grass, iron, smoke, and stone, sweet, sweet, clinging, cloying, silicone shards smashing, grating....

Have mercy and kill the alien filth, he thought, but there could be no smoothing for this one. It would be released, to take its fear back to the rest, where it would contaminate its kind with a weakening hatred...

He looked at the square frowning face, ape and snake alike, and saw big blue tears as he finished quickly with a shudder and floated between unfocused realities. Something bent inside him, as if closing deep cracks in the ground, and he let loose his own tears, stronger than ever, assuring him that his cause was just and the beast would never claim him. A guarantee as sure as a circle.

And the next city, a pale paradise of glass and onyx which had once been a pride of Idlot design, fell before the convenient machines that needed only a single success to see how the work

was done.

5.

Snake eyes must lose, Heilbronner said to himself, sweating. The double sunset bleached the horizon. Behind him lay five smashed cities, one red ocean, sand and hot winds.

The machines, folded at rest, had found no Idlots for over a week.

"Done," said Heilbronner, certifying victory with his word, recording, shaping his reality as he withdrew from the fear of the defeated.

6.

Now it came at him, forcing him to see and believe because it was part of the enemy's counter-offensive:

In black nothing, a dot—

•

•

A skipstone coming out of hyperspace.

•

A planetbomb, for his war zone.

"Divert," he said.

The machines obeyed.

Another came—

•

•

—to wipe Rath 5 clean, break it up into fine whispering dust—

To destroy a piece of matter in space was to push up the bottom of its gravity well, stretching space-time until it was smooth and flat, black and empty to Heilbronner's eyes.

"Divert!"

•

•
•
•

Closer—

"No time to divert," he said. "Evacuate."

Black.

War zone lost.

"Start again," Heilbronner said.

7.

Their infections take us, Heilbronner thought, and leave shells.

In the cross hairs: Idlot's home world?

Perhaps.

We must tear their bodies, crush their lives, before our fleshed-machines sit dead, and our egg tanks birth no more.

AFTERWORD FOR
"THE STANDARD CRISIS SCENARIO"

George:

Never published, and closely related to "OD" in its way, and perhaps foreshadowing my novel of the 1990s, *The Killing Star* (with Charles Pellegrino), depicting some deep-seated fears about the nature of intelligent life in the universe. Perhaps the apparent difficulty of interstellar travel is a quarantine we need; or the needs and means of spacefaring put a culture way beyond the psychology of this story, and we who write it just don't know any better.

* * * * * * *

Jack:

If memory serves, I was impressed with a story by Harlan Ellison called "The Region Between." The story centered around a wonderful concentric moiré graphic, and this *might* have influenced our "bomb-star" graphic in "The Standard Crisis Scenario." Although we never sent this story out for publication, we're including it here for completeness. It contains some jarring, jagged stuff in the almost stream-of-consciousness tradition of "Od" and "Faces Forward." We've left the clunkers unrevised in this story, for it is a representation—warts and all—of where we were, all those years ago. This is what the raw copy looked like. We have taken into consideration the idea that raw copy (like sausage-making) should not be revealed to the casual spectator. So it is with trepidation and tightly closed eyes that we put "The Standard Crisis Scenario" on the record.

* * * * * * *

George:

But in all truth, I rewrote this story for its first outing in this collection, conserving its original inspiration from Herman Kahn's eerie book on conflicts, *On Escalation* (1965), which also gave us our title. There are no clunkers in it now.

Sorry, Jack, I couldn't help helping it!

* * * * * *

Jack:

There you have it: the essence and wonder of collaboration. I had a few meals, watched some television, saw a movie, came down with a cold, and without even knowing it, rewrote an old story. Well, *I* didn't rewrite it, but it got done just the same. Now, isn't that a terrific way to write (or revise) a story? Take a nap, and when you wake up, there it is: a new story...and you don't have to sit over a hot laptop and perspire blood. But, alas, your collaborator does. Thanks, George!

And so concludes this diary of those green days of youth, creative passion, and collaborative partnership.

ABOUT THE AUTHORS

GEORGE ZEBROWSKI's more than forty books include novels, short fiction collections, anthologies, and a book of essays.

Science fiction writer Greg Bear calls him "one of those rare speculators who bases his dreams on science as well as inspiration," and the late Terry Carr, one of the most influential science fiction editors of recent years, described him as "an authority in the SF field." Zebrowski has published about a hundred works of short fiction and more than a hundred and forty articles and essays, and has written about science for *Omni Magazine*. His short fiction and essays have appeared in *Analog, Asimov's Science Fiction, Amazing Stories, The Magazine of Fantasy & Science Fiction, Science Fiction Age, Nature*, the *Bertrand Russell Society News*, and many other publications.

His best known novel is *Macrolife* (Harper & Row, 1979), which Arthur C. Clarke described as "a worthy successor to Olaf Stapledon's *Star Maker.* It's been years since I was so impressed. One of the few books I intend to read again." *Library Journal* chose *Macrolife* as one of the one hundred best science fiction novels, and The Easton Press included it in its "Masterpieces of Science Fiction" series. Zebrowski's stories and novels have been translated into a half-dozen languages; his short fiction has been nominated for the Nebula Award and the Theodore Sturgeon Memorial Award. *Stranger Suns* (Bantam, 1991) was a *New York Times* Notable Book of the Year.

The Killing Star (William Morrow, 1995), written with scientist/author Charles Pellegrino, received unanimous praise

in national newspapers and magazines. *The New York Times Book Review* called it "a novel of such conceptual ferocity and scientific plausibility that it amounts to a reinvention of that old Wellsian staple, [alien invasion]...." *The Washington Post Book World* described the novel as "a classic SF theme pushed logically to its ultimate conclusions."

Brute Orbits (HarperCollins, 1998), an uncompromising novel about the future of the penal system, was praised by reviewers for its characters, originality, and thought. Paul Di Filippo, in *Asimov's Science Fiction*, said that "Zebrowski never ceases to invest his individual characters with three-dimensional roundness...Startling, sobering, provocative", while *Publishers Weekly* called this novel "boldly speculative." The book was honored with the John W. Campbell Memorial Award for Best Novel of the Year.

Cave of Stars, a novel that is part of his Macrolife mosaic, was published by HarperCollins in 1999. *Skylife*, an anthology edited by Zebrowski with physicist and writer Gregory Benford, was published by Harcourt Brace in 2000. *Swift Thoughts*, a hardcover collection of his stories, with an introduction by Gregory Benford, came out in 2002. A second hardcover collection, *In the Distance, and Ahead In Time*, was also published in the same year. *Synergy SF: New Science Fiction*, the next volume of his legendary Synergy series of original anthologies, was published in 2004. *Black Pockets and Other Dark Thoughts* (Golden Gryphon), with an introduction by Howard Waldrop, came out in 2006, and a new edition of *Macrolife* was published in that year by Pyr Books, with an introduction by Ian Watson. Golden Gryphon published his horror novel *Empties* in 2009. *Sentinels In Honor of Arthur C. Clarke*, an anthology of fiction and nonfiction edited with Gregory Benford, was published in the summer of 2010 by Hadley Rille Books.

* * * * * * *

JACK DANN is a multiple award-winning author who has written or edited over seventy-five books, including the groundbreaking novels *Junction, Starhiker, The Man Who Melted, The Memory Cathedral*—which was an international bestseller, the Civil War novel *The Silent*, and *Bad Medicine*, which has been compared to the works of Jack Kerouac and Hunter S. Thompson and called "the best road novel since the Easy Rider days."

Dann's work has been compared to Jorge Luis Borges, Roald Dahl, Lewis Carroll, Castaneda, Ray Bradbury, J. G. Ballard, Mark Twain, and Philip K. Dick. Philip K. Dick, author of the stories from which the films *Blade Runner* and *Total Recall* were made, wrote that "*Junction* is where Ursula Le Guin's *Lathe of Heaven* and Tony Boucher's 'The Quest for Saint Aquin' meet... and yet it's an entirely new novel.... I may very well be basing some of my future work on Junction." Best selling author Marion Zimmer Bradley called *Starhiker* "a superb book...it will not give up all its delights, all its perfections, on one reading."

Library Journal has called Dann "...a true poet who can create pictures with a few perfect words." Roger Zelazny thought he was a reality magician and *Best Sellers* has said that "Jack Dann is a mind-warlock whose magicks will confound, disorient, shock, and delight." *The Washington Post Book World* compared his novel *The Man Who Melted* with Ingmar Bergman's film *The Seventh Seal.*

His work has been translated into over eighteen languages, and his short stories have appeared in *Playboy, Omni, Penthouse, Asimov's,* "*Best Of*" collections in Australia, the United States, and Great Britain, and other major magazines and anthologies. He is the editor of the anthology *Wandering Stars*, one of the most acclaimed American anthologies of the 1970s, and several other well-known anthologies such as *More Wandering Stars. Wandering Stars* and *More Wandering Stars* have recently been reprinted in the U. S. Dann also edited the multi-volume *Magic Tales* series with Gardner Dozois and is a consulting editor for Tor Books.

He is a recipient of the Nebula Award, the Australian Aurealis

Award (three times), the Ditmar Award (four times), the World Fantasy Award, the Peter McNamara Achievement Award, the Peter McNamara Convenors Award for Excellence, and the *Premios Gilgamés de Narrativa Fantastica* award. Dann has also been honored by the Mark Twain Society (Esteemed Knight).

High Steel, a novel co-authored with Jack C. Haldeman II, was published in 1993 by Tor Books. Critic John Clute called it "a predator...a cat with blazing eyes gorging on the good meat of genre. It is most highly recommended." Dann is currently writing *Ghost Dance*, the sequel to *High Steel* with Jack Haldeman's widow, author Barbara Delaplace.

Dann's major historical novel about Leonardo da Vinci—entitled *The Memory Cathedral*—was published to rave reviews. It has been published in over ten languages to date. It won the Australian Aurealis Award, was #1 on *The Age* bestseller list, and a story based on the novel was awarded the Nebula Award. *The Memory Cathedral* was also shortlisted for the Audio Book of the Year, which was part of the Braille & Talking Book Library Awards.

Morgan Llwelyn called *The Memory Cathedral* "a book to cherish, a validation of the novelist's art and fully worthy of its extraordinary subject." *The San Francisco Chronicle* called it "A grand accomplishment," *Kirkus Reviews* thought it was "An impressive accomplishment," and True Review said, "Read this important novel, be challenged by it; you literally haven't seen anything like it."

Dann's novel about the American Civil War, *The Silent*, was chosen as one of *Library Journal's* 'Hot Picks'. *Library Journal* wrote: "This is narrative storytelling at its best—so highly charged emotionally as to constitute a kind of poetry from hell. Most emphatically recommended." Peter Straub said "This tale of America's greatest trauma is full of mystery, wonder, and the kind of narrative inventiveness that makes other novelists want to hide under the bed." And *The Australian* called it "an extraordinary achievement."

His novel *Bad Medicine* (titled *Counting Coup* in the U.S.), a contemporary road novel, has been described by *The Courier Mail* as "perhaps the best road novel since the Easy Rider Days."

Dann is also the co-editor (with Janeen Webb) of the groundbreaking Australian anthology *Dreaming Down-Under*, which Peter Goldsworthy called "the biggest, boldest, most controversial collection of original fiction ever published in Australia." It won Australia's Ditmar Award and was the first Australian book ever to win the World Fantasy Award. His anthology *Gathering the Bones*, of which he is a co-editor, was included in *Library Journal's* Best Genre Fiction of 2003 and was shortlisted for The World Fantasy Award. His anthology *Wizards*, co-edited with Gardner Dozois and titled *Dark Alchemy* in the UK and Australia made the Waldenbooks/Borders bestseller list and was shortlisted for the World Fantasy Award. He has also edited a sequel to *Dreaming Down-Under*: *Dreaming Again*. The influential *Bookseller+Publisher* gave *Dreaming Again* a five-star rating and wrote: "Here are stories that engage with the building blocks of our culture and others that give shape to our shared darkness and light. *Dreaming Again* is at once quintessentially Australian and enticingly other. If you read short fiction you'll want this collection. If you don't, this is a reason to start."

His most recent anthologies are *Dreaming Again*, *The Dragon Book* (with Gardner Dozois), *Australian Legends* (with Jonathan Strahan), and *Ghosts by Gaslight* (with Nick Gevers), which just won the Aurealis Award.

Dann's stories have been collected in *Timetipping*, *Visitations*, and the retrospective short story collection *Jubilee: The Essential Jack Dann*. *The West Australian* said it was "Sometimes frightening, sometimes funny, erudite, inventive, beautifully written and always intriguing. *Jubilee* is a celebration of the talent of a remarkable storyteller." His collaborative stories can be found in the collection *The Fiction Factory*.

The *West Australian* called Dann's novel, *The Rebel: An Imagined Life of James Dean* "an amazingly evocative and utterly convincing picture of the era, down to details of the

smells and sensations—and even more importantly, the way of thinking." *Locus* wrote: "*The Rebel* is a significant and very gripping novel, a welcome addition to Jack Dann's growing oeuvre of speculative historical novels, sustaining further his long-standing contemplation of the modalities of myth and memory. This is alternate history with passion and difference." A companion James Dean short story collection entitled *Promised Land* has also been published in Great Britain as has Dann's most recent short novel *The Economy of Light*.

As part of its *Bibliographies of Modern Authors Series*, The Borgo Press has published an annotated bibliography and guide entitled *The Work of Jack Dann*. An updated second edition is in progress. Dann is also listed in *Contemporary Authors* and the *Contemporary Authors Autobiography Series*; *The International Authors and Writers Who's Who*; *Personalities of America*; *Men of Achievement*; *Who's Who in Writers, Editors, and Poets, United States and Canada*; *Dictionary of International Biography*; the *Directory of Distinguished Americans*; *Outstanding Writers of the 20th Century*; and *Who's Who in the World*. His recently published autobiography is entitled *Insinuations*.

Dann lives in Australia on a farm overlooking the sea and "commutes" back and forth to Los Angeles and New York.

His website is jackdann.com. You can also follow him on Twitter @jackmdann